HIDDEN SECRETS

MEL SHERRATT

CHAPTER ONE

Saturday Evening

Kit Harper staggered down the path, realising that having his hands in his pockets was an unwise idea. He pulled them out to steady himself, inadvertently swaying to the left.

No amount of drink would make him stop thinking of the mess he was in. It was all going to fall down around him soon.

Saturday night with the lads hadn't gone to plan. First, he'd had words with Scott who'd stormed out, and then Ben had turned on him too, following shortly afterwards.

Within seconds, Aaron was giving him a lecture on what he should and shouldn't have been doing. Kit had told him in no uncertain terms to leave, which he had. And then he'd nursed a couple more pints sitting alone.

What was it with people nowadays? All he'd wanted was a fun night out. Yet, whenever Ben was with them, he always spoiled things. It wasn't as if anyone really liked him that much. He was just someone who tagged along because he was seeing Gemma, Aaron's ex-wife.

He wasn't welcome at their night outs, and well he knew it, but he always insisted on joining them. None of them had the heart to say no either. They tolerated him, because of Gemma. So, Ben turning up had put a dampener on the evening straightaway, no matter how much Aaron tried to laugh it off. Aaron wasn't over their breakup despite being with Tasha now.

Kit passed a house that had lights on in every room, windows and door open, and music blasting out. Several people stood out in the garden, singing and raising cans and bottles in the air. He dodged a teenager as she raced to the pavement and threw up in the gutter, her friend holding the hair from her face.

He chuckled, spotting a police car turning into the road. The neighbours had obviously had enough, and who could blame them with the choice of music.

His mood dropped once the noise quietened, and he scowled as he recalled some of the things that had been said earlier. Ben could be such a dick. It was as if he took real pleasure in winding them up. One minute he was as friendly as anything, the next he could turn on you in an instant.

Kit had seen that first-hand tonight. Since he'd started working with Scott, Ben had shown his face even more. Kit couldn't understand why. He, Scott, and Aaron had known each other since junior school. Now they were in their mid-thirties, he trusted them with his life. They had a history together. Sure, they all had hidden secrets, but they'd been there for each other through thick and thin.

The heat of the day was still hanging in the night air. Even so, it was surprisingly quiet once he'd passed the party.

He checked his watch: couldn't read the time despite drawing it close to his face. It was way past midnight, that was for sure. He hoped Nicky hadn't fallen asleep on the sofa waiting for him. If she saw him like this, there was bound to be another argument.

He was in no fit state to do anything but pass out when he reached his bed. He didn't have the energy to argue with her again. They had been married for two years, and already he knew it had been the wrong thing to do – something else he was constantly thinking about.

What a mess. Scott had turned on him, Aaron hated what he was doing, Ben wanted to cause trouble, and he and Nicky were practically over before they'd started. Maybe he'd be better getting out of Stoke-on-Trent, packing a bag, and leaving everything behind.

He laughed. Beer talk. There was nowhere for him to go in any case, nor had he enough money. That was the problem he'd been trying to solve, which had got him into this mess.

A few minutes from home, he spied a couple walking towards him. They stopped to kiss, walked a few metres, and then kissed again. Kit dropped his eyes as he drew level with them, letting them enjoy their moment.

He turned into the cut-through by the school playing fields. The branches of a tree on one side of the path rustled, a warm breeze washing over him. He lifted his face to it, relishing it on his skin. It was so hot. God, he was wasted and couldn't wait to get home now.

He stomped ahead, the light in the lamp post thankfully working, showing the way ahead without him having to watch where he was going too much.

Kit had lived in Stoke all his life, grown up with its people through work and play. How many times had he walked this path during the years? It must be pushing into the tens of thousands, the area so familiar to him. It had been on his walk home from school. He'd been dropped off there every night when he'd got his first job. Then it was a shortcut from the pub to where he'd lived with Brooke, and now with Nicky.

A noise had him turning suddenly, his eyes widening as he tried to focus.

'Who's there?' He stared but could see nothing.

A shadow fell across the path. Something hard caught him on his temple, and he went down like a ton of bricks. The back of his head slammed onto the concrete path, taking the full brunt of the force and making the most awful noise.

It didn't matter, though.

He was dead before he hit the ground.

CHAPTER TWO

Sunday

Allie Shenton stretched across to her bedside cabinet, feeling for the ringing phone which had rudely interrupted her sleep. Her head came up from the pillow, and she sighed when she saw it was barely half past six.

'Turn that thing off,' her husband, Mark, muttered, pulling the duvet over his head.

The morning sun shone through the edges of the curtains, framing the window in a fiery glow. After a week of glorious weather, it looked like another fine day was on the cards.

But it was her work phone that was ringing, which could mean only one thing.

If she wasn't busy with a case, Sunday mornings were always spent reading the newspapers, propped up in bed before they'd cook an oatcake breakfast.

After that, it would be time in the garden or a long walk somewhere. Perhaps shopping if she hadn't managed to get any food during the week. Allie ordered most of her groceries online, or she or Mark called at the local shop on their way home. But when she wasn't too busy, she loved to browse around the supermarket.

'DI Shenton,' she said, her voice hoarse after sleep. Then she was wide awake, pulling back the covers and sitting on the edge of the bed. 'Okay, I'm on my way.'

'Why, why, why on a Sunday?' Mark protested.

'Because lots of people lose the plot on Saturday nights.' She gathered together some clothes before heading for a shower. 'Things escalate a lot in summer, too. The sun brings out the best, and worst, in some. Add in drink and recreational drugs and it's a recipe for disaster, over and over.'

'What's happened this time?' Mark removed the duvet from his head and looked at her.

'A man's body has been found with head injuries.'

'I'll do the shopping then.'

She turned to him with a smile, but his eyes were closed.

Since they'd got over their rough patch, the last few months had been incredible. They were firing on all cylinders as a couple once more, going through the rounds of interviews and training required to become foster parents.

They still had a few weeks to go before a decision could be made. Even so, Mark had brought champagne home one evening, in anticipation. He'd wanted to keep it chilling in the fridge, but Allie had insisted it should stay in the garage until they had a definite yes. She didn't want to tempt fate, in any way.

'Thanks,' she replied. 'We can make up for it next weekend.'

'I hope we hear from the council by then.' His eyes were open now, and he rolled over to face her. 'I can't bear the suspense.'

Allie sat down on the bed beside him for a moment.

'We're going to make great foster parents.' She leaned forward to plant a kiss on his lips. 'Now, go back to sleep.'

'Oh, I intend to.'

Thirty minutes later, Allie was driving towards Caverswall traffic lights. She was on her way to Fenton, one of six towns that made up the city, where the man's body had been found. It was next to Richmond Academy, on the edge of the Seddon Estate, a school that was now doing well in the league tables after a terrible couple of decades.

Despite the early hour, emergency vehicles were already in situ, and she pulled in as near as she could. At least there weren't many people about to rubberneck yet. Allie hated that the public got to see so much nowadays. With the advent of the smartphone, anyone could be a roving reporter, shooting video and uploading it to social media within a matter of minutes.

As she got out of her car, she spotted a familiar vehicle coming towards her and waited for its occupant to park up and get out.

'Morning, boss,' DS Perry Wright greeted her, sunglasses already on. He was dressed in a short-sleeved shirt, the top button undone but sporting a snazzy tie, and navy suit trousers.

'Morning, Perry. I can't believe we got here at the same time.' She smirked. 'It's obviously because it takes you less time now to do your hair.'

Perry had been touchy about losing his trademark blond-spiked style until his wife, Lisa, had likened him to Jason Statham. Allie couldn't see the resemblance herself and thought that Lisa was being kind.

But Perry had taken it to heart and embraced his baldness. He said it suited his all-year-round fake tan. Thankfully, that had gone as well. No more of the orange glow he'd been known for.

And although she wouldn't admit it, because she'd rather have something to tease him about, he did look much better for the loss of them both.

'Get much grief from Lisa?' she questioned.

'The usual. I was relishing family time over a long lunch, though. I got Alfie the latest Port Vale shirt, and one for myself, so we were going to play footie in the garden.'

'I was looking forward to a bottle of wine and a barbeque. Mark was ready to play chef. Inconsiderate of the public.'

They shared a smile before sombre faces were needed at the crime scene.

Arriving at the cordon, Allie didn't recognise the officer on guard so held up her warrant card.

'DI Shenton, and this is my colleague, DS Wright.'

'PC Goodwin,' the officer acknowledged.

'Has the pathway been cordoned off at each end?'

'Yes, Ma'am,' he replied.

'Who found him? The usual?' Most suspicious deaths, or victims of assault who lay unconscious, that happened overnight were found first thing by dog walkers or runners.

'A young woman out jogging.' He pointed to the other end of the pathway. 'She lives in one of those houses there, with her parents; found him here and called us.'

'Is she at home now?'

'Yes. My colleague is with her.'

Allie nodded her thanks. She and Perry signed into the logbook and prepped in forensic gear. Then they dipped under the tape and walked towards the murder spot.

It was a beautiful morning, not a cloud in a deep-blue sky and the temperature was already hitting double figures. She cursed inwardly.

They were going to ruin someone's weekend.

CHAPTER THREE

The body was already covered by a white forensics tent. The path ran next to the school football pitch, leaving their investigation open for anyone to see due to link-chained railings down part of one side. Allie hoped there were no matches on that weekend as more people would notice the crime scene.

Ahead stood the senior crime scene investigator, Dave Barnett, suited up like a snowman, sweat dripping down his brow. He was showing Christian Willhorn, the pathologist, something on his phone.

Spotting them, Dave raised his hand in acknowledgement.

'Morning, gentleman,' Allie greeted as she and Perry drew level. 'What have you got for us?'

'Male, white, thirty-six according to his driving licence,' Christian said. 'Goes by the name of Kevin Harper. Blunt force trauma to the side of his head, plus a heavy hit to it once he'd fallen.'

'Dead as a result of the second?'

'It's possible even from the first. Our killer and victim could have had a fight that went wrong.'

'Or perhaps he didn't see a fist flying at him in time to dodge it,' Christian remarked.

'A fist, you say?' Perry raised his eyebrows. 'Not come across a one-punch kill before.'

'It's just a theory, but that's where you come in.' Dave pointed downwards. 'His head took a right walloping on the concrete path.'

'Drunk, perhaps, so fell heavier than normal?' Allie suggested.

'We'll know more when the toxicology results are back,' Christian replied. 'Either way, it was no accident.'

'You say you have his driving licence?' Allie glanced around for evidence bags but saw none.

'Yes, it's inside the tent,' Dave told her. 'His wallet and phone were found on his person, although the phone took a bit of a battering as he fell on it. It's still working, even though the screen is smashed. Needs a passcode.'

'Is the address nearby?' Christian asked. He'd recently transferred from up north.

'Yes, not far,' Dave told him. 'My next assumption is he was on the way home from a night out when he was jumped.'

'But not robbed,' Allie added, almost as an afterthought.

'Any murder weapon found?' Perry asked.

'Nothing yet.'

'Thanks, guys.' Allie took a deep breath. 'Let's take a look and we can get on with piecing together what happened. Are Frankie and Sam on their way in, Perry?'

Frankie and Sam were the two detective constables who made up the rest of the immediate team.

'Yes, boss.'

'Okay, thanks.' Allie stepped forward to follow Dave, Perry behind her. 'Timeline, Dave?'

'He wasn't dead long before he was found. A few hours ago at the max.'

The temperature inside the tent was unbearably hot. There was a collapsible table set up to the right, several items already on top of it. Jordan Munroe, the forensic photographer, was taking photos of the body and moved aside to let them get closer.

'Hi, Jordan.' Allie smiled.

'Ma'am.' He nodded a greeting.

Jordan had only recently joined the team. In his thirties, with short black hair, model features, and a strong, firm physique, he was always a sight for sore eyes. However, Allie liked much more about him than that. He was meticulous at his work, spotting things before anyone else, and giving feedback on theories that led to great leads.

Sweat dripped down the middle of Allie's back. She was going to be drenched by the time they got outside again.

The victim was flat out and almost untouched by injuries. The only thing indicating his attack was the large pool of blood at the back of his head. He was dressed in a T-shirt with the slogan of a local band across its front, dark-denim shorts to the knee, and white trainers. Two tattoos were visible on his forearm and hand. At least that would make him easier to identify, despite having his details.

Allie took Jordan's place and stooped beside the body to get a better look. Hazel eyes stared ahead, olive skin tanned from a recent holiday or time outside. His dark hair was short, tidy, and he was clean-shaven, although signs of a shadow were already coming through.

From what she could see of him, he was lean and fit and, on the face of it, healthy. Was this a disagreement that had got out of hand? She wondered if he'd been walking home with his assailant or had met his fate on the way.

Or had he simply been in the wrong place at the wrong time? Even though it didn't look like he'd been robbed, something could have been taken, and whoever attacked him left the rest behind to throw them off the scent.

First thing they needed to find out was where he'd been the previous evening, and who with.

'You say he lives local?' she asked Dave.

'Yes, Berrisford Street.'

'It's a ten-minute walk, I reckon,' Perry replied.

Allie nodded, standing up. 'We'll be off soon.'

Now out of the tent, Allie glanced around. Two properties, back to back, bordered the cut-through. One had a six-foot fence; the other a row of conifers that were even higher. Maybe one, or both, had security cameras they could view, although they probably wouldn't cover the path. It was worth checking out, nevertheless.

At the far end, an elderly couple with three dogs at their feet, were talking to PC Goodwin.

'Since when did they become a couple?' Perry rolled his eyes as he joined her again.

'Who?'

'Dave and Christian. They were practically finishing each other's sentences.'

'It's good to have people who work together well.' Allie thrust her tongue into her cheek. 'Whereas I get stuck with you.'

Perry rolled his eyes in jest.

DC Frankie Higgins was coming their way, looking fresh and... so young. How Allie longed to be his age again. At twenty-eight, she'd still been on the beat. Having said that, age was nothing but a number. Apart from her knees creaking, and a dodgy back every now and then, she couldn't complain.

It wasn't yet seven a.m., too early for house-to-house. For the next hour or so, she'd set him on talking to the locals who appeared and scoping out the area.

She updated him on everything they'd discovered so far.

'I don't want to disturb the residents in the houses that run adjacent to the path yet but, equally, I know they'll be drawn to what's going on outside and will come to see for themselves. Keep an eye out for that when it happens and have a chat with them then.'

'Yes, boss.'

'The search team will be here soon, plus Sam is starting the operation off at the station. Perry, let's be on our way.'

It was time to deliver bad news.

CHAPTER FOUR

They left Perry's car at the crime scene and headed to the address they had for Kevin Harper. In the car, it would take less than five minutes, especially this early on a Sunday morning.

'It was a great night last night, wasn't it?' Perry said to Allie as she drove. 'We should do it more often.'

Allie and Mark had been out with Perry and his wife, Lisa, a rare occurrence that she'd enjoyed immensely. Perry's son, Alfie, had stayed with his grandparents overnight, so none of them had been driving. Luckily, neither of them had had too much to drink.

'It was,' she said, 'and really nice of Lisa to chat to us about fostering, too. She must get really bored of talking about work all the time.'

'She's happy to help. We both think what you and Mark are doing is amazing. Although I will be surprised if you share any Maltesers with the kids.'

Allie whacked him playfully on the thigh, keeping her eyes on the road. 'I am not *that* precious about my chocolate!'

'Yeah, you are.'

A few minutes later, they turned into Victoria Road, one of the main thoroughfares through the city. Allie puffed up her cheeks and then blew out her breath.

Berrisford Street, the next right, was a line of terraced houses. There were no gardens, the doors opening to the pavement. Hanging baskets hung proud from umpteen properties, no doubt fixed to the walls securely. Blues, yellows, reds, and whites caught Allie's eyes as she drove down the road.

Rows of cars were tightly packed together, with hardly any room for errors of judgement.

'Number eighteen is where we're after.' Allie manoeuvred the car into one remaining space a few metres along.

'I hate this, don't you?' Perry pointed to a navy-blue door as Allie killed the engine. 'Going to ruin someone's Sunday.'

'I hate going to ruin anyone's day.' Allie sighed. 'But it is what it is.'

Considering the number of cars that were lined up, it was quiet. The curtains were closed at the house they were visiting. She glanced at the clock on the dashboard: five minutes past nine. She hoped she wasn't getting anyone out of bed.

She knocked on the door, first fishing out her warrant card.

A woman answered, peeping around its frame.

Allie held up her ID. 'Mrs Harper?' she tried first.

'Yes.'

'DI Shenton and DS Wright. Could we come inside for a moment, please?'

The woman's face dropped. 'Has something happened?'

'If you wouldn't mind?' Allie urged.

She let them in, showing them through to the back of the room.

Originally the terraced property would have had two sitting rooms but, like many others, the space had been turned into one room with open-plan stairs running up its middle. The house was cosy: a three-piece suite, coffee table, and a TV crammed into one end, and a table with four chairs at the other. A pile of clothes sat on top of it, folded up, ready to iron or put away.

Allie's heart sank as she spied a wedding photograph of the couple on the wall. There were six people, all smiles in a line. Two women and two men stood either side of the bride and groom. All three men had matching suits; the two women wore the same floor-length dresses in a shade of deep pink to match the bride's flowers.

'Are you alone, Mrs Harper?' she asked.

'It's Nicky, but yes, why?' She wrapped her arms around her torso, as if already sensing something terrible was coming.

'Could we sit down?' Allie dropped into a chair before she replied.

Perry followed suit, prompting Nicky to do the same.

There was no putting it off any longer.

'I'm afraid we've found a body of a man this morning, who we believe to be your husband,' Allie told her.

Nicky stared at them both in turn.

Used to the shock that often accompanied the silence, Allie continued. 'Kevin Harper, he's your husband?'

Nicky nodded.

'He was on the cut-through between Fenton Road and Victoria Road. I'm afraid he was pronounced dead at the scene.'

'He was on his way home?' There was a quiver to her voice.

'It looks that way.' Allie sensed things starting to sink in.

Nicky's shoulders dropped, her face ashen. Tears poured down her cheeks.

'Can you tell me when you last saw Kevin?' Allie asked gently.

'It's Kit,' she said. 'No one calls him Kevin. He's been known as Kit since he was in his teens.'

'Ah, okay. So you'd prefer us to call him that, too?'

Nicky nodded. 'He was out with the lads last night. I thought nothing of it when he didn't come in. I assumed he'd grabbed a takeaway and gone home with one of them. That's what usually happens.'

'Would that be a regular occurrence, out with the lads?'

'We go out often as couples, but they all meet every month on a Saturday night.'

'Who is they?'

'Scott and Aaron. Scott Milton and Aaron Clarke. I think Ben was with them last night, too. Ben Grant.' Her face crumpled again. 'Oh God, how am I going to tell them?'

'We can do that for you.' Allie leaned across and rested a hand on her arm. 'We need to concentrate on you right now.'

'What happened to him?'

'He suffered a head injury.'

'You mean he fell and hit it?'

'No, we don't think so. It seems he was struck with something first.'

Nicky drew in a breath. 'So somebody hurt him deliberately?'

'We don't know for sure. It could be a fight that got out of hand.'

Nicky sobbed loudly. 'Please tell me he didn't suffer out there all alone.'

'I would imagine he wouldn't have known too much about it,' Allie soothed. 'I need to ask you some questions to establish Kit's whereabouts last night. In the meantime, is there anyone I can call to come and sit with you?'

'My mum lives in Cyprus. There's only my friends, Leanne, and Gemma.' She reached for her phone, hands shaking. 'Leanne is married to Scott, and Gemma is dating Ben.'

Allie sensed they were dealing with a group of close friends, already wondering if that would help or hinder their enquiries.

'I can do that for you, if you unlock it for me.' Perry took it from her. 'Are the numbers stored under their names?'

Nicky nodded, and Perry left the room.

Allie turned back to Nicky. 'Can you tell me where the men went last night? Did Kit say before he left?'

'They go to The Wheatsheaf pub, on Arnold Street. They always do.'

Now they knew where Kit had been to and from. 'They don't go anywhere before or after?' Allie asked.

Nicky shook her head. 'They find a seat and stay there all night.'

'What time did he go out?'

'About half past eight. He walked. It takes about twenty minutes.'

'Was where he was found the way he normally would have come home?'

'Yes.'

'So he was at the pub from approximately ten to nine? Do the other men usually get together at the same time?'

'Yes. Leanne rang me after Scott had set out – Kit goes past their house – and we had a chat for a few minutes.'

'About anything in particular?'

The way Nicky shook her head in reply made Allie wonder what she was keeping to herself. It was too forced.

'And you said earlier you never thought anything of him not coming home? Is that a regular occurrence, too?'

'Sometimes. If they ordered in a takeaway, they'd most likely go to Leanne and Scott's as they live the closest. He'd crash there if he fell asleep.'

'Can you tell us what he went out in?' Even though Allie

was certain they had the right man, she wanted to be sure until the official identification was completed.

'He was only casual with it being so hot. Long denim shorts and a white T-shirt.'

'Does he have any distinguishing marks, tattoos, birthmarks?'

'He has a raven on his left forearm, and a pair of dice on the side of his right hand. Did you see them?'

Allie's heart sank at the look on Nicky's face, eager for her to reply in the negative, to be wrong. But instead, she nodded.

Nicky burst into tears again, and Allie knew she'd have to stop soon. But for now, she had to press on.

'I'm so sorry for your loss, Nicky. But we have to get a big enough picture of Kit, his family, his friends, his life. So I need to stick with the questions for now. Are you okay for me to continue?'

CHAPTER FIVE

Gemma Clarke's knees almost gave way when she took the call from the police. She dropped down onto the settee, her hand to her mouth.

'What happened?' she asked the detective on the line.

'He was attacked on his way home last night. I can't give any more details, but Nicky would like you to come and see her. I'd also like to speak to Ben Grant. I believe he was out with Kit last night? Is he with you?'

'Yes, he's here.'

'Can you ask him to come with you, too, please?'

'Of course.' Gemma stood up, her mind already on the task of getting ready. 'Will you tell Nicky I'll be with her in half an hour? There's also Leanne Milton to call. Her husband was with Kit, too. My ex-husband as well. I can ring him if you like. Ask him to go to Gemma's?'

'Thanks, but I'm calling them next anyway.'

Gemma disconnected the call and sat for a moment, unsure of what to do. She hadn't taken in what had been said, never mind what had happened.

Kit was dead? How could that be possible?

words. It wasn't the right time to think about it, but all she wanted was for him to hold her, comfort her in his arms.

'Shall I meet you at Nicky's?' he said, breaking into her thoughts.

'Thanks. I'll see you there.' She disconnected the call, sighing with relief, glad she wasn't going to be alone to cope with Ben. Their relationship hadn't been too good lately, and it was the last thing she needed to worry about. If the police hadn't asked for him to attend, she wouldn't have taken him with her. Nicky needed her friends around her, not someone she barely knew. And she needed Aaron.

Her tears fell freely then.

'Was that your ex?' Ben said.

She jumped, not having heard him come into the room. His tone annoyed her, but she didn't let it show.

Instead, she nodded her reply.

'So you're meeting him at Nicky's? That's going to be awkward, seeing as I'll be there, too.'

'The police have asked to see you both.'

'Oh.' He paused. 'Your friends have never liked me.'

'That's not true.'

'Of course it is. I can't take the place of your precious Aaron among them.'

'Please don't start.' She wiped at her tears. 'I'm barely keeping myself together as it is. I loved Kit as if he were a brother. And poor Nicky will be inconsolable. I want to help as much as I can.'

'I think Leanne has been doing some consoling of her own.'

'What do you mean by that?'

'Oh, nothing.'

Gemma couldn't work out what he was insinuating, and quite frankly, she didn't want to think about it right now either.

CHAPTER SIX

'When did you meet Kit?' Allie asked Nicky.

'We've known each other since junior school. We all have, except Ben. Ben started going out with Gemma after she and Aaron divorced. Not straightaway, after a couple of years.'

'Have you been married long?' Allie suspected not because the wedding snap looked like a recent edition.

'Two years. Kit was married before to Brooke. He has a daughter, Danielle. She's eighteen. Someone needs to tell them as well.'

'We can do that for you, too. Does she see her father regularly?'

'Yes, but more outside the home. They meet in the pub, or he takes her out for something to eat.'

'You never go with them?'

'Sometimes, but we don't get on that well. Danielle blames me for the breakup, but Kit and Brooke were over way before we started seeing each other.'

'Okay, thanks. Where does he work?'

'At Car Wash City in Longton. He'd been there a couple of months, with Scott.'

Allie bristled at the mention. 'What do they do?'

'Scott was asked if he wanted a job there and if he could find someone to work with him. They were after two people to work together as managers.'

Allie parked that information for later. She wondered how involved they were with the back-end stuff she suspected to be happening behind closed doors.

'Did he enjoy it?' she continued.

'I think so. He didn't really talk about work that much. But he seemed happier.'

'What did he do before?'

'He was a security guard at the garden centre. You wouldn't believe the things people nick from there.'

Allie smiled. 'So he wanted to do something different?'

'Kit was always dreaming of bettering himself.' She flicked her hand around. 'Who'd want to live here for the rest of their lives? It didn't help that I lost my job six months ago.'

Allie didn't know what to say to that. It was obvious from her tone that they were struggling.

'Did Kit have family that live local?'

'Both his parents are dead, and he's an only child. His dad had a heart attack when Kit was seven, and his mum died last year. Cancer.'

Allie grimaced, hoping Nicky's friends were keen to look after her. She didn't like to think of people on their own after such a tragedy. Often, she found it hard to walk away after she'd given bad news, especially the death knock. It was hard to switch off from their pain, despite her training. It was also what made her good at her job, the fight for justice ever strong.

'Do you know the passcode to his phone, by chance?'

Nicky's eyes widened. 'He had it on him?'

'Yes, along with his wallet. That's how we identified him.'

'So it wasn't a robbery? It doesn't make sense.' Tears rolled down her cheeks again.

'We're not certain, but nothing seems to have been taken from him.'

'I don't know his unlock code.'

'Not to worry. We can take care of that.'

Perry came back into the room, nodded at Allie, and gave the phone back to Nicky.

'Your friends will be with you soon,' he said.

'Do you have a recent photograph of Kit that we could use, please?' Allie asked next.

Nicky scrolled on her phone until she found one she liked. 'Will this be okay?'

Allie glanced at it. Kit had taken a selfie, a beach and the crashing waves of the sea behind him. There wasn't anyone else around. She wondered where it was: it could easily be somewhere down south as much as a Greek island. Kit seemed so happy, not a care in the world.

He would never set foot on a beach like that again.

'Thanks. It's a lovely photo.' Allie smiled. 'That will do fine, if you can email the image to DS Wright?'

'I—' Nicky looked at her helplessly.

'Let me help.' Perry took the phone from her again.

'There will be a family liaison officer appointed to you as well.' Allie handed Nicky another tissue. 'They'll be here to help you if you have any questions when we're not here, to keep you in touch with what's going on, and also tell you about any breakthroughs we have. In the meantime, let's make you a cup of tea. Have you eaten this morning?'

'I'm not hungry.'

Allie couldn't blame her, but she needed to see that she was okay before leaving. She decided to wait until her friends arrived. PC Rachel Joy would be here within the hour, too.

She couldn't leave Nicky alone until then.

CHAPTER SEVEN

'Scott!' Leanne raced upstairs and banged on the bathroom door. 'Scott, you have to come out right now.'

'What's wrong?' It was a few seconds before he opened the door, a towel around his waist, his hair wet.

'It's Kit.' She burst into tears. 'He's dead.'

Scott frowned, unable to take in what she was saying. 'But I only saw him last night.'

'The police have just called. He was attacked on his way home, that's all they'll say. They said for us to go to Nicky's house. They want to talk to you.'

'What about?'

'I don't know! But we'd better get around there.' She paused. 'Ohmigod, I can't believe it. It can't be true.'

'Give me ten minutes and I'll be ready.'

'Okay.'

The door closed, and he was gone. Leanne took a deep breath to steady herself, but it didn't work. She rammed a fist in her mouth and sat down on the top stair to stop herself from screaming.

The door opened again, and she got to her feet, wiping at

her eyes. Scott flew past her into the bedroom, the argument they'd had only minutes earlier now forgotten.

Scott had come home in a rough mood last night, and when she'd moaned about it that morning, it had set them both off. She was fed up with him taking her for granted. He was fed up with her nagging him, apparently.

All that faded into the background now. It was trivial stuff compared to the news she'd delivered.

'I'll tell Amy to go to Mum's house for dinner,' she shouted through to him. 'I know she'll want to be with us, but it'll be too upsetting for her at Nicky's.'

Amy was their fourteen-year-old daughter. She was sleeping over at her friend's house.

'Yeah, good idea.' He appeared on the landing, tears welling in his eyes. 'Is he really gone?'

'I'm so sorry.' She rushed to comfort him, wrapping her arms around his waist and resting her head on his chest. 'Nicky's going to be devastated.'

'It doesn't seem real.'

'I don't think I'll ever believe it. I'll never want to, I know that.' Leanne hugged him tightly, knowing how much they would all miss Kit in different ways.

Half an hour later, they pulled up near to Nicky's house, unable to find a space close by. They walked back in silence, in worlds of their own as Leanne willed the news not to be true.

A woman in her mid-thirties opened the door. She was wearing a smart pale blue summer dress, her blonde hair tied in a ponytail.

'Leanne? Scott?' she asked.

They nodded.

'I'm PC Rachel Joy. I'm a family liaison officer for Staffordshire Police. Come through.'

They stepped inside, Leanne almost having to force her

feet to keep moving. If she stayed outside, she could pretend it hadn't happened. Put off the inevitable.

At the far end of the room, Nicky was sitting on the settee, Gemma by her side. Nicky's short red hair was a mess, as if she'd run her fingers through it continually. She was still wearing pyjamas, slippers on her feet, her hands around a mug.

Gemma's makeup had run down her face, rivulets of mascara in tramlines. Leanne hadn't bothered to put any on as she knew she would cry it away.

Spotting her, they stood up, and she rushed into their arms. In the middle of the room, they broke down together, friends shouldering the grief for a man they all loved.

'What am I going to do without him?' Nicky sobbed.

A man and a woman stood to the side, with the officer who had shown them in. Leanne assumed them to be police officers, too. They were waiting patiently, showing respect while they comforted each other.

When they broke apart, the older woman stepped closer.

'I'm DI Shenton,' Allie said. 'I'm the senior investigating officer for Kit's death, and this is DS Wright. We're so sorry for your loss.'

'Do we know anything else yet?' Scott asked, his face ashen. 'How he... how it happened?'

'We are working hard to find that out, but there is nothing we can share yet.' She pointed to the kitchen. 'Ben and Aaron are here. Perry, could you take Scott through to the others?'

The three women sat down, Nicky in the middle. Leanne reached out a hand to comfort her. None of them spoke.

Their silence didn't concern Allie. She surmised that shock was setting in, Kit Harper seemed to be well liked.

They were obviously good friends, but persons of interest who they would look at closely. They could be hiding a plethora of things between them. Even close friends hurt each other, especially after a night on the ale.

Or there could be nothing to hide at all.

'I need to check your whereabouts last night, please, Leanne,' Allie said, taking out her notebook.

'I was at home. I live at number seventeen Calvin Avenue, Fenton.'

'Were you by yourself?'

'Yes. My daughter, Amy, was staying over at her friend's house.'

'What time did Scott come home?'

'About midnight? He woke me up getting into bed.'

'And there seemed nothing out of the ordinary wrong with him?'

'No. I asked if he'd had a good night, he said he had, and then he was asleep in seconds.'

Allie took a note of everything she'd been told. 'And you, Gemma? You were at home alone, too, last night?'

'Yes. I live in Smallwood Avenue, number seven. It's my ex's turn to have my daughter. Charlotte gets on well with his new partner, so I'm happy for her to watch her.'

'Do you always stay in?'

'Sometimes we get together when the men go out, don't we?' The other women nodded. 'But I wasn't feeling up to it.'

'Do you know what time Ben came in?'

'I didn't hear him. I was asleep. He said just after midnight, though.'

'Does he stay at your house often?'

'Yes, most weekends from Friday teatime until mid-afternoon on Sunday. He works away during the week, in Birmingham.'

'And was he acting strange in any way when you saw him this morning?'

'No.'

'How about Scott?' She spoke to Leanne.

'No.'

Allie noticed she lowered her eyes, a slight blush appearing. She left that to recall later if necessary.

'Can I ask how it happened?' Leanne said then. 'I wasn't told.'

Allie sighed inwardly. She didn't really want to repeat it again in front of Nicky.

'I'll update you in a bit,' Gemma told her.

Allie smiled at her gratefully. 'Do any of you know who might have wanted to harm Kit in this way?'

Gemma and Leanne shook their heads emphatically. Nicky, however, didn't.

'Nicky?' Allie pressed. 'It's important that you tell us anything that is worrying you.'

'No. There's nothing. I don't know who would do that to him.'

Allie left them for now. She had enough details and wanted to get to The Wheatsheaf to speak to the landlord before she went into the station. While she waited for Perry to finish, she chatted things through with Rachel in the hall.

CHAPTER EIGHT

Four Months Ago

After a long and boring day, Kit was looking forward to a quiet night in. He hated his job and wished he could do something else. If only he wasn't so much in debt, then it would be easier to walk away. But he couldn't afford to lose a single penny.

When he opened the front door, his wife came running into his arms.

'Hey. What's up?' he asked, a worried expression on his face.

'I've had a visit from someone, and he threatened me,' Nicky sobbed. 'There was a knock on the door earlier. I just thought it was you, forgetting your key. When I answered it, I saw a man standing on the pavement.'

'Did you recognise him?'

'He was lanky and stick-thin, about thirty. He had short

dark hair and greasy skin and he was skittish. I'm sure I've seen him before.'

Kit stiffened. It sounded like Davy Lewis, one of the Seddon Estate's loan sharks.

'What did he say to you?' He pulled her away from him at arm's length and scanned her face. 'He didn't hurt you, did he?'

'Not really. I told him you were still at work, and he barged past me and into the kitchen before I could stop him. He told me you owe him money. Is that true?'

Kit's face drained of colour, and he closed his eyes momentarily. Why did this have to happen now?

'He said he'll be back soon,' Nicky continued, a tremor to her voice. 'That if you don't come up with the goods, he'll be after payment in different ways.'

'He said *what*?' Kit's blood boiled.

'He'll be back on Friday for this week's payment. And the loan's gone up another fifty quid because you're late. What do you owe him money for?'

'I borrowed a few hundred to pay some bills.'

'But we don't have anything spare. Why didn't you tell me you'd gone to him?'

'I ran into him one day, we got chatting.' Kit brushed a hand through his hair. 'I needed money, and it seemed an easier option. I can't keep scrounging from Scott. I still owe him.'

'He would have waited. He always does.' She scowled. 'You should have told me.'

'I'm sorry.' He sighed dramatically. 'What the hell does he think he's playing at, threatening us? The cheeky bastard.'

'He won't come back, will he? This is just his way of intimidating us?'

The look on her face made him feel like a right git.

'Of course not, babe.' Kit shook his head and then plonked a kiss on her lips. 'Why don't I finish off the tea and we can watch something on Netflix later? You go and sit in the front room.'

Kit closed the kitchen door after her, took off his jacket, and sat down at the table. He covered his face with his hands and then rubbed at his eyes.

Davy Lewis had no right to barge into their home and threaten Nicky. It had been awful to see her so scared, especially as it was his fault. He thought he'd be able to keep up with the payments, but last week had been a tough week. What was he going to do?

Kit was tired of never having any money. He and Nicky were barely covering the bills coming in each month, especially since Nicky had lost her job and was temping whenever she could get work.

But he'd been so much in debt from his first marriage that he was still paying off loans for things he didn't own anymore. One by one, they added up, meaning the money they had to run their home wasn't enough. There wasn't anything spare, although he was damned if they were giving up their nights out.

There was only one thing for it. He'd have to call Davy and lord it up, see if he could get more time.

'What the fuck are you doing coming round to my house?' Kit barked down the line when Davy finally answered his phone.

'Easy, tiger. It's not me who hasn't been paid what he owes.'

'I told you last week that you'd get double this Friday. There was no need to threaten my missus.'

'I think you'll find there's every reason. If you don't pay in cash, I'll make you pay *another* way. Let's just say it was an affable warning.'

'There was nothing friendly about it.' Kit paced the room. 'Leave her out of this. It's my debt.'

'Then you'd better pay up before it gets out of hand.'

The phone went dead before Kit had a chance to reply. He slammed his hand down on the table.

Nicky came rushing in. 'Are you okay?'

'Just angry,' he replied. 'He could have hurt you, Nick. And it would have been my fault.'

'Hey, I'm fine.' She smiled to reassure him. 'Maybe I over-reacted, and he wasn't that bad after all.'

He smiled back but he wasn't happy. There was no way he could get out of this mess. He couldn't ask anyone for a sub as he owed a bit to everyone here and there.

But no one threatened his family and got away with it. If it took violence to sort Davy out, then so be it. He was tired of being the nice guy all the time. And he knew Scott would help him out if necessary. That's what mates were for, after all.

Although he was far from being a good friend to Scott at the moment.

CHAPTER NINE

Sunday

Perry took Scott through to the kitchen where Ben and Aaron were sitting across from each other at the table. It had been clear to him on meeting them both that there was some animosity between them, so he hoped Scott appearing would be better for all concerned.

The room wasn't really big enough for four grown men. He waited in the doorway for them to comfort each other before pulling out a chair and urging Scott to do the same. He moved his knees when they bumped into Ben's.

'Would you like a drink? Tea? Coffee?' Aaron asked Scott.

'I don't think I can stomach one.'

Perry got out his notebook ready to take down the first account. It was always good to get things written up as soon as possible. That way, any discrepancies could be ironed out or picked up at a later date. For now, they needed to ascertain as quickly as possible which one of them saw Kit last. There were too many shifty glances passing between them for his liking.

All three men had aged well, Scott being the only one who had lost his hair completely. Perry imagined his piercing blue eyes would usually be hidden within laughter lines, but not today. The grief was clear on his face, the pallor of his skin a sickly grey.

Aaron's curly hair was tight to his head, his skin dark and eyes brown. His hands had a weathered look about them, clear to Perry that he was a grafter.

Ben seemed a tad more... polished, dare he say. His almost black hair was immaculate, and his aftershave a tad overpowering. His designer T-shirt was pristine, almost as if he was wearing it for the first time, whereas Scott seemed as if he'd thrown his on, having left it on the floor overnight.

Of the three, Ben was the only one who was clean-shaven. Perhaps the other two had rushed from the house after hearing news of their friend.

'I obviously need to speak to you about last night,' Perry began. 'We have to find out as much as possible about what happened to Kit.'

'It wasn't any of us, if that's what you're thinking,' Ben chimed in. 'Kit's a great guy.'

Perry held up a hand, ever playing the good cop. 'I just want a run-down of what happened, for now. What you did, who you spoke to, what time you left, that kind of thing.'

'We met around quarter to nine?' Aaron glanced at the others for confirmation, and they nodded. 'In The Wheatsheaf. We always do. We take the corner table and if it's not free, we wait for it to become empty, and then we pile around it and stay put.'

'And the night was a good one?' Perry glanced at them all. 'Plenty of laughter and beer?'

The atmosphere in the room changed as eyes flitted everywhere.

'I want to be honest,' Ben spoke first. 'There was an argument. Kit threw a punch at me, but I blocked it.'

'Can you elaborate?' Perry asked, making a note.

'He was talking some crap about me and Gemma. He said he didn't think I was good enough for her.'

Both Scott and Aaron were now gazing at the table. Perry recalled Allie had said something about Ben seeing Aaron's ex, so perhaps that was it. A bit of animosity.

'Anyway.' Ben shrugged. 'It led to me leaving.'

'What time was that?'

'Half past eleven. I was in the house for midnight.'

'And you two?' He looked first at Scott, then Aaron.

'A few minutes after Ben,' Scott replied. 'I was in at around midnight, too.'

'I stayed for about half an hour and then left,' Aaron said. 'The mood was gone after the argument.'

'And Kit was still in the pub?'

'He wouldn't leave. Said he wanted another pint.'

'Did anyone else give him grief in the pub?'

They shook their heads.

'What's Kit like as a person?'

'He was a good mate,' Scott said, affection in his voice clear. 'He would always have your back.'

'Yeah,' Aaron agreed. 'A reliable soul, always guaranteed to cheer you up. A joker, liked a laugh with us.' He turned away for a moment. 'I can't believe he's dead.'

Scott placed a reassuring hand on his shoulder. 'Me neither.'

'What about you, Ben?' Perry enquired. 'What was Kit like with you, when he wasn't in fighting spirit?'

'I didn't see him enough to know him that well, but we never had a problem with each other. Kit seemed quite affable. People took to him. I can't understand someone wanting to hurt him like this. It's just... shocking.'

Perry let a pause hang in the air, to see if anyone would volunteer anything. But no one did.

'So none of you knew of anything that was bothering him?' he added. 'Or someone?'

Shaking heads again, and still no talk coming forward.

Perry wasn't quite sure why, but he was getting nowhere. As this was an informal chat, until they'd checked out more details, he stood up to leave.

'I'll get someone to go through all this again with you. PC Joy – Rachel – will type it out, and then you can all sign it. If there's anything you need to tell us, something you remember later, you can let me, or DI Shenton know. Rachel will also be Nicky's point of call for the next few days while we make enquiries. We'll need you all to stay close by.'

'I work in Birmingham during the week,' Ben said. 'I'll call my manager and work from here tomorrow.'

Perry left them to it and rejoined Allie in the hall where he found her with Rachel. Two uniformed officers had arrived.

'Can you take down the statements with the men in the kitchen?' she asked one of them. 'And can you be the first point of contact by the front door?' she said to the other.

They both nodded and went ahead.

She turned to Perry.

'Let's chat in the car.'

Perry followed her out. He couldn't get a handle on the men, but gut feeling? He'd take a bet on them knowing more than they were letting on. People remembered most things said in the heat of the moment rather than conveniently forgetting them.

Could the blame lie with either one of them? Or even all of them?

. . .

Once Perry was gone, there was an audible sigh of relief from the three men in the kitchen. But Scott was furious with Ben. Even though he was finding it hard to keep it together after the news of his best friend's demise, he couldn't hold back his temper.

'Why didn't you tell the truth?' he whispered loudly. 'They're bound to find out sooner or later. The pub has security cameras!'

'It doesn't matter.' Ben shook his head. 'Sure, there was a punch thrown, but no one else will know why. It stays between us, right?'

'But you've misled the police. I can't see how that's going to come good. Why didn't you say it like it was? We still could have said nothing.'

'You had your opportunity to correct me. But you didn't, did you?'

Scott scowled at Ben and folded his arms.

Aaron rubbed at the back of his neck. 'I think we need to discuss what to say when they come back to us.'

'They won't,' Ben reiterated.

'What are you, a cop all of a sudden?' Aaron snapped.

'Well, I'm surprised you're not more concerned about how Kit was killed. And who did it.'

'I didn't follow him home and beat the crap out of him,' Scott hissed. 'I would never do that.'

'Neither would I!' Aaron cried.

'I know.' Ben raised a hand. 'So you need to have a good think about who wanted to hurt him. Do either of you know of anyone?'

Aaron shook his head.

Scott did the same. But then he thought about Davy Lewis. He'd seen Kit and Davy having words in the corridor earlier in the night, and they had history. But he kept that to himself.

'Perhaps you're right,' he conceded. 'The less the police know the better. Besides, the only person who will get into strife is me.'

'Relax.' Ben patted his shoulder. 'I've got your back. As long as we stick together, we'll be fine.'

Scott said nothing, hating the feel of Ben's hand on him. He shirked it off and went out into the garden. He didn't want to be near him right now. He didn't want to be near anyone.

He needed some time by himself to get his head around the loss of his friend.

CHAPTER TEN

Berrisford Street was busier now. Several people had come out to see why there was a police presence. A couple of men were washing their cars and shouting a conversation to each other. A child on a bike pedalled along the pavement.

'Anything interesting, Perry?' Allie asked once they were out of the Harpers' home.

'There was some sort of fracas in the pub. It might be something and nothing, but I'm sure that my lot were bending the truth. How about you?'

'They seem to be a close bunch of friends. Gemma and Aaron have been divorced for four years, Ben came on the scene a few months ago, and Kit has an ex-wife and daughter. Lots of secrets and grudges to iron out, perhaps?' She got out her keys and pressed the fob. 'Let's check out The Wheatsheaf.'

Allie caught up with Sam first on hands-free. Sam had been into the station first thing and then joined Frankie at the crime scene, sorting out house-to-house enquiries and questioning the witness who had found Kit Harper's body. So far, their findings had brought up nothing of significance. Allie advised her to continue with Frankie.

'I'm not sure Nicky is telling me everything either,' she went on to Perry. 'She was a bit quick with a couple of her answers, especially when I asked her if there was anyone who might have wanted to harm Kit.'

'You think she's holding back?'

'Possibly. I'll go and talk to her again, perhaps when she's on her own and we've seen the CCTV. That might tell us more. Jeez, is the air-con on? I'm melting here.' She pulled her blouse away from her skin.

'It's on!'

The Wheatsheaf was on the corner of Arnold Street and Johnson Road, attached to the end of another row of terraced houses. They went inside, the dingy air a relief from the heat. It was an old man's pub, dark wooden stools and tables with deep-red velvet seating, and beams on the walls that felt as if they were holding the place up. It seemed disturbingly dark after the light of the day.

The woman behind the bar was in her mid-fifties, with short, bleached hair and huge brown eyes. She welcomed them with a smile.

Allie and Perry introduced themselves. 'We're investigating a serious crime, and our victim was in here last night. Do you have any CCTV we can view, please?'

The woman nodded profusely. 'Yes, of course. Come through, and I'll show you where it is. Can I ask what happened?'

'I'm afraid a man has died.'

The woman's hand shot up to cover her mouth momentarily. 'Is it someone I'll know?'

Allie didn't really want to start the rumour mill just yet, but she knew the woman would guess when they asked for the timing of the recording.

'No formal identification has taken place yet, but we believe it is Kevin Harper. You might know him as Kit.'

'Oh, dear Lord.' The woman balked. 'It wasn't on the premises?'

Allie shook her head. 'You have nothing to worry about where that's concerned.'

The relief on the woman's face had Allie feeling guilty. She should have put her mind at rest straightaway.

'But it might have happened because of a fight that took place?' the woman went on. 'There was a bit of fuss around eleven-thirty. Is that what you're referring to?'

'Yes, that will be it. Do you know anything about it?'

'Not really. It was over before it had begun.'

They walked through a side door into a hallway, stairs leading to the first floor.

'Do you live here?' Allie asked.

'No, I work the bar, six nights a week and all day on Sundays. I'm staying here at the moment, though. I'm Helen Savage, by the way. The landlord, Nigel Barker, rents the pub from the brewery. Nigel's on holiday, hence me doing more hours than usual.' She pointed to a door. 'It's through here.'

Helen led them into a small office. She clicked a few buttons on a computer, fast forwarded the recording to the time they were after, and pointed to the screen.

'There you go. It seemed like a bit of something and nothing to me, but then again, I'm used to this sort of thing. Most arguments fizzle out rather than escalate. Do you think someone from here took it outside afterwards?'

'That's what we're trying to find out.' Allie stepped aside while Perry sat down. 'You know the group of men well, I imagine? They tell us they're regulars.'

'Yes, I've known most of them since their teens. Stopped them sneaking in on many occasions when they were under-age, threw them out on many, too. But once they were a legal

Her phone went. It was the sergeant on duty at the control room. 'DI Shenton.'

'Hey, Allie. It's Mike.'

'Hey. Don't tell me you drew the short straw this weekend, too. What's up?' She listened and then hung up with a grimace. 'We've got another suspicious death. A man's been found murdered in his bed, Jessop Place.'

'The Bennett Estate this time?' Perry raised his eyebrows. 'Must be something in the air.'

'Yeah, one case is hard enough to work, never mind two at the same time. We'll have to head there straightaway to see what's what.'

CHAPTER ELEVEN

Four Months Ago

Kit had received a text message a few minutes earlier that had him all fired up. Quickly, he splashed more aftershave on and jogged down the stairs.

'I'm just nipping to the shop,' he said to Nicky. 'We're out of milk. Want any chocolate?'

'A Twix, oh, and a packet of salt and vinegar crisps, please.'

He shook his head, not surprised when her eyes never left her phone. He could never understand why she was always messing with it. Talking to online friends, she'd tell him. It was a pity she wasn't more tuned in with what was happening in real life.

She had become so boring lately. All she talked about was having a baby, and yet there wasn't much possibility in that as the sex had dried up a lot recently. Talks of optimum times had put them off the spontaneity that he used to love.

The cold night had kept lots of people in, which would

work out to his advantage. Whistling, with a spring in his step, he crossed Victoria Road and took the cut-through to the shops, pulling in his jacket against the bitter wind.

Halfway along, he jumped as a shadow caught his eye.

'Bloody hell!' He clutched his chest. 'You scared the living daylights out of me.'

She laughed. 'Why? You knew I'd be here.'

'I sure did. I've been thinking about it all day.' He stood in front of her with his goofy schoolboy grin.

All it took was one step forward and they were in each other's arms, kissing as if they never wanted to stop. Her hands ran through his hair, making it stand on end. God, she was out of bounds but so fucking sexy.

When they finally drew apart, their smiles were shy but huge.

'We've crossed that line again,' she whispered.

Out of sight behind the bushes, the kids had walked a path through the grass as a shortcut to school. He took her hand and pulled her further back.

He was glad when she didn't stop him. Not even when his hands were all over her, her legs were wrapped around his waist, and he was fumbling with his belt. She held onto the railings as he pushed inside her.

It was over far too quickly. They stayed together as long as they could, then rearranged their clothes and went back out onto the path.

'I wish you didn't have to go,' Kit said. 'I wish we were going home together.'

She paused before replying. 'Me, too,' she said eventually. 'Although we said we'd never do this again.'

'We are so bad.' He kissed the tip of her nose and pointed towards the next road, the streetlamps illuminating their way. 'I need to go to the shop. I tipped the milk down the sink and said we'd run out.'

She giggled.

He leaned forward to kiss her again, one last taste of her before breaking away. 'I'll walk with you to the main road.'

Their chatter was comical small talk after they'd been so intimate. Kit was making her laugh while he told her about a shoplifter at work that day. He glanced at her surreptitiously. Why did she make him feel so good? And how could what they were doing be so wrong?

They came out on the street.

Kit stood with his hands in his pockets. 'When can I see you again?'

'I'll try to get away in a couple of days.'

'I could come to yours.'

'It's too risky.'

'It's worth it.'

She smiled. 'I'll text you.'

'You'd better.'

He watched her walk away, unsure if he was happy or disappointed in himself because of what they'd done.

Sleeping with her again wasn't part of the plan, but sometimes his every waking moment was spent thinking about her. She consumed him, despite the wrongness about what they were doing. How two families would be ruined if they were ever caught out. It still didn't stop him, nor her. It was as if it lit them both up to do it in secret.

Once out of the shop and back in the cut-through, Kit was still thinking of what had just happened. He didn't hear footsteps behind him. A fist cracked the side of his head, and he turned to see Davy Lewis's hand coming at him again. He ducked that one but copped for the next one, rendering him to his knees. Then Davy kicked him in the chest.

Kit managed to curl into a ball, the only way he knew to survive what was to come. Davy had already got the better of him.

'Don't ever threaten me,' Davy seethed, kicking out with every syllable. 'I want my money by Friday or there's more where this came from.' He gave one final kick before stepping over Kit and going on his way.

Kit groaned. He attempted to sit up, wondering if he might have broken a rib or two. Pain coursed through him and, even though he knew he deserved it, Davy had no right to hit out like that. He would have paid eventually.

He pushed himself to standing, thinking maybe he'd been lucky this time. But there was going to be a lot of bruising, and pain from it. Thankfully, the one punch to his face might go unnoticed, so at least he'd be able to go into work.

Why had he got involved with Davy? He knew he was a hard bastard, yet Kit thought he'd be able to handle the payments. Fifty quid for twelve weeks, paying back a five-hundred-pound debt with interest. But money had become tighter, and he'd failed to pay as agreed.

Now he'd taken his punishment to buy some more time. Hopefully, he could get some dosh soon. Put this matter to bed once and for all. Because Davy would do more damage next time.

Holding on to his side, he retrieved the shopping he'd dropped and made his way home, slowly but surely, dreading having to explain to Nicky. What on earth was he going to tell her? Perhaps he should say he'd been mugged. No, she wouldn't fall for that after Davy's visit last week.

Nicky was in the kitchen when he got home. Kit checked out his reflection in the hall mirror and groaned. His eye was already bruising, and swelling by the minute.

Nicky's jaw dropped when he went into her.

'Ohmigod!' she cried, rushing to him. 'Are you okay? What happened?'

'Davy Lewis caught up with me.'

'You can't let him get away with this.' She shook her head. 'You have to call the police.'

'I'm not doing that.' Kit winced, feeling his eye swelling. He hoped it wouldn't get any worse. 'At least I got the warning instead of him coming after you.'

'He said we could pay him more each Friday.' Nicky's face dropped. 'You did pay him, didn't you?'

Kit glanced away momentarily. 'I paid him half.'

'But you said—'

'It's all we could afford! There are bills going out this week. We have to pay those first.'

'I know, but... He's hurt you. He shouldn't be allowed to get away with it.'

'And you know as well as I do that no one grasses around here.'

Nicky folded her arms. 'We'll have to come up with a new plan. I hate to see you like this. I'll see if Mum will lend us some money to pay him off and we—'

'No,' Kit cut in. 'We can't ask her for more. She's given us enough.'

'But I don't want this to happen to you again. He's an animal!'

'Just leave it, okay? I feel bad enough about taking a beating.' He stormed out of the room.

Guilt washed over him, but he couldn't stand her sympathy after what he'd done before bumping into Davy. One minute he was having fun, and the next he was on the floor getting a good kicking. He still had the debt to clear and now he was taking it out on his wife. He was as much of a bastard as Davy Lewis.

He'd have to talk to Scott, see if there was anything on the cards he could do to earn some money. Just a one-off job to get Lewis off his back. Sure it was two-faced, and he didn't want to get into all that again, but what choice did he have?

CHAPTER TWELVE

Sunday

Allie parked the car in Jessop Place. It was one of the nice areas on the Bennett Estate, mainly due to it being a row of bungalows. Their occupants had to be over the age of sixty to have a tenancy. Some were clearly past their prime when they'd moved in and had already settled down to a quieter life. But, as people were living longer now, with less severe medical or physical problems, neighbours were getting to know each other and creating communities once more. Jessop Place was one such area. It was a lovely thing to see.

They donned forensic gear again, signed the log sheet, and went inside.

The bungalow was semi-detached, and from the off, Allie didn't have to be a detective to see it was occupied by a single male. She popped her head around the living room door, spying a black leather settee and dark wooden furniture. Soft furnishings in bland beiges and browns; not a plant or a flower arrangement in sight.

Drawers from a sideboard had been riffled through, one pulled out on the floor. Doors were open on the TV stand, old CD cases thrown on the carpet. They'd never be able to find out if anything had been stolen now they had a body.

It was stifling inside, too. Dave Barnett was in the kitchen, stretching his back as he stood next to Jordan who was taking shots.

'Not much for two in one day, Allie,' he admitted. 'I'd only just finished off on the cut-through when this came in. Christian is still there and will be with us shortly.'

Allie knew he wasn't complaining as such and grinned at him. 'You should get double time for a double job, Dave. What've you got for us?'

'Male in his sixties. Someone broke in through the back and suffocated him with a pillow. The place has been gone through, too.'

'He woke up while someone was here?'

'I don't think so. Having said that, your killer either found him on his back or turned him onto it before popping a pillow over his face, so it could have been pre-meditated. I reckon it would have been all over within a matter of minutes.'

'A break-in gone wrong?' Perry suggested.

'Come on through and I'll show you.'

They followed Dave into the bedroom. The victim was lying on his back, in Y-front underpants and a white vest, arms flopped to his sides.

The curtains were open in this room, the duvet on the floor where the paramedics must have thrown it off as they'd tried to resuscitate him.

Despite having had a pillow on his face, the man's mouth

was wide open, his eyes bulging. It was clear he had struggled before he'd given up.

'He'd obviously tried to flail out with his arms so the killer must be pretty strong to hold him down,' Perry noted.

'Not necessarily.' Allie moved closer. 'We'd all get rushes of adrenaline when we're doing things this physical. Perhaps psyched up, even more.'

'The only thing out of place was the rug that had been flipped over at the corner.' Dave pointed to it. 'Perhaps our killer's foot slipped while the victim was fighting for his life?'

'Not a nice way to go,' Allie stated. 'He wouldn't have suffered for long, but it would have been unbearable not to get your breath.' She opened the bedside cabinet drawer, peering inside. It was empty except for several chocolate bar wrappers.

Other than the corner of the rug being rolled up, there had been no signs of any foul play in the bedroom. In the kitchen, she looked for identification among the mess, this, too, being turned upside down. Cupboard doors had been opened, revealing barely any food on their shelves. A few tins and packets of rice, the odd box of cereal.

Two kitchen drawers had been emptied onto the table. There were several photos of their victim, a woman and four young children, perhaps going back to the millennium. Soon she found a pile of post addressed to a familiar name.

'Do you remember Jack Fletcher?' she said to Perry as she rejoined him.

'As in the Fletcher family who left Stoke years ago?' He turned to her.

'The very one. He's our man.'

'Well, that's a blast from the past. He's changed, a lot.'

'It has been a good number of years.'

Both Allie and Perry knew of Jack Fletcher. They'd met him several times out on the beat, as well as attending lots of

domestics. He hadn't been very nice to his family, in particular his wife.

'I haven't seen hair nor hide of him for well over a decade,'
she added. 'I thought he'd moved out of the city.'

'Clearly someone didn't like him coming home.' Perry
went back into the bedroom.

'Knock, knock.'

Allie turned. Christian stood in the doorway.

'The residents of Stoke have been busy overnight.' He
came into the room.

'Thank goodness most of them behave themselves.' Dave
chuckled. 'Mind, it does make for an interesting job.'

'Ma'am,' a uniformed officer shouted from outside.

Allie went out to him.

'A woman wants a word with you. Says she has some
information.'

Allie pulled down the hood of her suit and went towards
her. She looked to be in her seventies, silver hair braided in a
long plait that was flicked over her shoulder and reached
halfway down her chest. Her sundress was bright pink, and
her kitten heel slip-ons, that Allie found charming, almost
the same shade.

'Can I help you?' she asked.

'Are you in charge?'

'I am.'

'Only I'm not talking to anyone but the boss,' the woman
went on.

Allie ignored her remark. She never got annoyed when
someone thought she was the wrong sex or, sometimes, not
even old enough to do the job, even at her age. It was the
twenty-first century, though.

'What seems to be the problem, Mrs...?'

'Nancy Wilshaw. I saw him, last night. Jack. He was off
his tree, coming home singing at the top of his voice. I told

him to shut his trap and, well, I can't repeat what he said to me.'

Allie tried not to smirk. 'What time was this?'

'It was well past midnight. He's like this most weekends. It's a right pain getting back to sleep again. Has something happened to him?'

'We'll be giving details out shortly.' She turned to go back inside.

'Wait!' Nancy cried. 'I haven't finished. He was with someone last night. A man.'

That stopped Allie in her tracks. Had this been set up to look like someone had broken in rather than Jack Fletcher being attacked at home by a visitor?

'Can you describe him?' she asked. There was a lamp post directly outside the property. She hoped it had done its job and illuminated the man enough. 'Was he old, young? Colour of his skin? Clothes he was wearing?'

'I'd say thirty-ish, and white. Dark hair, wearing shorts and T-shirt.'

That sounded like a lot of men out last light, she mused. 'Had you seen him here before?'

'Not that I know of. But I couldn't see him that well.'

'I'll get a uniformed officer to come and take a statement from you, thanks.'

Allie went back inside to rejoin Perry. The bedroom was empty, giving her time with the deceased. It never failed to amaze her how a human could take the life of another, no matter what the circumstances.

Who had wanted to murder Jack Fletcher? How did he get to die in his own bed?

Or was it a burglary gone wrong? The back door had been forced, and the place done over, suggesting an intruder.

Allie took a deep breath once outside again, removing her gear and bagging it up for evidence. Once more, her shirt was stuck to her back. She should have brought a spare with her. At least she had one in her locker at the station to change into later.

She glanced around. There was quite the crowd gathering, on doorsteps, a few people sitting on the wall opposite. But it all seemed calm. Word would get out soon, more people would come, and Stoke would hear about another person's life being taken before its time.

All she and the team had to do was work out who had done this to him. Even if it was a coincidence, Jack Fletcher could have a lot of enemies. Kit Harper might have, too.

Every one of them would need looking into.

CHAPTER THIRTEEN

Frankie met DC Sam Markham in The Wheatsheaf car park. The area was small, only two more cars beside their own able to fit in. He assumed most punters left theirs on the road outside – hopefully most of them arrived on foot so as not to drink drive.

'What I'd give for a pint of something cool right now,' he said to her. 'It's too hot for murder.'

Sam laughed. 'When has the weather ever stopped anyone committing a crime? It takes all sorts, and they're never bothered about any repercussions.'

'I know, but they could be more considerate. I was hoping for a weekend off.'

'Me, too.' Sam sighed. 'Craig was a bit pissed off this morning.'

'Lyla was, too, and I'd been in her good books because we had the weekend to ourselves. Ben has stayed over at her mum and dad's.'

'Ouch. You'll have to make it up to her.'

'I guess we both will.'

'I don't have to charm Lyla.' She smirked.

Frankie laughed. 'You know what I mean.'

Inside, they introduced themselves to Helen Savage, who pointed out who had been here the night before. There were a group of men, a couple, and a few single men who were outside sitting on the picnic benches.

'Let's tackle the ones inside first,' Frankie suggested. 'I bag the old blokes by the bar.'

'I'll take the two in the corner.' Sam nodded in their direction.

Frankie stepped over to join the three men who were perched on bar stools. They had a pint apiece, each pushing seventy at a guess, and wearing the most outrageous shorts and coloured T-shirts.

He flashed his warrant card along with a big smile. 'Hi, gentleman. Mind if I ask you a few questions about last night?'

'Depends what time you're referring to, son. I was rat-arsed by half past nine.'

They all laughed, and Frankie joined in.

'The name's Bob.' The man who had spoken offered a hand to Frankie. 'This is Trevor and Steve. What is it you'd like to know?'

'There was a fight in here, about eleven thirty.'

Bob huffed. 'Call that a fight? It was just lads having a barney. There was no blood.'

Frankie liked Bob. His tone assured him he was joking, rather than being obnoxious.

'You mean the lads who sat over there?' Trevor was pointing to the far corner.

Frankie looked to where he'd said, then back again. 'Yeah, that'll be them. We heard one or two punches were thrown.'

'Ach, it was over before it began. We saw it, watched for a second or two, and were then straight back to our pints. There was nothing to it.'

'You didn't happen to hear them saying anything?'

Bob took a sip of his pint. 'Not a word. It was busy. You could hardly hear anything over the band. Do you like Bruce Springsteen?'

Frankie shrugged. 'Can't say I listen to him much.'

'Young whippersnappers,' Terry spoke out. 'They don't make music like they used to. It's all just noise nowadays.'

'I'll take your word for it.' Frankie rolled his eyes in jest and got out a contact card. He popped it on the bar between them. 'Thanks, fellas. A pleasure to meet you. I'll let you get on with your pints, but if you recall anything, do let me know. Have a good day.'

Spotting Sam deep in conversation with the young couple, he made his way outside.

Sam had sidled over to the man and woman who were sitting in the corner where the fight had taken place. They were in their thirties, their table laid out for a meal. They seemed fresh, as if they'd not long got up. The woman was wearing a pink strappy dress, the man a short-sleeved white shirt, open at the neck, and beige shorts.

'Hi there. Hope I'm not interrupting your Sunday lunch,' Sam said, flashing her warrant card. 'Can I join you for a few minutes? Nothing to worry about.'

'Yes, of course.' The woman gestured for her to sit across from them.

'Helen, from behind the bar, said you were in here last night?'

'Yes, we only live around the corner, in Sampson Street.'

'Do you mind if I take your names?'

'Chris Doyle and Melissa Frampton.'

Sam noted them down and then smiled. 'There was an

incident, and we're looking into a suspicious death to figure out if they are connected.'

Melissa's hand shot to her chest. 'Oh dear. Do we know the victim?'

'We can't divulge details yet. But we're interested in a particular group of men. Apparently, a fight broke out at about eleven-thirty, and I wondered if you saw or heard anything?'

'Oh, that lot.' Chris nodded. 'Wait, is it one of them?'

'I'm afraid so. You were saying?' Sam moved him on swiftly.

'I was coming back from the bar. They nearly knocked the drinks out of my hand. One of them hit out at another. They'd been having a good night until then.'

'Did you see who hit who?'

'No, sorry.'

'Did you hear anything said?'

They shook their heads.

'It was too noisy in here,' Melissa said. 'Saturdays are always lively.'

'Wait, I did hear a snippet, come to think of it,' Chris added. 'I was in the men's toilets. Kit was talking to Scott.'

'You know them all?'

'From here, yes. Kit was saying something about being stitched up by Ben. He said he didn't trust him.'

Sam noted that down, her interest piqued. 'Anything else?'

'No, sorry. That's all I remember. I'd had a lot to drink by then.'

'It's his birthday today,' Melissa explained. 'We're not always in here.'

'I wish I could join you, to be fair.' Sam smiled. 'Although, I don't think I could stomach a beef dinner. Too hot.'

'Neither can we. Sandwiches and a bowl of chips today.'

'Well, I'll leave you to it. Thanks for your time.' Sam stood up. 'Happy birthday. Enjoy the rest of your day.'

She chatted to a few more people in the bar before joining Frankie outside in the beer garden. Spying him talking to someone, she rang Allie to update her on things.

''We're not getting anything here,' she said. 'People remembered them, saw a punch thrown, but don't know why they were arguing.'

'Okay. Can you tell Frankie to come to Jessop Place, and then you head back to the office to continue setting things up, please? It might be a while before we can get there now.'

'On it, boss.'

Frankie came over to her when he'd finished. She relayed what Allie had said and told him of the other suspicious death.

'Have you ever worked two cases before?' he asked.

'No, but I suppose it's only like dealing with a lot of kills from one person. It's going to be challenging, but we'll crack it.'

'I'm sure we will,' he agreed. As ever he was confident that someone would slip up, or they'd be given some vital piece of information to help them along.

CHAPTER FOURTEEN

Four Months Ago

Kit was dreading catching up with Scott after his beating. He'd told Nicky not to mention it to Leanne, but now the bruising was more prominent on his face, he couldn't keep it from prying eyes. Luckily, his manager at work had been okay about it. He'd told him he'd tripped down the stairs, catching the wall at the bottom, and he'd believed him.

He still hadn't got the money to pay Davy, nor was he sure he could get it in time to stop another beating. The money would go up if he didn't pay a token, too.

Trust him to bump into Davy at the shops one night when he was at a low point. If he hadn't seen him then, he wouldn't have taken a loan. But Davy had got chatting to him and before he knew it, Kit had been telling him his troubles. Davy offered him a way out, and it had been too tempting to refuse.

That was the thing with loan sharks. They preyed on you,

making you think they were the good guys, then when they had you in their claws, pow. They would get you at your lowest and make things far worse than you'd ever imagined. And he had fallen for it, thinking he could easily pay Davy back.

Scott picked him up on the way to the gym. Kit could have done without it today, but there was no way he could put him off forever. He'd missed two sessions already.

Scott's eyes widened as soon as he spotted Kit's face.

He whistled. 'That's some bruiser you have there. What happened?'

'Had a run-in with Davy Lewis.' Kit held his head down momentarily, knowing the grilling he was going to receive. He'd thought about lying to Scott, too, but knew he'd see right through it.

'For fuck's sake.' Scott shook his head. 'You took money from him, didn't you?'

'I was desperate! You know we've fallen behind when Nicky lost her job. I had bills to pay.'

'You could have come to me. I would have helped and—'

'I can't keep borrowing from you. I'll never pay it back, and it gets to me. You're my mucker.'

'I'll always loan you. You know that.'

'Can we just get going?' Kit pointed to the road ahead. It was bad enough being broke, without having a mate who could always afford to sub him.

'Okay, okay.' Scott started the engine and drew away from the kerb. 'You know if you want to make some money, I can always—'

'I've thought about it and it's a no,' Kit cut him short, knowing what he was about to say. He'd heard it so many times before.

'You don't have to do it forever. Just do one or two jobs.'

For the past two years, as well as collecting scrap metal,

Scott had been running a county line to Derby every other week for Kenny Webb. He'd often told Kit that the boys he had working for him were good lads. They did their jobs and, in turn, he got treated well by Kenny, the next one in the chain.

Kit had watched from the sidelines, envious when Scott was flashing the cash. But as long as the money kept coming in and the police weren't pounding down their door, Scott was always game.

'What would Leanne do if she found out what you were up to?' he queried.

'She'd glue my balls to the wall.'

'So why do it? You could face time if you're caught.'

'They'd catch the young ones first.'

'They'll land you in it.'

'No, they won't.'

Kit glanced over at Scott. He really believed what he'd said. Then again, he had been doing this kind of thing for years now and had never so much as received a caution from the cops.

'What are you going to do about Davy?' Scott interrupted his thoughts as he pulled into the gym car park.

Kit shrugged. 'I don't know.'

'Do you have *any* money that you can buy yourself some time with?'

'You know I don't.'

'How much do you need?'

Kit couldn't bring himself to admit how much he'd borrowed. And he knew Davy would want more if he continued to miss payments. He should never have gone to him. He should have stuck with his friend.

'How much?' Scott persisted.

He sighed in resignation. 'Seven hundred quid.'

'When do you need it by?'

Kit noticed he hadn't batted an eye at the amount. 'This Friday.'

Scott reached for his bag off the back seat. 'Don't worry, then. I'll sort it.'

Kit sniggered. It was easy for him to say that. Because even though Davy would be out of his hair, he'd still have to pay Scott back. He shook his head.

'I can't take your money, not again.'

'The way I see it, you don't really have a choice.'

Kit knew he was right. He was well and truly screwed if he didn't pay the money he owed.

'I'll get some for this Friday and settle up with the remainder on the next,' Scott went on. 'I'll come with you when you pay Davy, too, make sure he knows he's getting full and final payment soon.'

Despite his embarrassment, Kit knew when he was on to a good thing. 'Cheers, mate. I owe you one – again.'

CHAPTER FIFTEEN

Sunday

Nicky Harper was taking a breather in the kitchen. She'd asked to be alone. So many people to deal with was making her head spin.

She still couldn't take in what had happened. Sure, she knew it was true, she just didn't want to believe it.

She wanted Kit to walk through the front door, a little worse for wear but okay.

She wanted him to have been so leathered that he'd fallen in someone's hedge, passed out, and spent the night asleep there.

She wanted it all to be a mistake. Because she wasn't sure what she was going to do without him.

Nicky had loved Kit since she was a teenager, despite only getting together with him a few years ago. He'd been five months older than her. They'd been married nearly two years now, but half of that had been spent disagreeing about having a child. Nicky had wanted to start a family straight away, but Kit hadn't been that keen. He already had his daughter, Danielle.

He and his ex, Brooke, had split up after being turfed out of their home for rent arrears when Danielle was eleven. There were other monies owed, too, that had landed on his doorstep because he'd taken them out in just his name. Even now, the loan companies wanted more and more money from them to pay off what he owed.

It was a never-ending circle, and it meant their home was always the last priority. Now she wanted to hate him for it and wondered if she would in time. It just wasn't fair.

She stepped across the floor covering that desperately needed replacing and opened the door below the sink unit, being careful as it was loose at the hinge and often fell off.

There were so many mugs that needed washing. She squirted washing-up liquid into the bowl, no dishwasher for her. Even if they could afford it, there was no room in their minute kitchen.

Running the hot water, she sank her hands into it, almost wanting to inflict pain on herself. She felt numb, like her life was stuck in some sort of time warp, Groundhog Day. How had it come to this?

Scrubbing at the dishes didn't make her feel any better either. She blew air on her face, puffing under her fringe that was almost in her eyes, and gazed out of the window at the tiny garden area. There was a lawn, a few slabs for a table, and a fence that next door peered over whenever they sat outside.

Her eyes welled with tears, knowing she would never sip a glass of wine out there, with Kit by her side.

'Nicky, Carmen is ringing.' Leanne came into the room with her phone. 'Would you like me to tell her you'll call her later?'

Carmen was another friend of Nicky's.

'No, I'll speak to her now.' She wiped her hands on a tea towel. A moment later, the phone was passed to her.

'Nicky, I'm so sorry. I can't believe it. This is terrible news.' Carmen's voice had a tremor to it. 'How are you coping?'

'I'm not really.' Nicky ran a finger up and down the worktop as she stared out on the garden again. The afternoon was shaping up to be as pleasant as the morning, the sun high in a cloudless sky. Not that she'd see much of it in here.

Not that Kit would ever see a day like this again. She squeezed her eyes closed to stop the tears.

'I'm in Manchester now,' Carmen said. 'Typical Jeff wanted some clothes for the golf tournament. But I can be home for about six. I'll come straight to you.'

'Thanks.'

There was a pause down the line. 'I'm so sorry, Nick. I just don't know what else to say.'

They ended the call, and Nicky went upstairs to tidy herself up. But all it did was depress her more. The bathroom was a hideous mink colour that had been in for years before she'd arrived, and although it was always clean, it looked considerably mucky. The tiles were dirty with years' old grout. It was the only bathroom in the house. They didn't even have a downstairs loo.

She dropped to the floor, annoyed that her mind was being flooded with inconsequential things. Material items didn't mean anything if you hadn't got somebody to love.

She let out a huge sob. What was she going to do without Kit? She couldn't comprehend a life on her own.

There was a knock on the door.

'Nicky, are you okay?'

It was Gemma.

'I'm hunky-dory. How do you think I'm feeling?'

'Can I come in?'

'Leave me alone.'

The handle went down on the door.

'I said leave me alone!'

'I'm not going anywhere.' Gemma came in and sat next to her. 'You can scream and shout and swear and fling things around, but I'm here to stay.'

Nicky crumpled then and let Gemma embrace her.

'I'm...' She couldn't bring herself to say the words so changed the subject quickly. 'Why did they leave him to walk home alone? It was their fault. He was too drunk to defend himself.'

'You don't know that.'

'He was alone! If he'd been with Scott or Aaron, he would have been fine. They left him.'

'Oh, Nicky.' Gemma started to cry, too.

'Kit's gone.' She broke down again. 'What am I going to do without him?'

'You have me, and Leanne, and Carmen. We'll take care of you.'

'It's not the same and you know it.'

'I do, but I don't know what else to say.'

Nicky held onto her as she let it all out. She was so lucky to have such good friends. She had a feeling she would need them all over the next few days, weeks, months even. Because this was one thing she couldn't face alone.

And they had lost Kit too. She was now a widow, but there would be a Kit-shaped hole in all their lives.

CHAPTER SIXTEEN

It was half past two when Allie got back to Nicky's house. She was hoping to talk to Leanne and Gemma as well.

'The men have gone, but the women stayed,' Rachel informed her as she let her in. 'They're in the living room with Nicky.'

Allie liked Rachel. She was a really good family liaison officer and had worked with her on a case a few months ago. She'd been a great asset to the team, and she was glad she'd been allocated to this case, too. Allocating family liaison officers was a central role, one she had no control over, but she would definitely put in a good word to ensure she might get Rachel again in the future.

'How is Nicky?' she asked in a hushed voice.

'Not good. I'm glad she's not on her own. It seems they're a great comfort to her.'

Allie went into the living room, her heart almost breaking at the expectancy written on Nicky's face.

'You have news?' the younger woman queried.

'It's far too early to tell yet, I'm afraid.' Allie sat across from them. 'I wanted to ask you a few more questions, if that's okay?'

Nicky nodded.

'Do any of you know if there was any animosity between Scott and Kit?'

'No,' Nicky said. 'Why?'

'It seems that they were arguing last night. Earlier, Ben told us that Kit had tried to hit him over something he'd said about you, Gemma.'

'Me?' Gemma frowned.

'Kit had said Ben wasn't good enough for you. Do you know what he meant by that?'

'That's probably to do with him protecting Aaron.' Gemma gave a half-smile. 'Kit, Scott, and Aaron had their noses put out of joint when I started dating Ben. And Ben could never understand how close we all are as friends at times. He had trouble fitting in at first, especially with Aaron being my ex and still hanging around with Kit and Scott, but it was fine in the end. At least, I thought it was.'

'We've just reviewed the CCTV at The Wheatsheaf, and the fight seems to be between Kit and Scott.'

'You think it was Scott who did this to Kit?' Leanne whispered.

'That's not what I'm saying.' Allie reassured. 'I'm trying to understand why they were having words. It was only for a couple of minutes, but they weren't happy about something. I wondered if you, any of you, had anything else to add?'

'I don't know,' Nicky replied.

Allie studied Leanne and Gemma in turn.

They both shook their heads.

'Can I ask you how Kit knows Davy Lewis?'

A flash of fear crossed Nicky's face, but she righted it quickly.

'I wasn't sure if it was important, that's why I didn't say

anything earlier,' she said. 'Kit borrowed some money from Davy. He came to the house threatening me because Kit hadn't paid him back in time.'

Allie glanced up from the notes she was writing. That could be an interesting development.

'When was this?'

'A while ago now. Three or four months perhaps. I've only just thought about it because it seemed to have blown over.'

'Have you seen him since?'

'No, Kit said it was all sorted. But they didn't like each other, that was for sure. Do you think it might have been him?'

'We'll look into everything, and everyone, Nicky,' Allie reassured her. 'Do you know why Kit had been drinking so heavily? Apparently, he'd drunk a lot during the evening and had sat alone after the other men had gone and drunk a further two pints.'

'That doesn't sound like Kit.' Leanne shook her head. 'He's usually very sociable.'

'I expect the argument spoiled the mood,' Gemma remarked.

'What was he like before he went out?' Allie posed the question to Nicky.

Nicky lowered her eyes momentarily. 'We'd been arguing,' she admitted. 'Couple stuff, you know.'

'It might help if you elaborate.' Allie raised a hand. 'I don't want intimate details. Just a few facts.'

'We're struggling to cope after I lost my job, that's all. I was upset about not being able to find anything else yet. Neither of us were in a good frame of mind last night. Now, I feel that it's my fault because if he hadn't got as drunk, he might never have walked home alone and—'

'Please don't torture yourself about "if onlys",' Allie soothed. 'Life is anything but predictable.'

'So you don't think the argument in The Wheatsheaf was anything to do with what happened to Kit?' Gemma asked.

'We're looking into every eventuality at the moment. I promise we won't stop until we have done everything we can. We'll be holding a press briefing soon when we will give out Kit's name and appeal for witnesses. It was a warm night. Lots of people would have been taking advantage of that, so he might have been spotted. We're also checking CCTV around the streets where he walked.' She stopped a moment for all that to sink in. 'We need someone to identify Kit's body. It may be later this evening, most likely first thing in the morning. Would you be able to do that?'

Nicky nodded fervently. 'I want to see him.'

'We can come with you, if you like?' Gemma said.

Leanne nodded her reply.

'Thanks,' Nicky said. 'I'd like that.'

'Rachel can drive you there when it's time,' Allie finished.

She said her goodbyes, ensuring lots of reassurance, and assistance if required, and then left.

Back in her car, she thought through the conversation, recalling in particular what had been said about Davy Lewis. Davy was known to her, for many years, doing a bit of this and that. Seldom did his name come up without him being in trouble for something or other.

He'd been inside twice if her memory served her right. The last time she'd nicked him was for a fight where he'd beaten the landlord of The Ruby Stone pub with a pool cue because he'd been refused another pint.

She decided he'd be worth talking to later. First, she needed to touch base with her team and DCI Jenny Brindley.

CHAPTER SEVENTEEN

Four Months Ago

Kit took a quick look around before knocking on the door. He wasn't sure why. Even if anyone did see him, he visited the house so regularly that no one would bat an eyelid. But even so, he didn't want a nosy neighbour getting him into trouble. Best to be forearmed if someone had spotted him.

It was half past two. He'd finished work early because she was off for the afternoon, faking a doctor's appointment so he could see her.

She answered the door and dragged him inside quickly. Her smile warmed his heart, and as soon as they were in the kitchen, his arms were around her, his lips finding hers.

There was something exciting about having sex in someone else's home. As well as the fear of being caught, which no doubt heightened the senses, it felt indulgent and risky all mingled into one. It made it quick, fast and furious, but equally satisfying.

Kit's hands were all over her. Her face displayed lust and exhilaration. She was doing this for him, no one else. Just him. And it felt so good. Not at all wrong, just fantastic.

It was over way too soon, but they'd both got what they were after. Afterwards they adjusted their clothes and she grinned. He returned it, a flush across his face, too.

'Just like old times.' He pulled her near again. 'I wish it didn't have to be so quick, but it was worth it. God, I've missed you.'

They kissed again, this time slow and lingering. They'd learned over the years their affair had been on and off, to take their chances with the sex first. It wouldn't do for either of them to be caught out.

She grabbed two bottles of lager from the fridge, and they sat down at the kitchen table. Just like two people in a relationship, they began to tell each other about their day.

Sometimes he didn't want to speak at all. He wanted to stare at her face, every line he'd seen evolve since they'd first met. Back then, he'd been a cheeky chap with homemade tattoos, which he'd since had covered with new designs, and a penchant for fast cars he didn't have the money for. He still couldn't afford them, but he didn't want to think about that.

The first time they'd got together, when he was married to Brooke, he'd told her he loved the thrill of the chase. Made out he'd been a player but then he'd realised that he'd loved her from the sidelines for years. And no matter how many times they ended the affair, it was hard to resist starting it up again.

'You're like a drug.' Kit interlinked his fingers with hers. 'I think I've cracked the addiction and given you up, but one look from you and I'm off the rails.'

She nodded. 'We said we'd never do this again after nearly getting caught the last time.'

Kit grimaced. They'd been at a restaurant. It wasn't often

they went out for a meal in case they were seen, but they'd both had an afternoon off and driven to Buxton for a treat. He'd chosen a small country pub off the beaten track where they could be themselves without fear of being seen.

But they'd bumped into someone Kit knew, an old friend of his father's. Luckily, he hadn't met Nicky, so he introduced her as his wife instead. It had been close enough for them both to think of what they would lose if their secret ever came out.

It still hadn't stopped them, though.

She checked her watch and sighed. 'I suppose you'd better go. Although I wish you could stay longer.'

'Me, too. I don't want to go home just yet. If Nicky is—'

She leaned forward and put a finger to his lips. 'No mention of her name when we're together,' she admonished. 'We agreed.'

He said nothing for a moment and then nodded before getting to his feet. He held out a hand to help her up. 'Come on. Another snog, and I'll be on my way.'

She slapped his backside, then followed him into the hall-way. His lips found hers one more time, and he didn't want to let her go.

Finally, they broke apart.

'You make me feel so horny.'

She laughed. 'Well, you'll have to save it until next time.'

'When will that be?' he asked. It was the same question every time they parted, and he couldn't give a toss if it made him seem desperate. He *was* – frantic to be with her for the rest of his life. To wake up next to her every morning, not to only enjoy her whenever she could fit him in. It wasn't enough. It hadn't been for a long time now.

'I'll message you,' she said.

'You'd better.' He grinned.

Outside, he strode down the drive. Even with his

thoughts of being with her all the time, there was another fine line between taking a lover and then wanting them to go once the deed had been done. He hated how she pushed him out, but equally he knew he had to leave. They were always on borrowed time.

Yet, even as he tried to convince himself it was only sex, it was much more than that now. He only hoped she felt the same way.

CHAPTER EIGHTEEN

Sunday

Once he'd seen everything was under control at the crime scene, Perry went next door to the bungalow which was joined to Jack Fletcher's home. The door was opened, and an elderly man peered at him.

'DS Wright,' he said, holding up his warrant card. 'I was wondering if I could have a word with you about your neighbour. I believe you rang for the emergency services?'

'Yes, of course, lad. Come on through.'

Perry stepped inside and wiped his feet, wary of the pale carpet he was treading on.

'I'd fetched him a paper, you see. I always leave it half in and half out of the letterbox, so he doesn't have to bend down to get it. When I went out at lunchtime, I noticed it was still there.'

The man pointed towards a door, and Perry followed him into the living room.

'That's when I checked,' he continued. 'I saw the back door was ajar, and the glass in the windowpane was broken, and found him in his bedroom. It gave me a shock when I saw him, I can tell you. I'm Joe Meredith, by the way, and this is my wife, Flo.'

'Pleased to meet you,' Perry greeted the woman sitting on the settee.

The room was welcoming, a fan on full, blasting air straight at them.

Joe and Flo looked to be in their eighties. She had curled white hair and was wearing a floral summer dress. Her feet were bare, swollen, perhaps from the heat, with bright-pink painted toenails.

Joe wiped at his brow with a handkerchief. His shirt was open at the neck, and he seemed uncomfortable in long trousers. His wiry hair was sticking up. Perry gazed at it wistfully. Despite his comments to the contrary, he'd loved to have kept a full head of his own.

Flo smiled at him. 'Sit yourself down, lad.'

Perry smiled back, guessing that the couple had been married since their teens, would have wonderful children and grandchildren, and most probably die within weeks of each other, the one left behind of a broken heart. They were like two peas in a pod. It was lovely to see.

Joe sat beside Flo. 'He's dead, isn't he?'

'Yes, I'm sorry,' Perry replied. 'Did you know him well?'

'He's lived there about two years, kept himself to himself, if I'm honest. He was never one for socialising with the neighbours.'

'He wasn't any trouble, though.' Flo put her point forward. 'He was quiet, really.'

'Another neighbour says he often came home drunk and made a lot of noise?'

'Oh, that will be Nosy Nancy.' Flo giggled. 'I'm right, aren't I? I bet she's having a field day.'

Perry smiled. He'd had worst days when talking to neighbours.

'It wasn't very nice seeing him like that,' Joe added. 'I told Flo he looked as if he'd been in pain. I can't imagine what it must be like to die all alone.' He patted her hand, and she gave him a kind smile. 'Was it a heart attack, because someone had broken in, perhaps?'

'I'm afraid Jack has been murdered.'

'Murdered?' Flo glanced at Joe. 'By the burglar?'

'We're not certain of that yet.' Perry dodged the question. 'We have a forensic team working to establish that right now. It's why I'm here, to see if I can find out anything that will help with the inquiry.'

'Did you ever go into his home?'

'No, that was the first time. Oh, wait, I went into his kitchen once when he had a problem with the electric meter. It was soon sorted. I used to be a sparkie, you see.'

'And a fine electrician you were.' Flo's voice was full of pride.

'I was going to ask if you could see if anything was missing, but not to worry,' Perry said.

'Ah, sorry. I only saw the kitchen and his bedroom before scarpering, so I wouldn't know. Was the front room a mess, too?'

'Pretty much. I wonder, did you hear anything last night? I assume your windows would have been open?'

'Not in a bungalow. Flo wouldn't sleep. We keep a fan on instead.'

'Anyone could climb in while we're asleep.' Flo was all of a dither as she looked at him for reassurance. 'You don't think someone will come here, after us?'

Perry held up his hand. 'I'm sure everything will be fine.

Please don't worry. There will be a huge police presence over the coming days. Can I ask you not to say anything, though, until his next of kin have been informed, please?'

'Of course.'

'Do you know any of his relatives?'

'Never seen him have a visitor.' Joe glanced at Flo. 'Have we?'

Flo shook her head. 'Not that I can recall. He was a bit of a loner. It's so sad. I can't believe someone would want to harm him.'

Perry stood up. 'Thanks for your time. I'll leave you to it now, but if you remember anything that you think could help us, please tell one of the officers outside. I'll get someone to take a statement from you later. I don't want to disturb you too much. I know it must be such a shock to you both.'

'We won't be sitting out in the garden nosing like Nancy, that's for sure. It's too close for comfort.' Joe chuckled, then his face crumpled. 'Sorry, shouldn't joke at a time like this. It isn't fair.'

'I'm certain Jack wouldn't want you being all maudlin,' Perry humoured him.

He left them behind with a chuckle of his own. Joe and Flo, you couldn't make it up. But what a lovely couple. Despite joking about Dave and Christian earlier, he'd never met anyone who finished off each other's sentences so much.

Outside, the heat had built up as much as the crowd. They were noisy too, the sunny afternoon giving them an added incentive to stick around and gawp.

He needed to get these people out of here.

'Can you move the cordon further back, please?' he told an officer as a car pulled up beside him. It was Frankie.

'Two in one day, Sarge,' Frankie said, passing him a bottle of water. 'It's going to be a late one.'

Perry took the drink with thanks, updated him, and

pointed to the street. 'Let's start house-to-house. I'm particularly interested in anyone who saw Jack coming home with a man.'

'A partner perhaps?'

'No one's given me that impression, but yes, that's possible.'

'So it might not be a break-in gone wrong?'

'It may have been set up to look that way. We only have one witness's word for it, though, so I need to find an image of him. Did Sam go back to the station?'

Frankie nodded.

'I'll call her, get her to use her expertise to track down any camera footage she can find.'

CHAPTER NINETEEN

Leanne sat in the passenger seat of the car as Scott drove them home, her head resting on the window. It still didn't seem real that Kit had gone. She'd only seen him and Nicky the other day. His life couldn't be over just like that.

The streets were full of people out walking in the sun, having fun. When they passed the park, envy consumed her to see everyone's happiness. Their lives hadn't been ruined by a bereavement.

A murder.

'I'll give Amy another call when we get home, tell her she can come back. I'm sure my dad will probably drop her off.'

Scott nodded, but she could tell he wasn't really listening.

'Is this to do with Kenny Webb?' she asked him when her mind wouldn't silence the thought.

'It's nothing to do with work.'

His words were clipped, which annoyed her.

'Well, I can't see why he'd want to lash out at Ben. Are you sure you didn't hear what he said to Kit?'

Scott shook his head.

'Have you asked him?'

'He says he can't remember. We were all drunk.'

Leanne turned to stare at him, but he kept his eyes on the road. She wasn't sure if it was to avoid her guessing he was lying. Because she knew he was. She could read him like a book, knew that expression. Besides, it hadn't been Ben who Kit had hit out at.

'I'll have a word with him about it when we next see him,' she said. 'If there is a next time. Yesterday, Gemma told me she wanted to end things with him.'

'Did she say why?'

'Only that he'd become too intense, possessive she said specifically. She hasn't been happy with him for a while.'

'So that could be why he was so angry last night?' Scott said it almost as if it was something for him to think about.

'I don't know,' she replied. 'Maybe he sensed what was coming. One thing that's puzzling me, why didn't you stop Kit from drinking so much?' She didn't tell him the detective had queried the same thing, but it had made her think about it since.

'Because it was a balmy night, and I didn't want to stop drinking either.'

'That's not a good enough excuse.'

'There isn't an excuse needed.'

Again, he kept his eyes on the road.

Finally, they were home. In the kitchen, Scott reached for a bottle of whisky and two glasses. He poured large measures into each and passed one to her. She almost knocked it back in one go, the urgency to forget everything so overpowering.

He turned back to her, tears in his eyes. 'I can't believe he's dead, Lee.'

Leanne went to him and took him in her arms while they both cried. 'I can't believe it either,' she said between sobs. 'We're all going to miss him so much.' Then she pulled away from him. 'Nicky mentioned something about Davy Lewis bothering them.'

Scott was wiping at his eyes. 'Did she say when?'

'A few months ago. She said Kit borrowed some money, and when he didn't keep up with the payments, Davy came after Nicky. Did you know about it?'

'Yeah, but it was sorted, back then. Kit didn't owe anything after that, and I haven't seen Davy in a long time. Can't say I want to either. He's a gormless prick. I'm going to sit in the garden. You coming?'

She didn't like how he'd changed the subject but ignored it. 'No, I have a headache. I'm going to lie down for a while. I'll be going back to see Nicky soon. You don't have to come, but I want to be there as much as I can.'

'You can rest on the sun lounger for half an hour, surely?' He reached for her hand. 'Come on.'

Once they were seated in the garden, Leanne kept her sunglasses on. In the distance, cries of children playing could be heard, faint music coming from a couple of houses down. They were lucky to live in a nice street of semi-detached homes and to have an extra-large garden. She'd have hated to be stuck in Nicky's little house.

It was all down to Scott. Even though his scrap metal business had been doing well, his change of job to the manager of Car Wash City had suited him, and the pay had been better, less sporadic. It would provide them with a few luxuries, nothing special, but knowing they didn't have to worry about money was a bonus.

Leanne's parents had never been well off. As a child, she'd gone without on several occasions, never able to keep up with the fashions, having hand-me-downs instead of new, and certainly no designer or nice brands of clothes. It had been hard growing up with Nicky and Gemma being able to have what they wanted and for her to be the odd one out.

Because of it, Amy cost her a fortune to look just so. But she wanted for nothing, within reason, of course. She and Scott didn't spoil her. If she asked for something, she had to work for it, doing odd jobs to earn the pennies.

'We'll have to help out with the funeral,' she said. 'If it's doable. I'll check the bank and savings accounts in the morning.'

'If we can't cover it all, we'll pay for some of it.'

'I'm sure Gemma and Aaron will help out, too.'

'Yeah, best not to ask Ben for anything.'

Leanne frowned. His tone was harsh again. There was something Scott wasn't telling her, but it could wait. Now was not the time to ask.

CHAPTER TWENTY

Four Months Ago

Kit was in the passenger seat of Scott's old van, the one he kept hidden in a row of council-owned garages.

'Are you sure this won't conk out before the job is done?' he asked as Scott started the engine.

'Stop your whinging.' Scott set off. 'I'm only shifting a few knockoff TVs for a mate. You just keep your eyes peeled for anyone.'

Kit didn't like it, but he'd had no choice other than to say yes when Scott had told him there was something he needed help with. The money would be good, and go straight to Davy Lewis to pay off his debt. Davy had called him last night, demanding payments again, and Kit wanted him off his back.

They drew up outside a lock-up on the edge of Longton.

'Take the driver's seat.' Scott got out of the vehicle.

Kit watched Scott snap the chain and remove the padlock. There was a lamp post outside the gates, so he kept his head down. He beckoned the vehicle forward, and Kit drove around the back out of sight.

Once another chain had been broken, Scott disappeared inside a unit. A minute later, he appeared with a large-screen TV in a box.

'Open the back,' he whispered loudly. 'And then come and help. There are a ton of these inside.'

Kit did as he was told and then went into the unit with Scott. He wasn't averse to a bit of petty theft. He'd done it during his adolescent years, well into his twenties, too. More recently, he'd wanted to stay on the straight and narrow. He'd been lucky until now, and he didn't really want to chance it. But he could see no choice.

'That's the last we can fit in,' Scott said after about ten minutes and several boxes. 'Let's go.'

Kit sighed with relief when they pulled away onto the road. Twenty minutes later, the TVs had been dropped off for a fair price at Dodgy Derek's. He ran a pawn shop.

Scott fanned a wad of notes in front of his face and grinned. 'Money for old rope. Well, if no one saw us, that is.'

'No one *did* see us.' Kit glanced out of the window into the dark. 'Did they?'

'I'm joking with you. Those TVs were nicked from Dodgy Derek's in the first place. I'm just returning them to him, for a price, of course.' He counted out some money and passed it to Kit. 'Right, let's go. Time for business.'

They dumped the van back at the garage, swapped it for Scott's car and were off again.

'Cheers for this, mate,' Kit told him. 'It'll come in handy this week. I've got bills up to my ears.'

'I keep telling you there's plenty more money where that came from. I don't get jobs like that too often, but I can always do with a helping hand. Besides, once a thief, always a thief, you know that, youth.'

Kit couldn't help but laugh. 'How did you end up being such a Jack-the-lad?'

'Learned from my old man.' Scott grinned. 'And so did you.'

'Yeah, but—'

'Look, if all you want is to clear your debt with Davy, then that's fine. I'm just saying you could earn a bob or two more if you wanted to.'

'How much do you make a week?'

'If I do a drugs run out of town, it's an easy grand.'

'A grand in one go!'

Scott shrugged as if it was nothing. 'You never wanted to know before. I could have taken you on lots of jobs.'

'It feels risky, but… a grand each time?' Kit's head felt ready to explode at the thought. 'Does Leanne know?'

''Course not! She'd kill me – or divorce me.'

'Why don't you move off the estate? You're making enough money.'

'It's my cover for now. I'm stashing a bit away so that I can stay legal and, in a few years, we'll move to a new-build as far away from here as I can. But for now, I still need to get my hands dirty. Speaking of which.' He parked the car at the side of the road and got out. 'Let's go and pay someone a visit.'

In Alexander Place, Kit followed him up the path towards a house. Scott banged on the front door with his fist.

'All right, all right,' Davy Lewis hollered as he answered it.

Scott pushed past him and into the hall.

'Hey! What the fuck's wrong with you?' Davy cried.

'Oh, come *on*. You don't like people barging into your home and yet *you* do it whenever it takes your fancy?' Scott threw a thumb over his shoulder. 'I believe Kit owes you money.'

Davy nodded. 'Yeah, he's a shit payer, too.'

'Well, he happens to be a very good mate of mine.' Scott

took the notes he'd got from Dodgy Derek and gave them to Davy. 'This is half his debt, and you'll get the rest next week. Then you will never set foot near Kit, his wife, or his house, ever again. Do you understand?'

Davy smirked. 'You don't tell me what to do.'

Scott headbutted him. Davy went down to his knees. As he held on to his nose, Scott punched him in the stomach.

Kit stood motionless in the doorway, unsure whether to help Scott or let him do his worst. Scott loved a good scrap, Kit not so much. It was one of the reasons why he'd stopped doing jobs with him. At times, Scott became far more violent than was necessary.

Finally, Scott stopped his assault. Davy groaned, staying down curled in a ball.

'I'm a man of my word and so is Kit, so he'll pay his debt,' Scott finished. 'I'll get the rest of the money to you next week. But if you *ever* cross his path again, I won't be so lenient. Do you understand?'

Davy said nothing.

Scott kicked him again. 'Do you understand?'

'Yes! For fuck's sake, yes.'

'Excellent! Well, I'll be off then. See you at the same time next week.'

Kit followed Scott back to the car, unsure whether to laugh or cry. He really didn't want to be in this life again. But it looked like he had at least one more job to do next week before he could walk away.

CHAPTER TWENTY-ONE

Sunday

Gemma went into the house with Ben. It seemed alien somehow, as if so much had changed in a short space of time, and yet nothing was out of place. Things would never be the same, however. It added to the urgency she felt to change her own circumstances now. Life was too short to be unhappy.

She thought back to when she and Ben had met. He'd been so attentive then. Now it was almost as if he came to see her at the weekend for sex, and even that was waning.

For a long time, she'd wanted to finish things with him, but she hadn't managed to pluck up the courage. She'd talked to Leanne about how wary she was of what might happen if he became angry with her. Leanne had told her to get it over with as quickly as possible.

Until Kit had been murdered, the plan had been to do it that afternoon, before Ben went back to Birmingham. Once he'd left, she was going to get the locks changed so he couldn't call again.

It was the little things that had begun to worry her. Over the past month, Ben had become more controlling, and on one occasion had even hurt her. Gemma remembered closing the door behind Aaron after waving him off with Charlotte for the weekend.

She'd turned back, almost bumping into him as he'd been so close.

'Are you okay?' she asked.

Ben pushed her up against the wall. He covered her body with his own, pressing in so much that she became breathless for the wrong reasons. He held both her hands down at her sides and stared at her.

'It wasn't fun for me seeing you with him.'

His look was menacing more than lustful, and she gulped.

'I wasn't expecting him so early and I—'

She couldn't speak anymore because his mouth bore down on hers. His eyes were open, almost black with rage. She tried to bring up her hands, but he kept a firm grip on them.

The look he gave her when he stopped had her feeling uncomfortable, a little anxious even. What was going on with him?

'You're mine,' he said.

She gave a faint smile. 'Ben, I—'

'You belong to me.' His lips went to her cheek, her neck, her collarbone.

She squirmed, not feeling turned on in the slightest. But then she realised he was sucking at her shoulder.

'Stop that.' She tried to push him away, pain shooting through her as he continued. 'You're hurting me!'

Finally, his lips came loose. He didn't move, breathing heavily against her. Her chest rose and fell at the same time as his.

'Aaron left you a long time ago, and now I'm here instead.'

She grimaced, the sting of his bite flaring. Then she gathered her wits about her.

'Don't ever do that to me again.'

She'd walked away, trying not to let him see her hands were shaking.

Ben had been his usual self for the rest of the evening, even a little more considerate. If he'd noticed she was quiet, he'd never said anything. It had led her to so many questions the next morning.

Was she scared of him, the power he had over her? How bizarre that he'd mark her, claim her as his own, brand her even.

'I'll make coffee,' he said now, heading for the kitchen.

She rubbed the back of her neck, tension spiking in her body. She used to love waiting for him to ring her, the anticipation of hearing his voice, him telling her how much he missed her. Now it had all turned sour.

The more she thought about it, the more she realised she was a convenience to him. Add to that the fact that he often scared her, and she was done. Ben was suffocating her, and it was too much.

CHAPTER TWENTY-TWO

Allie was starving so stopped at a corner shop to grab a quick bite to eat. She didn't want her stomach rumbling when she spoke to her DCI. She pulled up in the car park and rang Mark first.

'Hey, you enjoying the day?' she wanted to know, envious of his time off.

'It's not so bad, but I'm bored on my own. I've done the big shop, though. Are you going to be having a late one?'

'I'm not sure. With it being a Sunday, I expect we'll have to wait on a lot of things for the morning, so we'll do what we can.'

'Great. I'll keep the BBQ hot.'

'It won't be that early. I'm just having my lunch.'

'It's half past four!'

'It's been hectic.'

'Well, I'll leave you to it while I get the au pair to put suntan cream on the bits I can't reach.'

Allie laughed. 'I'm hoping to be home by about eight, but you know I can't promise.'

She disconnected the call, grabbed her purse, and went

into the shop. Like The Wheatsheaf earlier, it was dark after the bright sun, cool, too. She headed for the fridges.

While she was choosing what to buy, she felt someone staring at her. She turned and saw Mallory, one of the teens from the Limekiln Estate.

'Hey, Mallory, how are you doing?' she asked.

'Fine, thanks. You?'

'Super. Fancy a can of Coke?'

'I'm not always on the cadge, you know.' Mallory rolled her eyes.

Allie reached out a can regardless. She wanted to know what the girl was after talking to her. There had to be some reason she would stop and chat. The kids on the estates didn't usually like the police.

'This is a bit away from your patch,' she said, popping the can into a basket, along with a meal deal for herself.

'We've been for a walk and ended up here.'

'We?'

'Me and Kelsey. She left the shop when she saw you coming in, but I expect she's waiting outside.'

Allie reached for another can, wondering why Kelsey was avoiding her. Three months ago, she'd helped the family out when her mother's partner had been murdered. She'd thought they were okay, but on reflection, she hadn't seen much of the girl since then.

She paid for the drinks, making small talk with Mallory, and they went outside. She was a nice kid. Allie hoped she didn't come to much harm, knowing how her family had been dragged up. But Mallory seemed to have an edge about her. At fourteen, she was a minor, but she had so much to put up with at home that she was very much wise before her time.

'Aren't I ruining your street cred, you talking to a copper?' Allie asked in jest.

'Naw, you're okay really.'

Allie raised her eyebrows in surprise. 'I'm truly honoured.'

Mallory gave her a shy grin. 'Well, you're better than most.'

'I'll take that as a compliment. It's nice of you to say so.' Allie removed the cans from her bag and handed them to her.

'Thanks.' Mallory tore open a ring can and took a slurp. 'I heard about that man who was murdered.'

Allie managed not to ask her which one she was referring to. The public didn't know about either suspicious death officially yet.

'Fancy being killed on your way home,' Mallory went on.

Ah, she was talking about Kit Harper. 'Have you heard anything on the grapevine?'

'No.' Mallory shrugged. 'It's not our patch, like you say.'

Allie smiled. Talking to teens was often trickier than adults, but they were always to the point.

Up ahead, Kelsey perched on the low wall that surrounded the grass verge by the steps. She turned away when she saw them walking towards her.

Mallory sat next to her friend and passed her the spare can.

It worried Allie that Kelsey was hanging around with Mallory. They were the same age, and pretty girls ripe for exploitation. Especially Kelsey because of who her mum had been involved with. Hopefully that was all behind the family now.

Allie smiled at Kelsey. 'Mind if I join you while I eat my lunch?'

'It's half past four.' Kelsey's tone was one of indifference.

'It's been a busy day. I could murder an oatcake, but it's too late, so this will have to do. Cheese and pickle.'

'I'd rather have an oatcake.' Mallory rubbed at her tummy.

Allie sat down next to Kelsey and opened the packaging.

It stung that Kelsey was being short with her, but she didn't let it show.

'How have you been, Kelsey?' she asked after a moment. 'I haven't seen you in a while.'

'I'm fine.'

'And your mum, and Riley?'

'Everyone's fine.' Kelsey looked away and then turned back with a sigh.

'Oh, there's Andy.' Mallory jumped to her feet. 'I won't be a minute.'

They watched her walk towards a group of boys, then proceed to chat with them.

'Mum's told me to stay away from you,' Kelsey admitted, after a moment.

'Oh, right.' Allie didn't know what to think about that. 'And is that what you want, too?'

'It makes life easier, I guess.'

'For who?'

Kelsey gave a slight shrug but didn't elaborate further.

'Are you still going to Grace's drop-in sessions?'

'Occasionally.'

'So, if I happen to pop in sometime, I might see you then?'

Kelsey offered a faint smile.

It was enough to give Allie hope. 'What have you been up to lately?'

'Nothing much.'

The friendly vibe between them had disappeared in an instant. Allie couldn't help but wonder why. Usually, it was bad news. It meant that Kelsey was hiding something from her, that she didn't want to talk to Allie too much in case she slipped up about it.

Still, she couldn't keep an eye on every teenager in the city that she came into contact with. No matter how much she would like to.

CHAPTER TWENTY-THREE

Four Months Ago

Kit was freshly showered, his hair still wet at the nape of his neck when he walked into the living room to find Nicky sitting on the settee.

'Where are you off to?' she questioned.

'I'm treating Scott to a curry while I sweet talk him into loaning me some money,' he fibbed.

Nicky rolled her eyes. 'It seems counterproductive to me. I thought you weren't going to ask him again.'

'I don't have much choice, but this is the last time. I should have asked him in the first place, and I wouldn't be in this mess.'

'You won't be too late?'

'Not on a school night.' He grinned. 'I promise.'

Scott was waiting for him at the bottom of the road. He got in the van and fastened his seatbelt.

'What are we doing tonight?' he asked after greeting him.

'I have to fetch and deliver some packages.' Scott pulled off from the kerb. 'I need you to be my eyes and ears.'

Kit was nervous about the evening, but he settled in for the ride. He tried to put out of his mind that someone might want to cross Scott of their own accord, get rid of him for revenge or another reason.

Yet, he felt safe with his mate. Scott was known as a loyal fella but someone you messed with at your peril. He would never do anything that would jeopardise his freedom either.

The night started off okay. Scott drove him to four pick-up places around Stoke. Kit waited for him in the car, keeping a lookout. Not that he was sure he'd be any good if anything did go down.

On the last visit, Scott parked the car.

'I need you to come in with me on this one,' he said.

Kit shook his head vehemently. 'You said I was only the lookout.'

'It'll take five minutes, tops.'

'Who is it?'

'Jed Jamieson.'

'For fuck's sake.' Jamieson was a crook with a reputation for violence. Kit wanted to stay as far away from him as possible.

'What the hell are you mixing with him for?' He turned to Scott. 'Are you mad?'

'Relax.' Scott didn't seem fazed at all. 'I'm only collecting a package for Kenny. Nothing to worry about. I just prefer to have someone with me.' He got out of the car. 'Come on, we won't be long.'

Kit wasn't certain about this. He followed behind him, almost dreading going into the property.

Bernard Place was known on the Limekiln Estate as the place not to live. If you were lucky, you never got to even step on the pavement. Scott pushed open the gate of number seven, Kit stopping it from falling off as he went through. The largest panel on the bay window was boarded up and he could hear the TV from the street.

Scott knocked on the door, and a blond-haired boy of about four answered, dangly legs peppered in playtime bruises on show.

'Your grandad in, Clinton?'

'Yeah, who wants him?' he asked, a scowl on his face.

'Tell him it's Scott.'

'Grandad!' The boy shouted and then disappeared.

Kit groaned inwardly, clocking another generation growing up into a life of trouble they had no control over.

Clinton came back within seconds. 'Come on in, then.' He beckoned them forward.

Inside the scratty living room, Jed was sitting on the settee pushed up against the back wall. His feet were on the coffee table, the rank smell of his trainers by the side coming up at them.

The woman with him had her arms around him, head on his chest. She had dreadlocks, tattooed eyebrows, and Botoxed lips. Kit wouldn't dare tell her his thoughts, that she looked like a clown wearing too much makeup.

Clinton raced over to the armchair and jumped up on it. His nose was in an iPad within seconds.

Never taking his eyes from the TV, Jed pointed to an envelope on the coffee table.

Scott picked it up and pulled a package from his pocket. He handed it to Jed.

Scott and Kit made to leave. As they got to the door, Jed spoke again.

'I hope there's nothing missing from that package.'

'It's all there,' Scott replied, deadpan. 'We never touch the merchandise.'

'Wise man.'

Kit had frozen. Scott nudged him in the back, and they made a quick getaway.

Once they were in the van again, Kit let out a huge sigh of relief. 'I said I didn't want to be involved in any drugs, and yet that was what was in the parcel, wasn't it?'

'Yeah, but it's gone now. We're clean.'

'Were they all drug drop-offs?'

'You wouldn't have come if I'd told you.' Scott started the engine. 'Look, you needed to get Davy off your back, and once we pay the final payment, that's all over. Fancy a pint after we've visited Davy?'

Kit sniggered. 'I have a choice?'

'Not really.' Scott grinned. 'Come on, let's get this business finished.'

Kit gave a half-smile. He was indebted to Scott for helping him out with Davy, and at least there was no one to repay now. But the money he'd earned, and the money he knew Scott was getting, was tempting.

Perhaps it would be okay to do a couple of jobs with him and get some dosh under his belt, rather than ask him for another sub.

CHAPTER TWENTY-FOUR

Sunday

Arriving at the station, Allie hotfooted it up to the second floor where DCI Jenny Brindley's office was located. Usually, you wouldn't find Jenny in at the weekend, but with two murders that morning, she'd come in. Verity, her secretary, however, was not, which Allie was glad to see.

Jenny was sitting at her desk. Allie knocked on the door and went in when prompted.

'Allie, good to see you, ignoring the circumstances, of course.' Jenny's smile was warm. 'How are you?'

'Hot and bothered, Ma'am,' Allie joked, glad she had a senior officer she could do that with. She and Jenny had worked together for a few years now and got on well.

Jenny urged Allie to sit across from her. 'Can I get you a drink?'

'I'm fine, thanks. I'm heading down for a team briefing so I can grab a cuppa there.'

'Okay, tell me what you know.'

Allie ran through everything she had done that day. The people she'd spoken to, the scenes she'd visited, and the information her officers had gathered.

'Jack Fletcher, you say? I thought he moved out of Stoke a long time ago.'

'He did, he's been back a while now. We've had no trouble from him, though, nor the rest of the Fletcher family, so I can only assume he's here on his own. Our investigations will focus on that first.'

'I'm confident you can run two cases side by side.' Jenny nodded afterwards.

'I'll put Perry as first port of call on the Jack Fletcher murder and I'll take on Kit Harper.'

'Yes, do what you can today. I'll get out an initial press release this evening, and then we can do a formal conference in the morning. I'd like you there, too.'

'Ma'am.'

Once back at her desk, Allie set to work on her emails. There was one from Christian to say the body would be ready to view in the morning. She sent back a reply with a time they could visit.

There was another from the digital forensic unit, regarding a hidden folder located on Kit Harper's phone. Sam had asked them to unlock it. A file had been sent over WeShare.

Allie clicked on the link, and the photos uploaded. They were of Kit and a woman in various selfie modes. Kit had his arms around her in one, kissing her cheek in another. They were holding up drinks in a bar, a further image of the woman alone. There was no denying they were an item.

Allie sat back for a moment, her fingers steepled while she thought of the ramifications. Because it was a woman she recognised.

And it wasn't Kit's wife.

CHAPTER TWENTY-FIVE

The team was gathered in the incident room.

'Okay, listen up,' Allie said on entering. 'I have a bit of news. There was a hidden folder on Kit Harper's phone, retrieved from the digital forensic unit. Recognise anyone, Perry?' She placed her laptop on the table, turned it towards him and opened the lid so he could see the screen.

Perry looked, raising his eyebrows afterwards. 'Leanne Milton.'

'Looks like our man was playing away with his friend's wife,' Allie told everyone. 'Leanne is one of the group of friends that Kit and his wife, Nicky Harper, are close to. She's married to Scott, and there's also Ben Grant and Gemma Clarke. Add to the mix an ex, Aaron Clarke, and that's a whole lot of suspects. Three couples, and a new man replaced by an ex.'

'And an affair. This is going to get messy,' Sam remarked. 'Their association with each other is enough for each one to have been close to Kit.'

'We'll revisit the men tomorrow. I have the appointment at the mortuary in the morning, and the press conference after Jenny does the initial release this evening.' Allie paused. 'I'll have a word with Leanne, I think, if I can get her alone. If she and Kit have managed to keep the affair to themselves, then I'm inclined not to say anything. However, if the argument then turns out to be because someone found out or suspects, then that could give us another motive, and a stronger suspect in Scott Milton, as well as Leanne. Perhaps even Nicky.

'So, welcome to Operation Stafford. Let's go through what we have. Our victim is Kevin Harper – known as Kit. He's thirty-six years old, married to Nicky, the same age. He was hit on the temple on his way home from the pub. The force of it caused him to land heavily, the back of his head taking the brunt. Christian should be able to tell us soon of the actual cause, but for now we're looking for a murder weapon like a bat or a piece of wood. Or it was a fist.'

'Do you think there was intent to kill?' Perry put a question out.

'It's possible.' Allie nodded. 'Although we can't be certain that it was no more than a fight that got out of hand.' She pointed to the photo of Kit on the digital whiteboard, the one she'd got from his wife. 'Kit was out with friends. There was a fracas in the pub, and we're not sure they're all telling us the truth.'

'What did they say?' Frankie asked.

'Perry, want to come in here?'

'Ben Grant said there was a punch thrown at him from Kit, that it was over something and nothing, but when we checked the CCTV, it was Scott who Kit came at. All three of them left a long time before Kit, so they were potentially the last people to see him alive.' Perry paused. 'That's not to say they are involved, but we need to look at them in more detail.'

'Sam, can I task you with that?' Allie said. 'See if there is any evidence to bring them in or eliminate them altogether. There's definitely something they aren't telling us.'

Sam nodded. 'I'm working on checking CCTV. There's nothing on one side of the walkway, only from the main road. I can see Kit going in but no one following him. I've also accounted for each man coming out of The Wheatsheaf at the times they gave to us. I'm checking out Jack Fletcher too.'

'Can you check what time Davy Lewis left, please? He was in the pub too, and almost in the middle of the fight at the time, although I can't be certain he was joining in or trying to break it up.'

'Yes, boss.'

'Thanks. So, Jack Fletcher, murder number two and Operation Churchill.'

Perry updated them about the time he and Frankie had spent in Jessop Place.

'For everyone who doesn't know – that's you, Frankie, still being a young pup.' Allie smiled at him. 'Jack Fletcher is known to us for being drunk and disorderly, and abusive to his family. His son, Peter, died in a fire almost twenty years ago. Him and his mates used to hang around a derelict shed on the spare land at the back of the shops on the estate. He was inside when someone lit it up. It was tragic.

'We suspected foul play by Jack at one point as petrol was used as the accelerant and we found a few cans at his home. But there was no real evidence either way. The case is still open. Perry and I were PCs at the time and were on house-to-house.'

'So the family were known to us?' Frankie asked.

'They weren't angels before Peter's death, but everything seemed to fall apart afterwards. If I remember rightly, their mum died a year later and Jack Fletcher left soon after, leaving two sons and a daughter to fend for themselves.

Stuart Fletcher was twenty-one at the time.' She looked at Perry for confirmation, and he nodded. 'Ricky was about fourteen by then, and Suzanne a couple of years younger. Stuart stayed for a few years, possibly until they could both fend for themselves. Having said that, I haven't seen any of them in Stoke for a long time.'

'I remember the sister,' Perry said. 'She was always in and out of the nick in her teens.'

'She was. Shoplifting and petty theft mainly. Ricky was into selling drugs, but as far as I can recall, he never took any. He had a good business head on him, all be it an illegal one. He ran small groups of runners from the city to the suburbs. He's been in and out of prison too. Last one was a ten-year stretch for armed robbery. Got out late last year, according to our records.' She paused again. 'Frankie, I'm going to put you on the Jack Fletcher case tomorrow. Find out as much information as you can about him.'

'Yes, boss.' Frankie sat forward like a peacock strutting his stuff.

Allie laughed inwardly. Had she ever been that keen herself?

'Also, see if there have been any burglaries in the area around Jessop Place, check a few streets out from it, too. Continue chatting to the neighbours tomorrow, and we'll go from there. Forensics for both cases might be back by then.'

'Will do.'

'Thanks.' Allie glanced around the room. 'In the meantime, if you can add anything you have to the system, and then get ready for tomorrow. It's going to be a busy one.'

CHAPTER TWENTY-SIX

Four Months Ago

Kit walked into The Wheatsheaf, waving to acknowledge he'd spotted Scott sitting with Aaron. Without asking, he ordered them drinks as well as one for himself.

'Three of the usual, please, Helen,' he said to the woman behind the bar.

'What are you lot doing out during the week?' She reached for glasses. 'It's not even a football night.'

'Do we need an excuse?' Kit laughed. 'There's always good company to be found in here.'

His drinks poured and paid for, he walked towards their table in the corner, holding all three pints in a triangle in his hands. He sat across from them, popping the glasses in the middle.

'Cheers.' Aaron raised his in the air.

Scott was looking at his phone but popped it face down on the table.

'What's up?' Kit asked him.

'Nothing in particular.' He sighed before taking a sip of his pint. 'Just fed up with getting nagged at.'

'It's that thing called life.' Aaron played with a beermat. 'It's always there to throw up something new for us to deal with. I've been meaning to ask you about this Ben who Gemma has started seeing. What's he like?'

'He's not bad,' Scott replied.

'He's a good-looking git,' Kit added.

Aaron tutted. 'Don't tell me that.'

'Do I detect a hint of jealousy there?' Kit knocked back more of his pint.

Aaron smirked. 'Actually, yeah. I still miss her.'

Scott shook his head. 'You should never have divorced.'

'I know that now.'

'You're happy with Tasha, though?'

'Yeah, I suppose.'

Kit finished his drink.

'Steady on,' Scott remarked. 'I'm only half done with mine. What's the rush?'

'I just feel like getting plastered.'

'Work still getting you down?'

'Tell me about it. I wish I could do something more... substantial. You have it so cushy, Scott,' Kit chided.

'Yeah, like collecting scrap metal was in my life plan as I grew up.' His smile was smarmy, his tone one of disdain. 'Leanne is always moaning at me to do more with myself.'

Kit rolled his eyes. He couldn't believe how much Leanne didn't know about what Scott got up to. Aaron didn't either. There were only the two of them who knew about his extra work.

'She's not the boss of you,' Aaron said.

'I don't know what I'd do without her, though. Yet she

doesn't half shut off from me at times, if you know what I mean.'

'So that's what it is.' Aaron laughed. 'You're not getting any?'

'Not lately. She's always too tired.'

'You should appreciate her more, then,' Kit snipped.

'What do you mean by that?'

Kit shook his head. 'Ignore me, I'm a grumpy bastard today. Do you want another or not?'

'I'm not done with this yet.' Aaron held up a half-full pint glass.

'Just get yourself one,' Scott added.

At the bar again, Kit turned back to look at Scott and Aaron, who were now deep in conversation. Aaron was probably talking about football as his arms were flying around. Laughter burst forth from them both. He wished he could join in with them, but he felt sick after what he'd been doing that afternoon.

His phone beeped. It was a message from Ben.

You up for a quick pint? I'm in the area.

Nicky had told him that Ben wasn't often around during the week. A smile played on Kit's lips. It would be nice to see Aaron squirm if he showed up. It was snide, but who cared.

I'm out with Scott and Aaron. We're in The Wheatsheaf. Come to us if you like.

Will do.

'I've had a message from Ben,' he said as he rejoined his friends. 'He's popping in for a drink.'

Aaron balked. 'You're not serious?'

'Yeah, thought it would be good for you to meet him, get to know him. Save you worrying about Gemma.'

Aaron picked up his pint, necking back what was left. 'What makes you think I want to spend time with someone who's screwing her?'

'I thought it would put your mind at rest.'

Aaron stood up. 'Not sure that would happen no matter what. I'll see you later.' He made to leave, but Kit grabbed his arm.

'Come on, sit down again.'

Aaron shrugged him off.

Kit sighed.

Scott glared at him before shaking his head. 'You are such a dick at times. How would you feel if someone had done that to you?'

'I thought I was helping.'

'Sometimes you have no tact.'

'Can't do right for wrong,' Kit muttered.

Scott knocked his drink back and stood up. 'I think I'll go, too.'

Kit raised his hands in the air and threw them down. He might have known Scott would side with Aaron. Kit often had his nose pushed out by the two of them. Served them right if he wanted to have another friend to make him feel better. Besides, he didn't want to go home yet.

He went to the bar to order a drink for them both.

Ben arrived a few minutes later. 'I thought you were with the others?'

'They've only just gone.' Kit slid a pint across to Ben.

'Cheers.'

He downed half of his drink in one go.

Ben raised his eyebrows. 'Bad day?' he asked.

'Work's been a bitch,' he lied.

Sounds like you need a change. I'm thinking about it myself, too.'

'Something more local? Because of Gemma?'

'Perhaps.' Ben grinned. 'I think the world of her.'

They sat in silence for a moment. Kit couldn't help but feel disloyal to Aaron when they talked about Gemma. He hadn't wanted to hurt the bloke and he felt terrible about it now.

A crowd of teenagers came in and rolled up to the bar. They took him back to the years he was happy and carefree. He stared at them for a while.

'Ever thought of going into business yourself, Kit?' Ben asked.

'Lots of times. I'd love to get out of the rat race but I'm not sure I have any skills.'

'Sure you do. What would you fancy?'

'Anything that would work my brain. I'm so bored.'

'What do you do now?'

'I'm a security guard at a garden centre. It's top-notch job satisfaction.' Kit rolled his eyes.

'You should think about what you want to do in the long-term. You've years ahead of you. No point wasting it doing something you hate.'

'I suppose.'

As their chat turned to a recent football match, Kit realised he'd much prefer to be with Aaron and Scott. Ben was okay, but he was quite full of himself.

And he'd pissed himself off. It wasn't like him to be cruel to his friends. What on earth was he turning into?

CHAPTER TWENTY-SEVEN

Sunday

Nicky jumped when there was a knock on the door. It was past eight o'clock, and all she wanted was for the day to end.

PC Joy went to the window, closely followed by Leanne.

'It's Carmen,' Leanne said.

Rachel went to let her in.

Nicky didn't know if she was looking forward to seeing her or not, but she was glad she was here, which sounded silly. Carmen often made her feel inferior. It wasn't intentional: Carmen was always so preened, even though she was often wearing too much makeup for Nicky's liking.

Despite the circumstances, Nicky knew she would feel dowdy in comparison. Hair, clothes, makeup – even the car Carmen was driving said she was in a class of her own.

But Nicky had seen a different side to her friend. They'd met about six months ago. Nicky had visited the doctor's surgery, and as she'd come out, she'd seen Carmen by her car. She was wiping at her eyes with a handkerchief.

Nicky hadn't been sure whether to reach out to her but, thinking she'd be okay if someone asked her if she was all right when she wasn't, she'd spoken to Carmen.

Carmen had said she was fine but then promptly burst into tears. And it seemed she *had* needed someone to talk to, someone she didn't know, to unburden herself on because she'd blurted out that everything in her life was going wrong.

After they'd chatted for a few minutes, Nicky was glad she'd stopped. Carmen mentioned going for a coffee, not wanting to leave yet. Over that, she'd revealed how she was having problems with her husband. She said he sometimes got a bit too abusive, that she was even frightened to leave him because of it.

At the time, Nicky recalled her shock at how quickly Carmen had trusted her with the details. It was clear to her that the woman was desperate to unload.

There hadn't been much she could do but listen, yet Carmen had seemed so grateful. They'd ended up swapping phone numbers and meeting once a fortnight since.

Despite her situation, the Carmen Nicky got to know was a lot of fun to be around. She was vivacious with a deep, dirty laugh that would have Nicky in stitches. It had been a tonic for her, too.

Carmen's dark hair tumbled in curls down her back, and she walked with a confident stride. Today she had muted her usual colourful and vibrant outfits down to cropped designer jeans and a black T-shirt. Blue eyes framed by brown mascara, and a slick of pale-pink gloss on her lips.

She came into the room, holding her arms out. 'Nicky, my love. I'm so sorry.'

It brought on a fresh set of tears as Nicky clung to her. They sat on the settee together.

'I'll make fresh tea,' Rachel said. She disappeared to give them space.

'Have the police got any idea who it might be?' Carmen asked, once she was out of hearing range.

Nicky shook her head, wiping at her tears with a fresh tissue. 'I don't know anyone who'd want to... to kill him. Everyone loved Kit.'

Carmen rubbed the back of Nicky's hand. 'I expect it's some random dickhead on the way home, after a fight. Kit was obviously in the wrong place at the wrong time. You just don't know nowadays, do you?' She looked across to Leanne who was now sitting across from them, and Gemma beside her, perched on the arm of the chair. 'How are you two doing? You must be devastated, too.'

'It seems so unreal,' Gemma said.

Leanne shook her head, tears welling in her eyes, but she couldn't speak.

'If there's anything I can help with, please let me know. It's going to be such an unsettling time for you all, especially while the police work to find out who did this to him.'

Rachel came back, and they helped themselves to tea. Nicky took a few sips and put hers down. Everything had no taste; her appetite had gone, too.

After half an hour of fielding messages, and phone calls coming in on all their phones, Nicky wanted to be alone.

'I'm so tired,' she said, emphasising it with a yawn. 'Thanks for being with me all day, and I'm glad you'll be coming to the mortuary with me, but please don't feel that you should be here all evening, too. I can't cry anymore today, and my mum will be here in the morning.'

There was an outcry of disagreement.

'We can't leave you on your own, not tonight,' Leanne protested.

'We can bunk down here,' Gemma added. 'Aaron has Charlotte with him.'

'But you need to be with Scott, Leanne. He'll be hurting, too. And, Gemma, Aaron might want to see you. We were all so close. It's not just me who needs to grieve.'

'Why don't you let me stay?' Carmen offered. 'I don't have children to get back to, Jeff can cope without me.' She looked at Leanne and Gemma and then back to Nicky. 'I can keep an eye on you. I'd like to help.'

Nicky nodded, if only to give in so they would leave. All she really wanted to do was get the evening over and go to bed. Then she could cry to her heart's content.

CHAPTER TWENTY-EIGHT

The press release had gone out and, after speaking to Jenny again, Allie went back to the team and trawled through the reports coming in. Finally, there was nothing that couldn't wait until tomorrow, which was good because her emotions had been all over the place.

It was always satisfying to bring justice to the family of a murder victim, but sometimes during it, the grief was hard to bear. She'd been informed by Rachel earlier that Kit Harper's daughter had collapsed in a heap of sobs in Nicky's living room. It had played on her mind ever since.

Tomorrow they would widen their net, see what the calls from the press release brought up. It all seemed so little at the moment.

She decided to check in with Rachel before she left.

'How's everything now?' she asked the family liaison officer.

'It's quiet. Leanne and Gemma have left. Another friend, Carmen, has arrived and is staying overnight. They don't want to leave her alone, which is good. And her mum has confirmed her flight lands at ten-thirty in the morning, so she'll be coming straight here from Manchester airport.'

'Thanks. You can knock off for the night now. You've done a great job again today.' Allie disconnected the call, gathered together her things, and headed for home.

The drive didn't take longer than ten minutes. She suspected most people were still out in the pubs or in their gardens, the roads fairly quiet.

It was such a mild evening, Allie wished she'd been able to enjoy all of it. Instead, she had a head full of things to check in the morning. That was the one problem with the job – her inability to switch off. But how could she in the middle of a case? Correction, two cases.

Mark was in the conservatory when she went through to the kitchen, the doors flung open to the garden.

'Hey,' he greeted her as she came through. 'How's it going?'

She flopped down next to him on the settee. 'Emotive. It'll be a while before I switch off. What're you watching?'

'Nothing in particular. *Twenty-Four Hours in Police Custody* has just finished on catch-up.'

'Good!' She couldn't watch any police programmes, but Mark enjoyed them, saying some of the better ones gave him an insight into how hard she worked.

'I like that I can view it without you moaning,' he added.

'You're such a charmer.' She hid a yawn.

'Want something to eat? A piece of toast? A mug of tea?'

'I'd love both, thanks.'

Mark jumped up, and she settled down, hoping she wouldn't be asleep by the time he'd prepared it. The sky was darkening now. At least there hadn't been a storm. Although it was needed after the heat of the day, she didn't want anything to contaminate the area around the first crime scene.

She glanced around the large area they congregated in most evenings and weekends. They had a separate living area, but once the conservatory had been added to the kitchen, they found themselves in there more and more. It was such a bright, airy space, looking over the garden.

Her eyes landed on the collection of photos on the side unit. When her sister died, she'd taken down the ones she'd had on the walls of her room in the residential care home. For six months, she'd kept them in a box, until one Sunday morning, she'd got them out again and put them on display.

She smiled at the one where she and Karen were sixteen and twelve respectively, sitting on Westie, one of Karen's friend's, trials bike as it stood on its stand. Back then, the two of them had been invincible. If only she'd known how little time they had, Allie would have spent more of it with her as they had grown up. But then, no one ever knows that.

Losing Karen after so long had been a blow, but in reality she'd lost her sister twenty-five years previous, when she'd been attacked. Still, she was always in her heart, no matter what. And she was looking forward to having a temporary family now, someone else to share her time with.

Since their talk about fostering, Allie and Mark had discussed it at length before applying. Doing it would be the hardest thing yet, she imagined. With Perry's wife, Lisa's, help over the past three months, they had completed the application form and had regular visits from their assessment social worker. Her name was Christine, and she was taking them through the following stages.

They'd decided on short-term fostering. It suited them to be around for kids needing emergency care at the drop of a hat. If Allie was working long hours on a case, Mark would be around to step in as Mum and Dad.

Allie and Mark had been grilled about their family history, their relationship, their work and home life. It had all been really friendly, one of many stages to assess if they were suitable.

They'd started training sessions – first aid for children, safeguarding, and a two-day Skills to Foster course, where they had met like-minded people and made friends to share the experience with.

They were now waiting to hear the date to attend a young person's panel. It consisted of several teenagers who had gone through the system as foster kids. Once that was done, their application would go to a board of professionals and then to an agency decision-maker for approval.

Not for the first time, she imagined a little girl sitting on the floor reading a book. A young boy playing with a set of Lego. They'd opted for one child at a time. They hadn't got room to give to siblings. Maybe in time, but for now, they were excited to see if they could take care of one.

Mark passed a plate to her and placed two mugs on the coffee table. Then he fetched a plate for himself.

'We might not be able to do this much more,' she said when he rejoined her.

'Stuff toast down our mouths at the end of the day?'

'No, silly! But we will have to be mindful of a sleeping child.' Allie beamed. 'In our spare room!'

'They're not going to hear us.'

'I'm joking.'

'I wonder how quick it will be if we're accepted.'

'*When* we're accepted,' Allie chided. 'I suppose there may have to be a child in peril beforehand. That's a sobering thought.'

'Yes, but we can give them respite if necessary. I can't wait.'

Allie looked at Mark's face, eager, excited. She was more anxious, but there was anticipation. She hoped they would get it right, that they would have the chance to change a child's life.

'It'll be fine,' she added. 'You'll have to learn to share your chocolate, though.'

Mark gasped. 'It's you who needs to do that, Ms Squirrel.'

'I just happen to like Maltesers more than you.'

'Do you think we'll have to get used to chocolate cereals? And going on lots of walks? Hey, we might have to get a puppy!'

'One step at a time.' She laughed.

'But it would complete the image of domestic bliss.'

'Shut up.' Allie knew he was teasing her. It wasn't a dog he longed for. Mark wanted – no, needed – to be a father, even if it was on a short-term basis. She had spoken to several foster parents who'd gone on to adopt children. Who knew what the future would bring for them?

It was something to look forward to, for them both.

CHAPTER TWENTY-NINE

Monday

Allie hadn't got much sleep last night. She wasn't sure if it was the heat, because Mark had been restless, too, or her mind going over the things she knew about the death of Kit Harper. It was half past six now, though. Time to get up and face another day that promised to be just as hot.

After a shower and a quick breakfast with Mark, she headed to the station. Once at her desk, she checked over things to see if anything important had come in. There was an email from Dave Barnett to say the footprints on the path were too dry to pick up, but they were more than likely a male boot or trainer that had been there for days. They weren't a match to Kit's, though.

No murder weapon had been found nearby, so it was probable the killer had taken it from the scene of the crime, or indeed used a fist. The search team would widen their perimeter today.

There were preliminary post-mortem results from Christian, too. She scanned them, looking for one thing in particular, sighing when she saw it. There had been no DNA found of the killer so far. They were none the wiser, which was rather frustrating.

She reached for her mug and went out to join the team.

'Anyone want a brew before the team briefing?' she offered, picking most mugs up before they'd replied. She knew her team, their foibles, their moods, their taste in hot beverages.

'We've had a call from a neighbour who has CCTV footage of Kit going past his house,' Sam said when she returned. 'I'll check with him later, see if he can email it to me. It won't mean much but we can cross reference the time.'

'Thanks, Sam.' Allie popped down the mugs at the relevant desks of their owners. 'What did you find out about the men yesterday?'

'Not much that we don't know, I'm afraid. Aaron Clarke is a brickie, working on the new-builds off Bucknall Old Road. He and Gemma divorced four years ago, and he's with a woman called Natasha Hope now. There's nothing on her, nor Gemma for that matter. All of them have clean records.

'Except for Ben, they all went to Seddon Junior and High Schools. Kit was working at the Chesterfield Garden Centre, and Scott had his own scrap metal business until they both started working at Car Wash City, Longton branch, a couple of months ago.'

There was a collective groan around the room.

Allie put up a hand. 'Yeah, the bloody thing haunts us, I know.'

'I can't find a Ben Grant in the army. Well, I've found one who's several years older than this Ben. He came from Essex. He died two years ago in a car accident.'

'Interesting. Keep digging. He must have a sub-contracting licence if he works for himself.'

'He's more into the property design,' Perry replied. 'He told me he doesn't get his hands dirty now. From the car he drives, I expect that's true. He's got a nice Range Rover, twelve months old tops.'

'Okay, let's speak to all three of them again.' Allie pointed to the board. 'See if we can get to the bottom of this fight. Can you arrange for them to come into the station this afternoon? I assume they're all around?'

'Yes, Ben Grant said he'd stay in Stoke for a couple of days, to be with Gemma Clarke.'

'Good. Perry, can you do the interviews? Make out they're general chats and then see what they might give us about why they were lying.' She paused for thought. 'Actually, for this round, let's talk to them in their homes. It's a bit unconventional, but if you sense there's more to it, bring them in. It shouldn't take long, but I think it will be worth it.'

'Sounds like a plan.' Perry nodded.

'More forensics will be with us this afternoon, but the preliminary is there's nothing of use, unfortunately. So for now, let's work on tracking Kit's movements and who exactly would have been the last person to see him.' She turned to Perry. 'Anything else we need to know about Jack Fletcher's case?'

'I'm not getting much, to be honest. Was hoping some forensics had come through, with more links.'

'Sam, anything else?'

'I found out Jack left the pub around midnight, and I can see him walking away but there are no cameras on the road. I'm working out from there, although I haven't seen anything yet. I'm wondering if someone gave him a lift, perhaps dropped him off near to his home. I'll keep on checking.'

'Right, then. I'm going to visit the mortuary for Nicky to ID Kit's body and then take her to see the crime scene. After that, it's the press release.' She clasped her hands together. 'And then I'm going to take great pleasure in calling to see Kenny Webb at Car Wash City.'

CHAPTER THIRTY

Three Months Ago

Kit was in The Wheatsheaf waiting for Scott to arrive with Martin Smith. At the weekend, Scott had thrown a curveball by mentioning a job offer that had come up. He'd told him about his plans to pack in with the scrap metal business and become a manager at Car Wash City.

Even though it was a chance to work with Scott on a full-time basis, Kit wasn't sure. It could either be a great move or a really stupid one, and right now he couldn't make his mind up which. The business had a reputation.

Kit had tried to warn Scott off at first.

'You'll get yourself in strife,' he'd said.

'I know what I'm doing,' Scott had insisted. 'It's a legitimate business, on the outside. Besides, Martin wants us both to work there.'

Kit had been flattered as well as apprehensive. He hated his security job but wasn't sure about this either.

'It could be a massive opportunity,' Scott went on. 'There are six branches now and there are going to be more. We could be managers at our own within no time.'

A new job could be the thing Kit needed to get himself on track. If it wasn't for Brooke bleeding him dry after the divorce, he wouldn't have ended up in so much debt. The thought of a larger salary kept calling to him.

Eventually, he'd told Scott he needed to hear more and then he'd decide if it was for him. He might as well hear what Martin had to say, to make sure there wasn't anything dodgy.

Kit supped his pint, the noise around him fading away as he thought through what Scott had talked about. He'd said he could do as much or as little as he wanted behind the scenes. He didn't even have to get involved at all, but he could earn some decent money if he did.

Both men arrived a few minutes later. He waved to get their attention, and they came over to him.

Martin was in his late forties. He had olive skin and a good head of hair, brown but greying at the roots. He wore dark jeans and a white shirt underneath a smart jacket and carried a soft leather laptop bag.

'Hey.' Scott shook hands with Kit. 'This is Martin.'

'Hi, Kit, pleased to meet you.' Martin offered his hand, too. 'Scott's told me a lot about you. All nice, I hasten to add.'

The jovial nature of his tone put Kit at ease. Martin pulled out his laptop and went through what he was doing with the company. He then explained what he wanted from him and Scott and why it would benefit them all round.

'It's a good job offer,' he finished. 'I know Scott is up for it, but I do need two men, preferably friends who know each other well.'

'It's nothing dodgy, is it?' Kit grimaced at his choice of words but wanted to be clear before committing himself.

Martin laughed. 'Of course not. Tell him, Scott – I only take chances on dead certs.'

'He's right.' Scott nodded. 'He's been trying to get me to work with him for a year or so now.' He pointed to Kit and then back at himself. 'Think about it, mate. You and me – working together. It'll be a blast. And no weekend work either. The lads will cover those shifts. We'll be in during the week only.'

It wasn't what Kit had expected from the conversation, and not having to work weekends was a real selling point. It pissed him off at times when they went out on a Saturday night, and he couldn't let his hair down because he had a shift the following day. He'd been able to get away with a mega hangover when he was eighteen, but not at his age. They were a nightmare to work though.

As Martin continued to tell them about the benefits, he warmed to the idea. To do something completely different, get a life again.

'Can you give me a few days and I'll get back to you?' he asked Martin.

There was a pause, and he thought he was going to flat-out deny him. But then Martin glanced at Scott before nodding.

'I'll need to know by the weekend.'

'Okay.'

Scott picked up his glass. 'I'll drink to that.'

'I'll get a round in for you on my way out. Same again, Kit?' Martin stood up.

'Cheers.' Kit grinned.

'What do you think?' Scott asked, once Martin had gone. 'Is it worth a shot?'

'I don't know.' He pulled a face. 'It sounds good, but I'll have to speak to Nicky first.'

'You know she'll talk you out of it.' Scott shook his head. 'For once, do something for yourself.'

'It's a big decision.'

'You're hardly giving up a job that you love. Besides, look how well Martin has done.'

'I suppose. What does Leanne think about it?'

'I haven't told her yet.'

'You can't just pack in your business without discussing it with her.'

Scott shrugged. 'I don't care what she thinks. I'm still going to do it.'

Kit frowned. It was typical of Scott to think of no one but himself. Nicky would go crazy if he did it behind her back.

'Definitely think about it,' Scott added. 'It will be brilliant with the two of us. We'd work well together, I'm sure. Come on, live dangerously for once.'

Kit was intrigued, enough to know that he'd regret it if he didn't have a go at something else. And it wasn't every day he was offered a job, especially working with his best mate. Nicky would have to put up with him doing something spontaneous for a change.

With that, Kit decided.

'I've decided to go for it,' he said.

'Fantastic. You won't regret it.' Scott swallowed a mouthful of lager and raised his glass in the air as a toast. 'I have a feeling we're going to enjoy this.'

'I like the sound of that.' Kit clinked his glass with Scott's. 'Here's to us, and Car Wash City.'

CHAPTER THIRTY-ONE

Monday

Nicky was surprised she'd managed to get any sleep last night, but the emotion must have drained her. She woke up sweating, the thin sheet she'd been using to replace the usual duvet due to the run of hot days, pushed to the floor.

She reached for Kit's pillow, pulling it into her chest and hugging it tight. The bed felt so different without him there. She was used to him lying beside her, cuddling up to her back in the mornings, then racing out of bed when the alarm went off.

She desperately wanted to be close to him again. She missed him, knowing that she hadn't really been nice to him in the months leading up to his death.

She wondered when she had lost her confidence. It was way before she'd been made redundant. Even before that, she was bored with the daily drudge, the routine. There was so much time to fill when she didn't have children to look after. It hurt, but there was nothing she could do about it.

She couldn't recall a time when she hadn't known Kit. In their teens, she'd often played gooseberry with Kit when Scott and Leanne, and Gemma and Aaron, were dating. He'd always called her the irritating friend back then, and she'd done everything to encourage that. But then he'd paired up with Brooke, she'd started dating a boy from a different school and forgotten about Kit until she was older.

When he'd been best man at Leanne's and Scott's wedding, Nicky had been the chief bridesmaid, and he'd ribbed her all evening about the bridesmaid getting off with the best man. She knew he fancied her back then, but he was still married. His daughter, Danielle, came along, and Nicky put her infatuation to bed and got on with her life.

It was six years before they were at another wedding, and this time, even though he was still married, they started an affair. A few months later, when she was totally head over heels in love with him, he and Brooke split up.

Kit hadn't taken much persuading for them to become a permanent item. Three years later, they'd married, and she'd taken Brooke's place in their group of six.

She couldn't stop thinking of the life Kit had lost, nor of the one growing inside her. The only part of him she had left. Kit would never see their child being born, or even know what sex it would be. He'd spoken about wanting a boy, not just because he already had a daughter. He wanted a son to take to football matches, to play games with, to laugh and giggle with.

Nicky had said at the time that she didn't mind either a girl or a boy, but she only wanted the one. At thirty-six, she didn't want to be an old mother, so one would be enough.

They hadn't told anyone they'd been trying for a few months. It had been a source of their recent arguments as her life had been overtaken by the need to be pregnant. She'd longed for a child so much that she'd obsessed about it, almost ruining what they had because of it.

Kit hadn't really understood, no matter how much he sympathised with her. He was already a father. But she wanted to be a mother, to grow a child inside her, carry it, nurture it. Now, she would have to do it without him.

Desperate for comfort, she pulled down the loft ladder and climbed into the attic. She shivered involuntarily. All the things she'd bought were stored at the back, away from Kit's prying eyes. They had cost her nearly three thousand pounds over the past year, and her credit card was maxed out because of it. But she hadn't been able to stop.

She reached for her latest purchase and smiled through tears as she took it from its packaging. A tiny duffle coat she hadn't been able to resist. She played with its toggles, fastening them and holding it up. It was so tiny. All the clothes she'd bought had been unisex.

She placed the coat next to her face, trying not to let her tears fall.

A few minutes later, about to leave, she turned and spotted a small box she hadn't seen before. She pulled it over and lifted the lid. Then she gasped.

The box was full of money, twenty pounds notes in four piles, red bands around their middles.

She picked one up. They seemed like they contained five hundred pounds each. That meant there could be two thousand pounds. How could that be possible when Kit said they had no money?

'Are you okay up there?'

She jumped at the voice. It was Carmen. Quickly, she shoved the box out of sight and scuttled down the ladder onto the landing.

'I was just looking at some stuff.' Tears formed in her eyes. 'I'm... I'm pregnant.'

'Oh, duck.' Carmen took her in her arms. 'Did Kit know?'

'I was going to tell him soon.' Nicky sobbed. 'I'll never get the chance now.'

She cried until she was spent, staying in Carmen's arms. Eventually, she felt calmer, her grief spent for now. Even though, there was lots of things to worry about.

'What am I going to do?' she said. 'I can't cope with a baby on my own.'

'Sure you can. You have three good friends, and your mum, to help out. In time, this will be good for you. You'll have a part of Kit with you for the rest of your life.'

'That's such a lovely thing to say.' Nicky smiled through her tears.

Carmen was right. She would hold on to that piece of comfort.

CHAPTER THIRTY-TWO

Allie pressed the buzzer to be let into the mortuary. Inside, they made their way to the chapel of rest.

It was another bad thing about the job, being with family as they identified their loved ones, but it was a necessity at times. Now, it was even more important as Allie wanted to gauge Leanne Milton's reaction, after what they had found out.

Nicky had wanted to bring her friends with her for support. Rachel had met Allie in the car park, bringing everyone with her. They wouldn't be allowed to view the body, but it was good they were there.

Nicky chose to go in the room with Allie, and once she'd identified Kit, fell apart in her arms. After a couple of minutes, she took her back to the waiting room, where Gemma and Carmen were.

'Where's Leanne?' Allie asked.

'She went to get some air.'

'I'll go and see if she's okay.'

Bingo. That had been easy – had Leanne left them purposely?

Allie found her, sitting outside in a makeshift garden, on a bench with a plaque celebrating someone who had died in 2014.

Leanne's shoulders dropped when she spotted her, and she looked away until she drew level with her.

'I think you know why I want to speak to you.' Allie saw no point in being anything other than straight to the point. 'We found some photos of you and Kit on his phone.'

Leanne's sob was raw and she tried to hold in her tears. But they fell anyway.

'Please don't tell Nicky,' she begged. 'It will destroy her.'

'If it's the reason the men were arguing, and something then turned sinister on Kit's way home, then it's all going to come out.' Allie sat down beside her. 'You have to be prepared for that.'

'I can't tell her! And what about Scott finding out?'

Allie raised her eyebrows. Leanne didn't seem to have been bothered about her husband up until now.

'How long had it been going on?' she wanted to know.

Leanne looked at the ground.

'Leanne?' she probed after an awkward silence between them, the traffic in the distance the only sound.

'A long time, okay. We saw each other on and off.'

'Was it the reason why his first marriage broke down?'

'No.' She sighed. 'Well, it might have been. We weren't always seeing each other, but it couldn't have helped.'

'Do you think someone found out about it? Could this have been why the men were arguing?'

'I don't know. We were always careful, but you never know.' Her skin reddened. 'Was he killed because of me?'

'We have to keep an open mind at the moment. I just wanted to clarify when the last time you saw him was again.'

'It was on Saturday when he stopped by for Scott.'

'I mean when you and he met in secret.'

'Kit came round to mine on Wednesday, on his way home from work. Scott wasn't due back at mine for an hour and Amy was at drama club.'

'And you didn't go out late on Saturday night to meet him?'

She shook her head fervently. 'I would never harm him.'

'You'd be surprised what people do in the height of passion and in a jealous rage. Could I see your phone?'

Leanne got it out of her bag. 'You won't find anything on it.'

'I'm trying to get a picture of Kit's life and why he might have been killed. If Scott had found out about your affair—'

'They've known each other since they were five years old! They were like brothers. Scott wouldn't have hurt him.'

'Not even if he found out Kit was sleeping with you? You have to admit, it changes everything.'

'No.' She shook her head again. 'He wouldn't.'

Allie wasn't convinced, but there wasn't anything more she could ask. She scrolled through the messages on Leanne's phone. There was nothing from Kit.

'I deleted every message he sent once I'd read it,' Leanne explained.

Allie handed the phone back to her, knowing she'd need to get a warrant to explore it further. Which she would do, if necessary.

'Are you coming back inside?' she asked.

Leanne stood up and followed her into the building. In a way, Allie couldn't help but feel sorry for her. No matter what the circumstances, Leanne had to hide her grief, and that was a hard thing for anyone to do.

And she couldn't condone Leanne's and Kit's actions; she didn't know their circumstances, even though she was trying to keep her own thoughts and judgments hidden.

She checked her watch: half past ten. They needed to make a move. Nicky had asked to visit the crime scene, and Allie wanted to ensure she had time to do that as well as be present at the press conference.

CHAPTER THIRTY-THREE

Two Months Ago

Kit sat in the living room watching the television. He was glad to have the house to himself soon. Nicky was going to see her friend Carmen. He liked Carmen, didn't mind if she came over, but they were going out for a meal. Apparently Carmen had insisted on paying, so that was good. And at least it gave him time away from the incessant baby stuff. Because he knew that was not a good thing if it happened.

Over the past few days, he had made his mind up to leave Nicky. He couldn't keep up the pretence of having feelings for her. It wasn't fair to string her along.

But it was getting the words out that he was having problems with. He didn't even know how to begin. So far, he'd tried twice. He wanted to be with Leanne, not Nicky. It made him a twat, but he didn't care. If he couldn't have her, then Nicky would always be second best.

He hadn't been truthful with her since before they

married, which made him a shit of the biggest variety. Yet, how do you break your wife's heart? At least when he split up with Brooke, they were at each other's throats all the time, so it had been easier to walk away.

A message flashed up on his phone and he reached across for it. It was from an unknown number, a video attached. The frame it was frozen on was of him and Leanne.

He sat upright, wondering briefly whether to open it or not. Then he clicked on the image.

The video was nothing sordid, but they'd been caught out. They were in his car, and they were kissing. It was clear to him it couldn't be mistaken for him and Nicky.

He remembered when it had happened. He and Leanne had met up two days ago. She'd come to the garden centre, and they'd gone round to the staff car park, around the back of the building. They'd only been able to have a brief kiss. How had someone caught that? Were they being followed or had someone spotted them on the off chance?

He checked the phone number it had been sent from. It definitely wasn't one he recognised, even though it had come up with no name. Should he call to see who it was? In the spur of the moment, he decided to.

But the phone rang out. He couldn't even leave a message.

Who the hell was playing games with him, and was it going to get them into strife? He quickly saved it to a hidden folder on his phone and deleted the message. Whoever it was might get in touch again but until then he'd be none the wiser.

But, strangely enough, after seeing it he wasn't sure he was bothered if it got out or not. He ran a hand through his hair. Fuck, he was tired of hiding his feelings.

While he could hear Nicky upstairs drying her hair, he rang Leanne. Scott was working late so there was no chance of him being home yet. And he needed to see if she'd received the video link, without mentioning it if she didn't.

'Hey, gorgeous,' he spoke in a low voice.

'What's up?'

Her tone was puzzling. She didn't seem pleased to be hearing from him. Wasn't she able to speak? Or *had* she received the video too?

'Nothing,' he replied. 'I just wanted to talk to you. Are you on your own?'

'Yes. Is Nicky there?'

'She's upstairs. Don't worry, she can't hear us.'

'Well, I'm glad you've rung because I wanted to speak to you. I can't do this.'

'Can't do what?'

'Us! It needs to stop.'

Kit froze. 'Why?'

'Because you'll be too close to Scott if you take the job at Car Wash City. It'll be harder to meet up, and also to keep it secret. It would crush him, and Nicky, if it got out.'

'But you can't just finish things!' Kit's voice rose. In a panic he looked towards the door, but he could still hear Nicky upstairs.

'I have to,' Leanne went on. 'I — I care about you but I can't have this on my conscience.'

Kit couldn't believe what he was hearing. 'So that's it? I just have to get on with my life without you?'

'Yes.'

'No! I can't.'

'You'll have to. Scott will find out and—'

'Shall I tell him *our* little secret? He might not think much of you then.'

'You wouldn't!' Leanne gasped.

He was calling her bluff. If he did say anything, a lot of

people would turn against him too. All he'd be doing it for was spite.

'I have to go,' Leanne said. 'Amy's home and I can't—'

'No, wait! Please, can we meet and talk about this more?'

'There's nothing left to discuss.'

The line went dead, and he swore.

'What was that?' Nicky came into the room, making him jump.

'Oh, nothing.' He put his phone down on the seat. 'I was just reacting to something on the news.'

Nicky sat down on the opposite end of the settee, her nose already in her phone.

Kit couldn't wait for her to leave. His mind was on Leanne. How could she want to finish it when *he* wanted them to be together permanently? At least she hadn't received the video clip. He'd have to speak to her again tomorrow. She was getting cold feet, that's all.

A message flashed up on his phone.

Don't ever tell her what's been going on.

He picked it up, glancing at Nicky to see if she'd seen it too.

She had.

'Who was that from?' she asked.

He pasted on a fake smile. 'It's something to do with work.'

When he didn't elaborate, Nicky nudged him along. 'And?'

'And what?'

'Why was it sent to you?'

'Someone hid Big Dave's boots and he was in a rage about it and had a go at Pat. There was nearly a bust up but they're fine now. The supervisor found out and said she'd report us if we didn't say who it was.'

'And was it you?'

He nodded.

Nicky rolled her eyes. 'Your so-called jokes will get you into real trouble one day, Kit Harper. Are you going to tell her the truth?'

Kit shook his head, glad that she believed his lies. 'It'll blow over before the end of the week.'

Nicky stared at him, but he didn't look her way. After a few moments, he glanced at her to see she was back looking at her phone.

He sighed inwardly. At least she didn't seem suspicious of anything.

CHAPTER THIRTY-FOUR

Monday

After an emotional time with Nicky Harper, Allie made her way to the station. The morning had the ability to wipe her out, but she'd bottled all that for later in the evening when she was on her own. She could never come away from a visit where someone had identified their loved one without feeling their pain. The tears, the anger; the frustration, the disbelief.

Afterwards, they'd driven to the crime scene, where flowers had been laid. There were already lines of flowers and cards against the opening to the cut-through.

Even though it was cordoned off, Allie had pushed the press back as soon as a few photos had been snapped, greeting them with friendly chit-chat and getting them out of the way quickly. She hated the sensationalism, even though she knew the journalists had a job to do. In some ways, it was just as important as her own. They gathered clues, information, and it had often led to a break in a case.

Jenny informed Allie it was only going to be a brief state-ment to the camera, on the steps of the station. There would be no questions at this stage, just another information briefing for the public.

'Our main focus will be on Kit Harper as I assume more people might have seen him out on Saturday evening,' Jenny told her. 'Plus, we don't have formal identification for Jack Fletcher yet. I'll be asking for further information, and then we can see what comes in.'

'Yes, Ma'am.'

Twenty minutes later, Allie took a deep breath as she stood by the side of Jenny and looked straight into the lens of the camera. She didn't particularly like being in the spotlight but knew that people often approached her when they'd seen her on TV. It gave a face to a name, she suspected, a more personal touch. Plus, it had got her known more in the city.

Jenny began the briefing.

'A murder investigation was opened after a man in his thir-ties was found with serious head injuries in the early hours of yesterday morning. The man was declared dead at the scene.

'Earlier this morning, the victim has been formally identi-fied as Kevin Harper, known to his friends and family as Kit. He was thirty-six and had been out with friends at The Wheatsheaf, Fenton.

'The investigation is in its early stages, but we are appealing to anyone who was in The Wheatsheaf on Saturday evening between the hours of nine and midnight, who may have seen or heard anything that might assist us with our enquiries, to come forward and contact the police. It may have been a snippet of conversation that you overheard, or you saw the argument that we know broke out.

'Or you may have seen Kit while he was walking home, having remembered something now you've seen and heard this statement. The helpline telephone number you will need is flashing on your screen below. Handouts will be given to all press.'

While Jenny took a deep breath before moving on, Allie scanned the crowd of journalists eager for information. Most of them were the ones she'd moved back earlier at the crime scene. They were holding up phones, some taking notes on paper the old-fashioned way. All of them were giving them their full attention.

'The second murder inquiry is of a man in his sixties,' Jenny continued. 'He was found in his home in Burslem. We believe him to be Jack Fletcher and are appealing to his family to come forward. When further details can be given out, we will do another update. I won't be taking questions at this time. Thank you.'

Allie waited for Jenny to retrieve her notes. She was about to go back into the station when she noticed Simon Cole, the crime editor for the local newspaper, *Stoke News*. He was waving for her attention.

'This might be something and nothing, Allie,' he said in a whisper. 'But I heard Kit Harper was working at Car Wash City, the Longton branch. I think Scott Milton was, too.'

'Yes, I know.'

'Damn, I thought I might be telling you something new.'

Allie raised her eyebrows. 'I'm a copper, it's my job.' She grinned. 'Although I appreciate the tip-off. You could do some checking for me, though. I'm after information on Martin Smith. He's in charge of the Stoke branch. I'd love you forever if you could find any dirt on him, under the radar, of course.'

'Of course.' He tapped his nose twice, the sign for secrecy.

Allie laughed as she sped off along the corridor. She was always glad to have Simon onside. They knew a lot about Martin Smith but equally they knew nothing.

CHAPTER THIRTY-FIVE

Allie rang Kenny Webb before she ventured over to Longton, wanting to ensure he was there. She wondered if he'd be his usual jovial self, hoping that his friendliness would throw her off the scent. It never worked, even though she'd left him thinking it had on many occasions.

The door to his office was open wide, to let some fresh air in, she assumed.

'We'll have to stop meeting like this, Inspector,' Kenny joked as she stepped inside.

'People you know keep dying,' Allie retorted with a shrug.

'Yeah, joking aside. I was shocked to hear about Kit. Anything I can do to help, consider it done.'

'As it's one of your employees, again, then I thought I'd stop by to get some background.'

Allie filled him in with the details she could. 'What can you tell me about Kit?' she finished.

'Him and Scott had worked here for a couple of months. They took over for me. Kit was a good worker, got on well with the lads and the customers. I liked him a lot.'

'Did he make any enemies while he was here?'

Kenny shook his head. 'He was one of the most affable blokes I'd met. Scott was the dodgy one. Kit always kept his nose clean.'

'When you say Scott was dodgy?' Allie encouraged him to say more, always keen to hear his musings.

'I don't mean in the illegal sense, Inspector. Kit was the better worker of the two. Scott would often be found out of office when Kit was doing the manual stuff. Kit never complained to me about it, though. Perhaps that's the way their working relationship was. I'll miss him. He was a great bloke.' He pointed to an envelope on the top of a filing cabinet. 'The lads have had a whip-round for his lady. Raised nearly a grand throughout all the branches. I'm going to add a couple of hundred to it.'

Allie nodded, liking his gesture. 'That's a lot of money for a collection,' she queried.

'*That's* how much we take care of our own.'

She stared at him pointedly. He was telling her that Kit was okay, they would have looked after him as a worker and that perhaps they had nothing to do with his death. But she knew from experience, it could all be for show. Still, she had no evidence to the contrary at the moment so she would keep her options open.

'Tell me why Kit and Scott,' she said.

'We're expanding the car washes, and I needed people in here I could trust while I set up two new branches.'

'Business that good?' She tried to hide the sarcasm in her tone. Knowing the scene behind closed doors, Allie wanted it to fold, to stop making them illegal money. But she had to bide her time until the drugs squad gave them the nod to raid it all. It was taking so long, though, each tiny piece of evidence being stored towards the bigger picture.

'I can't complain,' Kenny replied.

'Do you think Kit and Scott would have made a success of it here?'

'I do. Business had already improved. They'd fired a couple of the lads, hired a few more, and the dynamics changed. Everyone was working together as a team. I do hope Scott can continue that without him. I don't really want to put anyone in Kit's role. It would seem as if I wanted to replace him. It's going to be tough for the next few months, I expect.'

Kenny knocked on the window and beckoned in a man who was outside on the forecourt. Allie recognised him. It was Martin Smith.

'Allie wants to know how the branch is coming on,' Kenny said when he appeared in the doorway.

'It's doing okay, business building up again,' Martin told her. 'But we have a good team of lads working for us. Why do you ask?'

'I'm investigating Kit Harper's death.'

'Ah, yes, I was sorry to hear about it. He was a nice bloke. Do you have any leads on his murder yet?'

'We're following lots of them.'

Kenny chuckled. 'Police talk for we don't have a clue, more like.'

Allie rolled her eyes, ensuring Kenny saw. She really wanted to take a nosy around the place but, even with a warrant, she had no reason. No evidence to back it up, and there was no way they'd let her if she asked.

Instead, she'd wait it out. Something was always going down at Car Wash City.

'Does Kit have an office, or a locker, I can see?'

Kenny banged on the window again and shouted one of the lads in.

'Show the detective where the lockers are.' He passed him a key. 'She's after number nine.'

.   .   .

Kenny waited until he knew Allie Shenton was out of hearing range before turning to Martin.

'Well, that's put the cat among the pigeons,' he said. 'Just as we were leading up to everything.'

'Yeah, it's definitely bad timing.' Martin frowned. 'Do you have any idea who might have topped Kit?'

Kenny shook his head. 'If either of them was courting trouble, I would have put money on it being Scott. Kit seemed like a nice guy, which is why we hired him. No excess baggage.'

'I thought so, too. Maybe he had some we didn't know about.'

'Perhaps.' Kenny ran a hand over his chin. 'I don't like having the police so close. Go and watch her while she searches his locker.'

'I'm on it.' Martin disappeared.

'Fuck!' Kenny sat back. Things would have to be put on hold for now. And he knew one person who wasn't going to be happy about it.

CHAPTER THIRTY-SIX

One Month Ago

Kit had been on the forecourt of the car wash for half an hour. He'd been chatting to the lads and handing out freebies to customers flocking in to wash their cars. Even though it wasn't part of his remit, he enjoyed the banter and getting to know people. Giving them that extra service brought them back. Some regulars visited every week, and it was nice to see them. Luckily, they didn't know what was going on behind the scenes or they might never visit.

Recently, though, he'd been getting paranoid about the comings and goings in the office. He didn't trust Kenny Webb, much preferring to deal with Martin Smith.

'Have you seen the new screen washes to give out to...?' He stepped into the office, almost falling over Scott who was on his knees. His hands were inside a bag Kit had seen being dropped off earlier that morning. 'What are you doing?'

Scott visibly jumped. 'What are *you* doing creeping up on me?'

'It's a good job it was me. If it had been Kenny, you'd be for it. Were you skimming some off the top for yourself?'

'It's just a bit. No one else needs to know.'

'But *I* know, and you've put me in a right predicament now.' Kit shut the door behind him.

'Chill out, everyone does it.' Scott's skin reddened.

'Not me. And don't you get enough from the sideline anyway, without taking a risk? How long have you been doing it?'

Scott wouldn't look at him.

'And how much are you making?' Kit added.

'What does it matter? You were willing to take it from me when you needed it. Now you know how I was always flush.'

'You've been skimming for years?' Kit's tone was incredulous.

'How do you think I got so much? It wasn't just from fetching and carrying, and the odd drugs run on a county line. That's why I took the job here. It's easier pickings.'

'Have you forgotten who we work for?' Kit shook his head. 'And who *he* works for? If you get caught, I don't want you dragging me into this.'

'I won't get caught.'

'Too right, you won't, because I'm not going to let you. Unless I come in on it, too.'

'I had a feeling this would happen the minute you got comfortable here.' Scott sighed. 'It's risky, you do know that?'

Kit folded his arms. 'If Kenny finds out, you'll be kicked out on your arse anyway. You don't cross him, nor Ryder.'

'And you don't cross me either.' Scott came closer to Kit, pointing a finger in his face. 'I don't want to hear a word of this coming from you.'

'This is my livelihood, too!'

'And it'll stay that way if you keep your mouth shut.'

'Only if I'm in on it. I'm loyal and I actually do some work. Not like you, prancing off here, there, and everywhere, rather than do some grafting.'

'It's washing cars. Like that's hard.'

'You know that's not all I do.' Kit shook his head. 'But me doing that will take the scent off what *you're* doing.'

Scott stared at him for a moment, deep in thought. Then he nodded.

'Okay, as long as you know what you're letting yourself in for.'

They shook hands, and then Kit went back out to the forecourt. He cursed under his breath. He didn't really like double-crossing Scott, but when the likes of Steve Kennedy took you to one side and told you to find out what's been happening, no matter how, you just did it.

By next month, he had to tell Steve exactly what Scott was up to, and who he was supplying the drugs he was stealing to.

Kit had wondered why they'd been offered the jobs just like that, and now he knew. They were giving Scott enough rope to hang himself before tackling him about it. He couldn't warn him or else he'd be punished.

One thing was certain, he wasn't going down for Scott, nor was he getting into any strife because of him. Even if it meant selling Scott out to save himself.

Right now, he wished he'd never heard of Car Wash bloody City.

CHAPTER THIRTY-SEVEN

Monday

Scott had popped out for some fuel. The tank was three-quarters full, but he needed a reason to get out of the house. Not only was it oppressive because of tiptoeing around Leanne, he had business to attend to.

First stop was to see Davy Lewis. He parked up and ran along the path.

'What do you want?' Davy asked, answering the door in a pair of boxer shorts. His hair was a mess.

Scott almost growled at him. 'Get a good night's sleep, did you? It's nearly lunchtime, and Kit is lying in the mortuary.'

'Yeah, sorry to hear that.' Davy yawned. 'I'm not sure what you want with me, though?'

'Was his debt clear?'

There was a slight pause. 'He owed me a grand.'

Scott punched him in the stomach. 'I told you not to give him anymore.'

'He was desperate.' He clutched his torso. 'He was *always* desperate.'

'Never mind that. I need you to keep quiet about what happened on Saturday night.'

'You mean the fight?' Davy shook his head. 'What use would it be for me to talk? I still won't have the money. Unless...'

'I'm not giving you any of it, you cheeky fucker. The debt died with Kit.'

'But I'm out of pocket!' He raised a hand and then dropped it with a sigh.

'Consider it a good pay-off.'

'It's a pay-*out* I'm after. If you want me to keep my mouth shut, then I need my money.'

Scott threw another punch at him. He was about to do it again, but Davy's groans brought a woman out of the living room.

'Leave him alone or I'm calling the police.' She dropped to Davy's side.

'I'm okay, Mum. Go back inside.' He stared at her, but she didn't move. 'Piss off! This is business.'

She tutted. 'Please yourself.'

As she scurried away, Scott took a few deep breaths to calm himself down. His annoyance wasn't really with Davy, but it had felt good to vent his anger.

His phone rang, and he cursed when he saw who the caller was. Kenny. He had to answer it.

'I want to see you,' Kenny said. 'Get to my office ASAP.'

The call was disconnected before he had time to reply.

'Fuck!' Scott stared down at Davy, who was on the floor. 'I need you to do me a favour. I'll pay you money if you move a package on for me.'

'That's more like it.' Davy nodded.

'I'll be in touch this evening.'

Scott marched to his car. This was more important than a measly grand. He thought through tactics as he drove to Longton. The less Kenny knew the better. Either way, Scott might get a kicking, and it wasn't going to be pleasant.

He hotfooted it across to Car Wash City, finding Kenny in his office with Martin.

Scott swallowed. He was wary of the two men when they were together.

'Ah, the wanderer returns,' Kenny said when he spotted him.

'I couldn't get here yesterday,' Scott explained.

'What about first thing this morning?'

'Too many police around. It's too dangerous.'

'This isn't *Breaking Bad*,' Martin said. 'Where's the stuff?'

'It's hidden well.'

'From the police?'

'From anyone.' Scott stayed poker faced, lying through his teeth.

'Bring it to me.'

'I will, when it's safe to do so.'

'I've had a call from Davy Lewis.'

Scott cursed under his breath. He'd sold him out. He'd get him for that.

'He said you're trying to get rid of the package. Is that right?'

'Course it's not. Davy wanted a piece of the pie, so I told him a pack of lies.'

'You'd better not be lying to me.'

'I'm not, I swear!'

'So when can you get the package to us?'

'A couple of days. I'll get it to you then.'

'You'd better. And then, take the rest of the week off. You're bad for business with the police all over you.'

Scott nodded, thankful to get away unharmed.

'If you think of crossing me, I'll break every bone in your body.' Kenny glared at him. 'Do you understand?'

Scott faked a smile. 'Everything's fine. I just need to keep a low profile for now.'

Once back in his car, Scott screeched off, ignoring the blast of a horn from the car he'd cut up. His day was going from bad to worse. The package they were talking about had all but gone. He'd sold most of it on a week ago, and now he had no way of replacing it as he wouldn't be at work. He wasn't hanging around for Kenny to find out, though.

Scott wanted in with a bigger player in Stoke, to keep himself safe when the shit hit the fan. He needed to visit Steve Kennedy, get him to cover his back. He wasn't the only one who everything would go tits up for if the police found out what was going on.

He stopped as the traffic lights turned to red, then pummelled his fist on the steering wheel. Kit had caused him some hassle getting himself killed. He couldn't even grieve for him because he was in such a quandary. How was he going to get enough drugs to give back to Kenny?

What a fuck up. Kit had warned him, and he hadn't listened. Instead, he'd played the hardman, creaming a bit off the top here and there.

And now it was all falling down around him. He'd be mad to stay in Stoke, but he couldn't leave. The police would find out more about the fight soon and they'd be back to question him. What if he slipped up? He'd have to think of something to say.

The lights changed to green, and he sped off again. He wasn't sure what reception he'd get from Steve, but he had no choice but to find out.

CHAPTER THIRTY-EIGHT

The one thing certain about Perry's role in the police was that *nothing* was ever certain. Even without CCTV evidence showing they were lying, he knew that his chat with the three friends who had been out with Kit on Saturday evening would bring up something different than the day before.

He went to see Ben Grant first. Gemma Clarke lived in a detached house with room enough to squeeze one car in the drive. The black Range Rover, he knew belonged to Ben, was parked on the pavement in front of it.

Gemma opened the front door with a faint smile.

'How are you?' Perry asked, to put her at ease as he stepped inside.

'I still don't want to believe it.' Tears filled her eyes. 'Not even after visiting the mortuary and the cut-through this morning.'

'Throughout my time as a police officer, I've found people deal with grief in individual ways,' Perry replied. 'Some show it, some grieve in private. Some don't cry at all, bottling it up for months, years. Some go to pieces at the funeral when it all becomes final.'

Gemma showed him into the living room, warm and inviting. It was decked out in creams and Wedgwood blues, a style that was put together well and wouldn't seem out of place in a home renovation magazine. A collection of photos showed a baby girl growing into a toddler and then a little girl. Perry assumed the roller skates in the corner of the room belonged to her too.

The atmosphere was a little off, and he couldn't put his finger on why.

'You have a beautiful home,' he said, for want of a little small talk.

'Thanks.' She pointed to a chair and sat across from him. 'Ben will be down in a moment. Can I get you a drink? Something cold, perhaps?'

'No, I'm fine, thanks.'

There were footsteps on the stairs, and Ben appeared.

'Sorry, I was on the phone to work,' he explained. 'I might not be there in person, but I have to be available to contact. It's a big week for us. We have to finish one job and finalise a new contract.'

Perry noted there was no annoyance in his tone. He seemed low, shoulders drooping as he moved to sit on the arm of Gemma's chair.

'I need to go over your statement,' he said. 'When we spoke yesterday, you mentioned a punch was thrown by Kit to you?'

'Yeah, it was something and nothing. A bit of hot air.'

Perry nodded. 'We've viewed CCTV footage from inside the pub, and it seems Kit threw a punch at Scott and it was you who was trying to keep them apart.'

Ben's face reddened in an instant. 'Did I say it was at me? Sorry, I wasn't really thinking straight after what happened. Yes, it was exactly the way you told me.'

'And yet none of the others said anything to corroborate you either?'

'I think we were all shell-shocked, to be honest. I'd only known Kit for a few months, but they'd been friends since they were knee-high.'

'So can you run me through what happened again?'

Perry took down everything Ben said again, ready to check with the other statements he'd be getting afterwards. Apart from the moment with the punch, everything else seemed to be the same as he'd told him the day before, and what they'd seen on the footage from The Wheatsheaf. Which made him wonder why he'd lied yesterday.

He smiled at Gemma. She hadn't said a word, which surprised him. He'd spotted her glancing at the floor a few times too.

'And you say you were home by midnight?' His question was directed at Ben.

'Yes, that's right. Wasn't it, Gem?'

Perry looked at Gemma for confirmation, and she nodded.

'I think that will be all for now.' He stood up. 'Were you planning on going to see Nicky again today?'

'Yes,' Gemma said. 'I want to give her time with her mum first. They're really close, even though she lives in Cyprus now.'

Once outside, a quick phone call to Scott Milton revealed he and Aaron were at Nicky's home with Leanne, so he made his way there. Allie was parking up as he arrived, and they met Rachel on the doorstep.

'Any joy with Kenny?' Perry asked.

'Not really. Martin Smith was there, too. It was all about how they liked Kit and had a collection for him. There was nothing useful in his locker either. Just the usual crap.' Allie turned to Rachel. 'What about you? Anything we should know about?'

Rachel shook her head. 'Nicky's mum has arrived from Cyprus. She's nice, really upset, of course.'

'I think I might speak to Aaron and Scott together,' Perry said. 'There's something about Ben Grant that I'm not gelling with, although he is an outsider to the group because they've only known him for a few months.'

'Could it be a bit of animosity over a new fella and an ex still on the scene?'

'It seems more than that.'

Allie nodded. 'I'll sound out the women while you talk to the men.'

'More tea, then?' Rachel asked.

They shared a smile before going inside.

Once Perry had Scott and Aaron alone, he sat with them at the table. As soon as he asked them to go through it all again, it was Scott who cracked about who'd thrown the punch.

'Why didn't you mention this yesterday?' Perry questioned.

'I couldn't in front of Ben,' Scott replied. 'Kit had been adamant that he was trying to set him up for something.'

'That's a strange thing to say,' Perry remarked. 'Did he mention what?'

Scott shook his head. 'He had a feeling he wasn't being truthful with us, but he didn't really know why.'

'Do either of you feel the same?'

Perry noted they glanced at each other before each shaking their head.

'Ben was okay,' Scott said eventually. 'But we mostly put up with him because of Gemma.'

'So what was the reason for Kit taking a swing at you?' Perry said to Scott.

'I had a go about Nicky not being able to get a job, and Kit took it a little more personally than I'd intended.' Scott ran a hand over his head. 'It was stupid of me, really. She's trying her best to get fixed up. I don't know why I said it. Anyway, Kit didn't like it, and he hit out. It's unusual, to be fair. Even if we have words, we've rarely had a scrap.'

Perry stared at him. What was going on here? First, Ben tried to blame Kit for the punch, and now Scott was coming out with this? It didn't ring true at all, although it was feasible. Were they hiding something?

He decided to say nothing. Make them think he believed them. Even though things would probably need to become more formal if evidence came to light, he continued with his questions.

'Do you know why Kit would be wary of Ben?'

'I was suspicious of him, too,' Aaron admitted. 'Not just because he was going out with my ex, but the way he could change in an instant. One minute you would get nice Ben, having a laugh and a joke. The next you'd get a different Ben, someone who was having a dig and hinting at dark stuff in his past.'

'Like what?'

Aaron paused. 'It's hard to say, nothing in particular. Yet... I don't know. I often got the feeling he wasn't being truthful about everything with us. He was always bragging about what he had, what he'd done. His work in Birmingham; the time he spent in the Army. Of course, I couldn't say anything as it would seem like sour grapes. The guy is sleeping with my ex.'

Perry nodded, understanding where he was coming from. But he still wasn't getting a handle on the dynamics of the men's relationships. Scott, Aaron, and Kit had known each other since they were young. Ben hadn't been around for longer than a few months. Scott and Aaron were trying to put the blame onto Ben, yet it was Kit who had wanted to fight with Scott?

He left them to it then, letting the men think they were in the clear. But something was off.

Perhaps some secrets were best kept hidden until their owners slipped up entirely.

CHAPTER THIRTY-NINE

In the living room, Nicky was sitting with Leanne and Rebecca Morris. Although Rachel introduced them, it was clear she was Nicky's mother. Rebecca was similar in looks to her daughter, with short red hair and a slight figure. Her skin was weathered due to her time overseas, but she looked well for it.

Allie sat across from them all on the armchair. Rebecca asked her several general questions about Kit, and then Allie answered all her queries about what was happening, and what had happened, so far in the investigation.

Along with that, Allie updated Nicky on what she could. Which was more that they were waiting for things to come back to them, rather than them knowing anything. Despite the first twenty-four hours being the most important, they were only on the second day.

Then she got to the blunt questions.

'While I have you both here, Nicky and Leanne, I wanted to talk to you to see if there was anything worrying you. I know you're a close group of friends, but I also know that

Ben Grant has only known you for a few months. How do you find him?'

'He's okay,' Nicky said. 'It was hard at first to accept him, but he's nice. Always kind to Gemma and Charlotte, and that's the main thing.'

Leanne said nothing, so Allie prompted her.

'I wasn't going to say anything,' she spoke quietly, 'but Gemma told me she was going to finish things with Ben this weekend.'

'She never said anything to me,' Nicky said.

'Did she say why?' Allie asked.

'I guess she wanted someone to talk to, and as Ben had accused her of flirting with my husband, I suppose she wanted to set the record straight.'

'What?' Nicky frowned.

'That's exactly what I said. Do you remember your birthday, when I invited you all round for Sunday lunch?'

'Yes, but I don't recall any odd behaviour. We had a lovely afternoon.'

'It was afterwards, when Gemma was back at home. She said Ben had pushed her against the wall in the hallway. Then he'd accused her of flirting with Scott for most of the lunch.'

Nicky snorted. 'That's absurd!'

'So it wasn't true?' Allie asked.

Both women shook their heads.

'They were always teasing each other, but in a friendly manner rather than flirtatious,' Leanne went on. 'They do have a good rapport, to be fair, but I've never thought anything of it. They ware fun to be around when they bounced off each other.' She turned to Nicky. 'Ben said she practically had her tongue down his throat at one point. I never saw that. Did you?'

'No, because she wouldn't do that.'

'He said she had her hand on his knee, too.' Leanne was

on a roll. 'Gemma was so embarrassed when she was telling me. But she'd needed someone to talk to because she said he'd grabbed her chin, squeezing it hard, and told her not to show him up like that again.'

The hair on Allie's neck stood on end. Was that why Gemma had coloured yesterday? It didn't sound quite the happy relationship she would have them believe. To Allie, it seemed coercive. She'd check with Perry later to see how the couple were this morning. It could have been a one-off, but for Gemma to talk to Leanne in confidence about it, she suspected not.

'When was this?'

'About a month ago,' Leanne replied.

'And was it a one-off occurrence, do you know?'

'She hasn't mentioned anything else, but I've never been able to trust him since.' Leanne shook her head. 'Gemma would never do anything with Scott. She isn't like that.'

A blush spread over Leanne's cheeks, and Allie realised why in an instant. When Leanne caught her checking her out, she continued talking.

'Gemma wondered if it was Ben's past coming back to haunt him.'

'His past?'

'Ben was in the Army and suffered post-traumatic stress disorder. I think the incident showed Gemma how he could change in a moment from kind to volatile, and it worried her because she didn't know him well enough to wonder if it was a regular thing or not.

'And she was wary because of Charlotte, too. She needed to know exactly who her daughter was mixing with. If Ben could be nasty to her, then he could turn his temper on Charlotte. She wouldn't stand for that, so I assume he'd changed his tune. She said it brought a whole new element to their relationship, though, and she didn't know if she liked it.'

Allie took down a few notes, her mind going in lots of directions at the same time. Was Gemma in an exploitative relationship with Ben and scared to speak out?

She waited for Perry to finish with Scott and Aaron. It would be good to discuss their interviews back at the station.

Because something wasn't adding up.

CHAPTER FORTY

Frankie had got to work visiting the remaining properties in the vicinity of Jack Fletcher's bungalow. He didn't find it hard to engage as most of the residents were in their gardens or sitting on the boundary walls of their properties, due to the weather and the police presence.

In half an hour, without stepping inside a property, he had learned more gossip about Jack.

Apparently, he was a nice man, and a vile one.

He would speak to anyone or ignore them walking past on the street.

He was always foul-mouthed and drunk, or he was merry and smiling.

It seemed however long he'd been at the pub would determine how nice or vile he was, and how his neighbours would find him.

But he did get a nugget of information from one of them. Jack had often been seen visiting the woman in the bungalow at the head of the cul-de-sac.

As he walked towards it now, he noticed there was no one

in the garden and the front door was shut. So either the woman was out, or she didn't want to be sociable.

He opened the wrought-iron gate, closing it quietly behind him. The garden was laid to lawn either side of the path, which took him three strides to cover before he reached the property.

He was about to knock when the door was opened. A woman in her late sixties stood there. Frankie recognised the traits of grief immediately. Her hair was dishevelled, as if she'd been running her hands through it over and over, and her shoulders were drooped.

'I'm Detective Constable Frankie Higgins. I believe you knew Jack Fletcher?' He held up his warrant card.

She nodded. 'I didn't want to believe it yesterday, so I stayed in my back garden for most of the day, away from the speculation. Mary from number nine said he was strangled, and his eyes were popping out of his head.'

'That's not true.' He smiled to reassure her. 'May I come in for a moment, Mrs...?'

'Malpass. Isobel Malpass, although I'm a widow.' She stepped aside to let him in and then showed him into a living room, decorated in deep purple and silvers.

When urged, he sat across from her on the settee, being careful not to disturb the tabby cat curled up asleep.

'How do you know Jack?' he began, getting his notebook out.

'I met him when he moved in. I was at a birthday party at the community centre and he was there too. He held the door open for me and we got chatting. He said he recognised me from Jessop Place. When I was ready to go home, he offered to walk with me rather than me getting a lift from a friend. It's only two streets away, and it was a nice evening, so I said yes. After that, he started to pop round for coffee every now and then.'

'And had he confided in you about anything that was troubling him?'

'He told me his life had been traumatic, that his middle son had died in his late teens, and his wife a year later of a stroke, although she was an alcoholic. He liked a drink, too.' She smiled as if remembering something. 'I only saw his funny side really. We never went to the pub together. It was always here for coffee. Occasionally, I'd cook him a meal.'

'So neither of you wanted to be more than friends?' Frankie hoped his question didn't come across as too intrusive.

'No. But I did think a lot of him, Detective. No matter what people may say about him, he was kind, thoughtful, and very remorseful about his past.'

'Jack was seen with a man last night. Do you know of any family he has in the area?'

'He had other children, I think – grown up obviously, but he never talked about them. I didn't push him to either, it was none of my business. Although, come to think of it, he did mention meeting up with one of his sons.'

'When was this?'

'A few months ago, I think. He told me he doesn't live on the estate anymore. I can't remember his name, sorry.'

'Not to worry. That's a great help.' Frankie noted down her response. 'What was Jack like?'

'He was quite the loner. He hadn't been home in fifteen years but said he didn't want to leave when he came back. His mother died, you see. He never did say why he left, though. I assume he wanted a fresh start, but I could be totally wrong.'

'Do you know where he stayed during those years?'

'Blackburn. He never married again, nor moved anyone in with him. That's a shame if you ask me. I still can't think why anyone would want to kill him.' She gave a sad sigh. 'I'm going to miss him so much.'

It was time for Frankie to leave. 'Once we can give you more details, I'll get an officer to come and update you. It will be better hearing it from us before the grapevine makes it out to be much worse.'

'Thank you, young man.'

Outside, Frankie looked up at the sun and relished the rays on his face for a moment. It was hard to think that Jack Fletcher would never feel them on his again.

The crowd of people were still there. He hadn't the heart to move them on, knowing they'd be back again once he'd gone. And maybe he might get a snippet more of gossip if he went to chat to them again.

Because someone must know something that could give them a lead as to why Jack Fletcher was murdered in his own home.

CHAPTER FORTY-ONE

It was three p.m. The press release hadn't yielded anything worthwhile yet, but it had only been a few hours. Sam was keeping Allie up to date with anything important. Nevertheless, she was eager to get back to the office. She was having to keep her impatience at bay, both cases going slower than she'd have liked.

A worry was there had still been no relatives coming forward about Jack Fletcher. Perhaps Frankie would bring back something. If not, she'd put him to work with Perry, or take him out herself, while they gave it a little more time. She hated prioritising one case over the other, but it would be first come, first served with forensics, evidence, and leads right now.

On her way to the station, Allie spotted someone she knew. She slowed down, indicated, and pulled into the kerb. The man had gone past by now, so she glanced over her shoulder.

She had been right. Andrew Dale had just come out of a property on Victoria Road. It was a run-down terraced that stood out a mile, the others in the block clearly taken care of by their inhabitants.

She watched as he walked away, grabbing her phone to make a note of the property number to cross reference it later. Then she rang Grace Allendale.

Grace had transferred onto the Safer Estates team and was keeping an eye on Andrew after Allie had flagged him as a vulnerable adult earlier in the year. Allie was convinced he was being exploited by a group of teenagers, perhaps men further up the chain, too.

Her call was connected after a couple of rings.

'Hey, how's married life treating you?' she asked before getting down to business. Grace had married Simon Cole, the crime editor, three months ago.

'It's exactly the same as it was before.' Grace laughed. 'Should it be different? Am I missing out on something?'

'Not that I recall. Mind, it was so long ago for me that I can't remember. Anyway, I wanted to ask you about Andrew Dale. Have you managed to get in to see him lately?'

'Not for a few weeks now. He met with me once a fortnight to begin with, but the last time, he wasn't in. I've left two further cards with appointment details, but he hasn't been in for those either. Although I'm sure I saw him in the window. Want me to try again this week?'

'That would be great, thanks. I've just seen him coming out of a property in Victoria Road. I'll send you the details, but it was one I recall being found in Billy Whitmore's notebook, you remember? I wonder if someone has him collecting the money that Billy was responsible for before he died.'

'I hope not.'

Three months ago, after the death of Billy Whitmore, Allie had her suspicions that Andrew was being used as a cuckoo, a term given to a vulnerable person whose home was being used by others for crime purposes.

Billy Whitmore had been found with a notebook containing names and addresses of other vulnerable people in the area. Some of them had been questioned, offered help and guidance. Most had been too scared to speak out after being contacted. Grace had been keeping an eye on Andrew, knowing he might be a key to something more sinister.

'How's the flat been?' Allie wanted to know.

'Quiet, to be honest. I've had no noise complaints from neighbours.'

'Do you think the lads have moved on?'

The lads Allie mentioned were a group of teenagers who had been going into Andrew's home, often causing a nuisance of themselves outside beforehand and then inside with loud music and playing violent video games.

'It's possible,' Grace answered. 'But I doubt it. Let me see what I can do.'

'You're a star, thanks.'

Allie disconnected the call and went on her way. She, too, hoped Andrew hadn't been embroiled in something.

Her thoughts turned to Davy Lewis. He was seen around Andrew's flat, too, plus the comment from Nicky Harper yesterday instilled a reason for a quick visit before returning to base.

CHAPTER FORTY-TWO

The Seddon Estate was predominantly owned by the city council. There were approximately six hundred homes, a mixture of flats, town houses, and semis. Over the years, there had been a lot of right-to-buy sales which had left it a mishmash of owner-occupiers and tenants.

Some properties were built around large open greens that weren't good for today's needs. Not only did motorbikers race all over them, cars were continually parked on them, too, due to the narrow roads and lack of driveways.

To its advantage, though, the mixture of people had created a better community feel, and it was one of the quieter estates to police. While some residents would always do as they pleased, like in any other city, most behaved themselves and looked after what they had with pride.

Davy Lewis and his family, however, didn't. Allie pulled up outside a semi-detached property in Alexander Place. The garden, as ever, was a mess, the grass too high to attack with a mower. The front door was wide open, the windows in the living room, too, and rap music blared out.

Allie tutted. All it took was a bit of bloody sun and the morons came out to play, disturbing everyone else's peace.

Her attention was drawn to a man across the road, sitting on his front step. His bare belly hung down to his knees, showing bright-pink skin he'd suffer with later. The state of it, she mused. If he can't close his legs, he shouldn't be allowed to wear shorts.

She popped on a pair of sunglasses. At least she could grimace behind them and no one would see.

She trod carefully along the path of the property and banged on the open front door.

'Anyone home?' she shouted. When no one came to her, she knocked again, this time stepping inside the narrow hall and pushing open the living room door. 'Hello, police.'

'What do you want?' a woman sitting on the settee asked.

'Well, you can turn the music down for a start.'

The woman didn't move, so Allie strode over to the music deck and flicked a switch. The silence was almost as deafening.

'Hey, you can't do that!'

'Oh, stop your moaning, Carol.' Allie pushed her sunglasses up onto her head. 'We're after Davy. Is he home?'

Carol Lewis had lived on the estate all her life. She'd been brought up alongside three brothers and a sister, all of them either in trouble or shooting up in an alleyway somewhere local.

Allie had met her when she'd first been on the beat. Carol was five years older than her, and her own children caused trouble now. Back then, they'd been babes in arms, but two of her three boys were in prison at the moment. The eldest son was the one she was after.

'I haven't seen him in ages,' she muttered, folding her arms across her mucky T-shirt.

'Try recalling when it was.'

'A couple of weeks ago.'

'You mean he's moved out?'

'Yeah, shacked up with Lily Barker. I don't like her, the scrawny cow. She's the one who tells him to keep away from me. She thinks she's better than the rest of us just because the council have fitted her a new kitchen and bathroom. I can't believe she got one first. I've been complaining about mine for—'

'Do you have a phone number for him?' Allie was losing patience. It was too hot to be indoors, especially with the smell in the room wafting around her, a mixture of sweat, rotten food, and something she didn't want to think about.

Carol sighed, hauled herself up to sitting position, and reached for her phone. She scrolled for a moment and then passed it over to Allie. 'Here.'

Allie noted it down. She kept hold of the phone before releasing it.

'You sure you're telling us the truth, Carol? Because if I find out he's here, then I'm going to come down on you like a ton of bricks for obstruction.'

'See for yourself if you must.'

'Oh, I intend to.'

Carol shook her head in dismay. 'Can't I have any peace? He's not here.'

'I'll just check first.'

There was a noise in the kitchen. Allie ran through to find Davy tearing out of the back door. She raced after him.

Davy was off across the fields at the back of the property. Allie legged it over the wall, wondering what he had to hide. He could easily have spoken to her rather than give her the run around.

It was too hot to run far and she caught up with him quickly, pushing him to the ground and cuffing him.

'That was silly, Davy. I only wanted to speak to you. Got a guilty conscience?'

'I haven't done anything,' he cried.

'You don't know what I'm going to ask you.'

'I still haven't done anything.'

'So who gave you the shiner?'

'I walked into a door.'

They were silent while they caught their breath. Then she dragged him to his feet.

'We'll talk about this at the station.'

'Ah, man.' Davy groaned. 'That's not fair! I have things to do.'

Carol was on the doorstep when they got back to the car. 'I'm going to make a complaint about you,' she shouted to Allie. 'I told you, he's done nothing.'

'I'd keep quiet if I were you,' Allie snapped. 'I knew it didn't sound like your kind of music, Carol. I'll be seeing you shortly.'

As they pulled off, Allie glanced at Davy in the rear-view mirror and shook her head. She couldn't believe she had this moron to deal with. Still, at least they might be able to find out more about the fight.

CHAPTER FORTY-THREE

Leanne sat in the conservatory, her mind on Kit. Soon they would be attending his funeral. Well, that was if the police ever found out who had killed him.

She still couldn't believe he'd been murdered, never to walk through her front door and into her arms again. Although she felt selfish for thinking of herself, she had lost so much.

Their affair had been so on-off that she couldn't really remember a time when they hadn't been together. Occasionally, the guilt became too much, but they'd always been drawn back to each other, the pull irresistible.

She'd tried to finish it two months ago but had lasted only a week without him. Thankfully, she'd seen him a few times before he'd died. Because she'd hate herself forever if that hadn't happened.

Time after time, she'd questioned herself about ending her marriage, but everything coming out would have hurt too many people. There was Amy to think of, never mind Nicky.

And sometimes she wondered if all she really wanted was some excitement in her life. When things were going well with Scott, that was the time she'd want to cool things with Kit. When they were in a rut, arguing or not having sex, that's when she missed Kit and started the affair up again.

She grimaced. Selfish, selfish, Leanne. It was all about her.

Amy came in to her.

Leanne smiled as she sat down beside her, tucking her feet to the side. She was so much like her now that it was like seeing herself as a teenager again. Leanne's long blonde hair and wrinkle-free skin were a thing of the past, but the blue of her eyes matched Amy's.

'Hi, darling. Are you hungry?' she asked.

'No, I ate at Marnie's.' Amy turned to her, a worried expression on her face. 'Mum, can I talk to you?'

'Yes, of course. What is it?' Leanne prayed it wasn't too serious, unsure if she could cope with teenage angst as well as everything else.

'It's about Dad.'

'Oh.' Leanne hadn't been expecting that. She pressed the mute button on the TV remote. 'What about him?'

Amy looked at the floor for a moment but then continued. 'I heard him on the phone last week. He was in the garden, and he was arguing with someone.'

'Do you know who he was talking to? Did he say a name?'

'Kenny.'

The blood drained from Leanne's face, but she tried to stay calm. 'Could you hear what he was saying?'

'He said he wasn't prepared to store anything else. It was too dangerous, and he didn't like it. What did he mean by that, Mum?'

'I have no idea, sweetheart.' Leanne was being truthful, but she might have an idea. 'Did you hear anything else?'

'He said something about not wanting any more money. As if he was getting paid to do something. He sounded frightened more than angry. And then he turned and saw me and ended the call. Is he okay, do you think?'

'I'm sure he will be. I'd rather you say nothing to him just yet, though. Let me sort this out, okay?'

'Okay.'

'And, Amy, please don't say anything to anyone about what you've just told me.'

'I won't.' Her expression changed to one of concern. 'It's nothing to worry about, is it?'

'I don't think so.'

'It isn't anything to do with Kit's murder?'

'Of course not!' She pulled Amy into her arms. 'We'll sort it out, whatever it is.'

As she comforted her child, Leanne hoped Scott hadn't got himself involved in anything again. Years ago, he'd probably avoided a prison sentence when someone had been caught dealing drugs and luckily hadn't grassed him up. She'd sworn to leave him if he ever did anything like that again.

Even so, when Amy went to visit a friend, Leanne was left wondering. A few minutes later, she began to check through the house for signs of anything untoward.

She found nothing in the living room or kitchen and went to search the garage. Halfway through, she thought of something. There was a small metal box with a key under the bed. They kept their passports in it, along with a bit of spare cash and some euros leftover from their last holiday.

In a panic, she tore upstairs to her bedroom. She got to her knees and pulled it out, placing it on the bed. The key was in Scott's sock drawer, so she searched it out and opened the box.

Squashed inside were several large envelopes she didn't recognise. She took one out and looked in it.

The envelopes were full of wraps. Dealers' quantities. There were also several bundles of cash.

How dare he bring that into the house! The police could find it, and they wouldn't believe she didn't know anything about it, especially now she'd touched it. Her prints would be everywhere.

She took the envelopes downstairs and shoved them in a carrier bag. Then she left them on the kitchen table while she waited for Scott to get home.

CHAPTER FORTY-FOUR

After leaving Davy Lewis to be booked into custody, Allie checked in with Jenny and then slipped out of the back of the station, to the supermarket at the end of the street. Twenty minutes later, she dropped a carrier bag in the middle of their bank of desks.

'Here you go, guys. Grab them before they melt.'

'Ooh, ice lollies!' Sam cried. 'Is there a Fab?'

'There is. And a box of Magnums if you're quick.'

Allie laughed as hands dived into the bag, tearing the paper from the one she'd picked out for herself.

'How did you find Gemma and Ben this morning?' she asked Perry.

'They seemed a little off with each other, but I couldn't put my finger on the problem. Why do you ask?'

Allie relayed the conversation she'd had with Leanne. 'Their relationship doesn't seem to be as stable as they are making out.'

'You think they're covering something up, or just having problems as a couple?'

'I'm not sure, but something's bugging me.'

Once the lollies were gone, Allie began a briefing. She and Perry told everyone about their interviews with Kit Harper's friends.

'We know they're covering up something,' Allie finished. 'But we can't fathom out if it's to do with Kit's murder. Take Scott, for instance. He didn't say anything yesterday when Ben covered for him, saying Kit hit out at him, and yet today when questioned, Scott remembers it was *him* who Kit punched out at and then came up with something he'd said about Nicky that had upset Kit enough to retaliate.'

'I got the impression that Scott and Aaron don't care much for Ben, but nothing concrete about why,' Perry added. 'Just him going out with Aaron's ex doesn't cut it for me.'

'I know they're lying but I think it's best to keep them on their toes for now. The fight might be something and nothing and not necessarily linked to the murder. So we keep that line of enquiry between us for now. What about you, Frankie?'

'Nothing much to report, boss.' Frankie looked over his notes. 'I checked with the landlady at the Farmer's Arms, Jack's local where he'd been on Saturday night. He arrived on his own around seven-thirty, joined a group of men at the bar, and the last time she remembered seeing him was about eleven.' He told Allie about the visit to Isobel Malpass. 'I mentioned Jack being seen with a man, and the only thing she could think of was his son who he'd met up with a few times.'

'Which one?' Allie asked.

'She's not sure. He didn't talk about his family much, to be honest.'

'So no relatives found?'

Frankie shook his head.

'Okay. Thanks, Frankie. If no one comes forward today, we'll go out to the press again, and update the public on both cases. We can mention we saw him with a man this time.

Someone might have spotted them meeting up. Let's also see if we can get some CCTV from the nearest main road.'

Once Davy Lewis was ready to be interviewed, Allie went downstairs to question him. Her first line of attack would be to find out why he ran. Then she'd challenge him about Nicky Harper's comments.

She began the interview after doing the necessary things.

'Where were you on Saturday evening, Davy?' she started. 'Between the hours of eleven p.m. and one a.m. on Sunday morning.'

'In Manchester, why?'

'Can anyone vouch for you?'

'I was with a few mates. We were at a concert.'

'Who was playing?'

'Some local band that my friend was supporting.'

'Which friend?'

'No one you'd know.'

Allie sat forward, annoyed at his rapid-fire answers. 'Catch a train or go in a car?'

'Train.'

'So you'll have train tickets? And concert tickets, too?'

Davy's face dropped. 'I lost them.'

'That's all well and good, but I have footage of you in The Wheatsheaf at eleven thirty p.m. So, I repeat, where were you?'

Davy frowned. 'You're seriously not trying to pin Kit Harper's murder on me?'

'Please answer the question. What time did you leave The Wheatsheaf?'

'About twenty minutes after the fight. If you have it on camera, you'll see me leaving, too.'

'I'm well aware of that. Did you go straight home?'

'No, I went for a curry.'

'On your own?'

'Yes, I often do. At the Spice of Life in King Street. They do the best curries.' He leaned back with a grin. 'Satisfied?'

'Not yet. What time did you leave?'

'About half past twelve. I met up with some friends there.'

Allie knew if he was telling the truth, that put him out of the picture for Kit's murder. She would get Sam to check everything out once she went upstairs again.

'I was in the right place at the right time, if you ask me,' Davy said. 'All hell could have broken loose if I hadn't helped to hold Kit back.'

'So he wasn't angry with you over anything? You were trying to keep the peace?'

'Precisely.' Davy folded his arms.

'Rumour has it that you threatened his wife over some money Kit hadn't paid you back in time. Was that true?'

Davy shook his head. 'I might have lent him the odd twenty once in a blue moon, but he paid it back.'

'When?'

'When what?'

She sighed. 'When did he pay you back?'

'I can't remember. It was sometime last year.'

'You haven't been to his home in the past few months?'

'I don't know where he lives. I only bump into him in The Wheatsheaf. I'm not much for him. He whinges too much.'

'About what?'

'Being skint. Blah, blah, blah.'

Allie had heard enough. She had nothing to keep him here. And, although he was probably lying about the money lending and the threats to Nicky Harper, even Davy Lewis couldn't be in two places at once.

Unless there was something he wasn't telling them. She'd have to dig deeper before she brought him in again.

Upstairs, she sat across from Sam while she relayed the conversation.

'I wouldn't have put it past Davy Lewis to be involved either,' Sam told her afterwards. 'I'll check everything out once Spice of Life opens. I've had no forensics back yet. Have you?'

'I'll let you know when I've checked my emails.'

In her office, Allie thought about the events of the day so far. They were a small team for two murders, but the wider force would wrap their arms around them and help out, especially now there were two suspicious deaths to deal with. Frankie would fill her in soon on Jack Fletcher, but for now, her head was full of thoughts of Kit Harper, his wife, and his friends.

CHAPTER FORTY-FIVE

Kit's murder had hit Aaron hard, and he was sure something must have been going on between him and Ben. Why else would Ben try to get between Kit and Scott, and he wasn't talking about the fight the other evening? He'd seen it for himself over the months. Ben was always trying to cause trouble, often putting Kit down. Scott seemed to defend Kit all the time, too.

It put Aaron to shame now, knowing that he'd never stuck up for Kit. He hated how Ben lorded it up about being with Gemma as well. It was as if he took more pleasure in annoying Aaron than being with his wife.

On the occasions he'd met him, Ben had made Aaron feel welcome, giving him a best mate vibe. But he'd seen right through his act. A couple of times Ben had overstepped the mark with the sarcasm, clipped comments that had too much of an edge about them, and Aaron had caught him staring on several occasions as well, as if he was weighing up the competition.

He thought back to an earlier chat with Gemma.

'This is a bit awkward,' he'd said, standing on the doorstep to collect Charlotte one Friday evening.

'What is it?' Gemma asked.

He paused for a second and then spoke. 'I'm worried about you. It was something Charlotte said to me last weekend. About Ben. Charlotte said he can get a little... intense around you sometimes.'

Gemma laughed, he thought to hide her embarrassment.

'She's nine years old,' she said. 'She doesn't know the meaning of the word intense.'

'Well, no, that was my wording. Charlotte said scary.'

'That's ridiculous. Did she say anything else?'

'She'd seen Ben grab your wrist, and it looked as if it hurt you. I was making sure she didn't mean he was treating you bad.'

'Perhaps she meant that we were holding hands, squeezing them hard or something. I don't think she has anything to be worried about.'

They both watched the neighbours across the road arrive home and park the car in their drive.

'Are you fishing to see if the relationship is working?' Gemma folded her arms. 'Because if so, why don't you come out and ask me straight?'

'It's not that. I—'

'Look, I get it. This is new for Charlotte. She's had me all to herself since you left. Perhaps she feels threatened by Ben being around, but I'm very careful to see that she's included in everything we do. Besides, she doesn't see that much of him anyway. He only comes at the weekends because he works away during the week.'

'Oh, I thought—'

'You thought he was getting his feet under the table, and you don't like it.' She shook her head. 'I've never said anything about Tasha as I sat back and watched her move in with you. How do you think that made me feel? After being with you for so long, and then seeing you with someone else?'

Aaron tucked his hands into the pockets of his jeans. 'I hadn't thought of it like that.'

'No, that's your problem. You don't think at all.' Gemma sighed. 'I'll have a word with her about it.'

'That might make things awkward.'

'Even so, I'll do it.'

'I worry about you, that's all.'

'Well, you don't need to. We're not a couple anymore. I keep everything friendly because of Charlotte, but you and me, we were over a long time before Tasha came on the scene.'

Charlotte knocked on the car window, beckoning him to hurry.

'I'm sorry. I should never have said anything. But I can't switch off my feelings for you. I care about you.'

'And I can take care of myself.'

She'd closed the door, almost in temper, and the words had haunted him ever since.

Aaron knew that his relationship with Tasha wasn't working. He wasn't over the divorce because he'd never thought they would split up, not even when they were going through their roughest patch. Knowing Gemma since their early teens, he'd thought they'd be together forever.

But now, after Kit's death, it had become more poignant how much Gemma still meant to him. He wanted her back and he wouldn't let her go again. Which is why he was concerned about her relationship with Ben.

Last night, he'd spent the evening Googling Ben's name, trying to find out information about him. Gemma said he worked for a property management company based in Birmingham, but there was nothing coming up with his name on it. After an hour, he'd given up.

Now, he was parked at the bottom of Smallwood Avenue, opposite the house he used to live in, waiting for Ben to leave. Gemma had told him he was going back to Birmingham soon. Even so, it seemed strange to be a few doors down from his old home, spying on his ex-wife and her lover.

Finally, forty minutes later, the door to the house opened. He slid down his seat as much as possible, keeping out of view but still able to see.

Ben came out with an overnight bag. There was no kiss on the doorstep, thankfully, and Aaron wasn't sure if he was glad or not. It was weird to think he still wanted Gemma to be happy.

Ben drove off, and when he got to the end of the avenue, Aaron started his car and followed behind. It might not be possible to tail him all the way to Birmingham, but he was going to have a good go.

Fifteen minutes later, Ben pulled up in another street and then swerved into a driveway of a house. They were still in Stoke, on the edge of the Ivy House Estate.

Ben went inside and Aaron parked up. It seemed a pleasant enough street for him not to stick out too much. Up ahead, two children were playing in a small park, a woman sitting on a bench watching over them. A man walked past with his dog and gave him a nod.

An hour later, Ben was still there. Aaron decided to wait for a little while longer. Fifteen minutes passed and he was about to give up and leave when the front door opened. Ben came out of the house again, but he wasn't alone. He was with a woman, similar in age. Quickly, Aaron reached for his phone and took a few discreet photos.

They got into another car, laughing at something, before driving off. Aaron kept his head down as they passed him, looking behind when it was safe. Within seconds, they were gone.

Aaron frowned. Had Ben got another woman, pretending he was working away during the week when he was staying with her, and then vice versa with Gemma? He couldn't get his head around it. Surely not?

There didn't seem any point in following Ben now. But he would come back this evening, to see if his suspicions were true.

He sent a message to Scott, asking him to meet him in the pub. He needed to talk to someone about what he'd seen. He was certain Ben was lying to Gemma.

There was something he wanted to ask Scott about Kit, too.

CHAPTER FORTY-SIX

When Scott arrived home twenty minutes later, Leanne was sitting at the table, the bag now on the seat beside her out of view. One look at her face, and he'd know something was wrong.

He paused in the doorway. 'What's up?'

'Where have you been?'

'At work. I had to show my face sometime today.' He came in, checked the kettle had enough water, and flicked it on.

'After what's happened to Kit? Surely your boss should be more understanding.' She folded her arms.

'I'm taking the next two days off.'

'And is your *boss* happy with that?'

Scott turned abruptly. 'What's going on, Leanne? I've had a shit day and I don't want you giving me the third degree. If you have something to say, then just spit it out.'

She picked up the bag and put it on top of the table. 'I found this little lot in the box under the bed.' She resisted tipping it onto the table for fear of someone calling while it was on display. It would be just her luck to get caught with it.

Scott reached across, taking a quick look inside. His face darkened.

'What the hell are you doing with that? You should have left it where it was.'

'So that the police could find it? I don't think so. Tell me, exactly what have you been doing with Kenny Webb?'

Scott pinched the bridge of his nose. 'I'm really not in the mood for this.'

'Well, I want to know.' Leanne couldn't hold back her temper. 'There's two thousand pounds as well. You've been dealing, haven't you? You promised not to get involved again when you nearly went to prison. How could you!'

'It's just a bit of pin money,' he cried, holding his hands out, palms up.

'It's dirty money!'

'You've been happy enough to spend it over the past few months.'

Leanne caught her breath. 'Don't you dare turn this around to being my fault,' she snapped. 'I had no idea because obviously you tell me nothing. But you'd better start explaining.'

'Leave it alone. I have enough to think about with Kit, never mind that.'

'You're not using him as an excuse.' Her eyes widened. 'Did Kit know? Is that what the argument in the pub was about? Did he get killed because of something *you* did?'

'I don't know!' Scott pulled out a chair, but before he could sit, she slung the bag at him.

'Then you'd better find out. And take these with you. I don't want them in the house.'

'Fine. I'll leave, too. That's what you want, isn't it? Don't think I haven't noticed something's going on with you.'

Leanne froze. 'What do you mean?'

'You've not been yourself lately. You've been miserable,

moaning at the slightest thing. You've been distant with me, off all the time. Nothing I do is ever good enough either. So maybe I'll go and not come back.'

'Don't try to change the subject. I want them out of the house right now. And if there are any more, you'd better get rid of them, too.'

'I don't have anywhere to take them!'

'I mean it, Scott. Get them out of here.'

Scott grabbed the bag and raced from the room. In seconds, he left the house with the slam of a door.

Leanne burst into tears. What had Scott got himself mixed up in? Surely none of it had anything to do with Kit's murder?

And despite his accusations, she was nowhere near to blame as much as Scott. He'd kept her in the dark about everything.

But now she knew, and she had to decide what to do about it. She wouldn't put herself, or Amy, in danger because of him.

Scott sneaked down the side of the house and into the back garden, cursing under his breath. First, he'd had an interrogation from the police, then Kenny, and now he was getting it in the neck from Leanne. He'd only come home to get changed before meeting Aaron.

But Kenny was the one he needed to worry about. Scott didn't want to be fired but he didn't want to lose his liberty and end up inside either. He prayed Kenny wasn't setting him up to be raided because things with Leanne would really be over if that was the case.

Or maybe he could work this to his advantage. He needed to think of a way how to blame Davy Lewis. That would work in his favour. He'd have to keep the drugs nearby until tomorrow, until he'd seen Steve Kennedy anyway. He was due to meet with him first thing.

Making his way along the back fence, he raced up to the shed and slipped inside. He hid the bag behind a load of old tins of paint and crept out of the garden as quickly as he could, hoping Leanne hadn't seen him.

CHAPTER FORTY-SEVEN

Scott had arranged to meet Aaron in The Wheatsheaf. It felt wrong to be without Kit, but Scott was just pleased to be away from Leanne. The weather was still glorious, and they were sitting outside with a pint apiece. The picnic benches were full bar one, the noise quite jovial as everyone let their hair down in the evening sun.

'I've been meaning to talk to you.' Aaron took a sip of his drink and then put down his glass. 'Last week, I went out with Kit for a pint, and he mentioned he wasn't happy about something at Car Wash City.'

Scott glared at Aaron. 'What about it?'

'Well, you see, that's the point. I don't know because he wouldn't tell me. He said something was going on at work that he didn't like, that he was worried about, but when I asked him what, he wouldn't say. He told me to forget it. But I haven't been able to, especially since he's been killed. Do you know what he was going to say?'

Scott shook his head.

'You don't think anyone from work got to him?'

'You mean, murdered him? Come off it.'

'You've both been mixing with some faces lately. I just wondered if things had got out of hand and maybe—'

'Leave it,' Scott said.

'But, what if—'

'I said leave it.'

Scott's tone was enough to stop Aaron in his tracks. 'What's going on with you?'

'Is this why you asked me out for a drink, so you could interrogate me?'

'No, actually. I wanted to talk about—'

'You think I had some involvement in Kit's death?'

'Not directly, no.'

'I would never hurt him!'

'From what I hear, none of the management at Car Wash City ever do the hurting. They get other people to do it for them.'

'Don't be ridiculous.'

Aaron raised his eyebrows. 'Really?'

'Really.'

'So how come—'

Scott stood up, finishing his drink in one mouthful.

'I can't be bothered with this.' He slammed the glass down on the table.

'All I'm asking is what was going on.'

'And all *I'm* going to say is mind your own fucking business.'

Scott strode down the street, annoyed with himself for reacting to Aaron. But who the hell did he think he was, questioning him? And what had Kit been saying to him?

He slowed his place, annoyed now. He should have stayed and figured out what Aaron knew. Would Kit have said anything to him? Was Aaron testing him to find out if he'd tell him anything new?

Passing by the park, on the spur of the moment, he went

through the gate and sat down on a bench overlooking the lake.

How had everything gone wrong in a matter of days? More to the point, what was he going to do without Kit? He had let his friend down and now he was dead, he couldn't put anything right.

He didn't want to go home. Leanne would probably still be mad with him, and he couldn't blame her. He had become too greedy. And now it was his fault that Kit had died.

His phone went, and he cursed when he saw who it was.

'Hey, Kenny.'

'Where are you?'

'On my way home from The Wheatsheaf. Why?'

'Regarding your delivery. I want it first thing tomorrow.'

'Okay.' Scott sighed inwardly.

'You sure no one knows you have it?'

'Yeah, it's safe.' There was no point in telling him that Leanne had found everything.

'I'll be in at nine. Make sure you're there.'

Kenny hung up, and Scott went on his way again. Shit, he was screwed.

His dealing sideline had started as something and nothing. An odd package dropped off here and there; larger parcels being stored at the car wash until the next day before being moved on again. Sometimes it was cash, but mostly cocaine.

If truth be known, he'd be glad to see the back of the drugs. With the police close by because of Kit's murder, he hadn't slept much. But his job was to fetch, carry, and store. He just hadn't expected it to be at his home as well.

As he rounded the corner to cross the road, there was a loud noise. A vehicle revved out from a side street and came right at him. His phone dropped to the ground, and he went up in the air.

Landing heavily, he lost consciousness immediately. The vehicle was gone within seconds.

CHAPTER FORTY-EIGHT

Tuesday

Allie had been at her desk for ten minutes, going over the things that had come in overnight, when Frankie knocked on her office door.

'Morning, boss,' he greeted. 'Just been told on my way in that there was a hit-and-run last night. The victim was Scott Milton.'

Allie, who had been skimming through an email, gave him her full attention.

'Please don't tell me he's dead,' she said with a shiver.

'No, but he's in a bad way, apparently. He was thrown five metres, and his head hit a kerb when he landed. He was admitted to the Major Trauma Unit.'

'Thanks. I'll head up to see him after the team briefing.'

The Major Trauma Unit was an award-winning service, where patients with potentially life-threatening accidents or illnesses were assessed immediately by a large team and treated as quickly as possible, having better chances of survival.

Some of the casualties had been filmed as part of a documentary. Allie would never forget watching one of the first episodes and seeing someone she knew being rushed in for brain surgery, tears pouring down her face at the thought of him not surviving. Thankfully, he had.

Allie checked which ward Scott had been transferred to and made her way to the hospital. He was in a side room now, so that was good news.

She tapped lightly on the door and entered. Scott was asleep in the bed, a bandage around his head and a frame under the covers to protect his legs. Leanne was sitting by the side of him.

'Hi, Leanne. I'm so sorry to hear about Scott. How is he—?'

'This is all your fault,' Leanne interrupted. 'If you'd caught the person who killed Kit, this wouldn't have happened.'

'That's not how it works. It might not be the same person who committed these crimes. We need evidence to back up everything that we do.'

'Someone is out to hurt us! Can't you see that?'

'Us?'

'Me and my family, my friends.'

'I want to reassure you that we're working hard to ascertain if the two incidents are related,' Allie said. 'And we're trying to sort it out before anything else happens. In order to do that, I need to ask you a few questions and take a statement from you. But before that, how is Scott?'

'He's had an operation to pin his leg, and they're monitoring his head injury for concussion. He's going to be in for a couple of nights if all goes well, but he'll be out of action for a few weeks while his bones heal. He's only asleep now. I expect he's exhausted.' She stifled a yawn. 'I know I am.'

'That's good to hear. And how are you feeling?'

'How do you think? Kit is dead, and someone tried to do the same thing to my husband.'

'I wish him well, Leanne. It must have been awful to go through. Shall we grab a coffee somewhere?'

A few minutes later, they were sitting in the corridor, a drink apiece. Allie was glad to get the chance to speak to Leanne away from Scott. She couldn't blame her for being upset but, away from him, she might be a tad calmer.

'Where had Scott been, do you know?' she asked.

'He sent me a message to say he was meeting Aaron for a drink. Then I had the call from the police. I came straight here. Amy is beside herself. I've sent her to my mother's again.'

Allie could understand her worry. 'And you don't know of anyone who might want to harm him like this?' she asked gently.

'No! Do you?'

'We're checking through CCTV around the area at the moment. Hopefully, we can get a vehicle and a registration number and go from there.'

Leanne hesitated. 'Do you think someone is targeting me?'

'Why would you say that?'

'Because of... Kit and now it's Scott who's been hurt. Perhaps someone wanted to kill him, too.' She gasped as the reality hit her all at once.

Allie couldn't help but feel sorry for her. For all she knew, none of this was Leanne's fault. Here she was, losing someone she must have loved and now seeing her husband in so much pain after a possible attempted murder.

'But do you know why?' she asked.

'No, I don't.' Leanne shook her head to stress the point.

'The two incidents might not be connected,' Allie reiterated, trying to appease her. 'We're not linking them yet, but they are friends, who work together at a place we know might not be above board behind the scenes. I really did hope you'd be able to tell us something.'

Again, the shake of her head.

'Are you sure?'

'Yes.'

Allie stared at her, urging her to continue.

CHAPTER FORTY-NINE

Leanne stared straight ahead, willing her tears not to fall. There was so much that she could say to DI Shenton. She could tell her how screwed up her marriage really was. How she and Scott had been arguing, over finding the drugs and the money. About the worry she had that someone might come and find them. She could say all this and more. But that would make her feel like the guilty party.

'We're an ordinary family,' she said instead. 'I don't know why this is happening to us.'

'Okay. I'll be in touch when I have something to share with you.'

Once the detective had gone, Leanne washed her hands again and went back onto the ward.

She sat next to Scott, watching him sleeping. Her eyes brimmed with tears, and she pinched the bridge of her nose.

Whatever happened, she had to keep her affair with Kit a secret. Losing Kit had been unbearable, but seeing Scott in such a vulnerable state had sent her heart reeling in a direction she never thought it would. Her life would be so different without him. There was no way she could cope with that.

She thought back to some of the special times she'd shared with him. Their wedding day, which had been wonderful, despite looking back at Kit as the best man.

The day she'd found out she was pregnant, and the birth of Amy.

The times he'd come in of an evening with a packet of cheese and onion crisps and a bar of chocolate, knowing how much it would cheer her up.

There had been a lot of good times.

But there had also been a lot of rows over the past few months. Scott said she was a nag. Was she? Or was she looking out for him, or wanting so much more from him and showing her annoyance?

She ran a hand through her hair. It was funny what went through your head when you risked losing someone. Last night she'd been ready to finish things. Now all she wanted was for Scott to wake up and be fine again. Maybe they could save what they had, perhaps start afresh if he gave up the dealing.

Sitting next to him now, love for the man she had married and raised a wonderful daughter with flooded through her. She realised how much she cared for him, despite the drugs, and Kit, and how much they were in a rut.

How stupid she'd been, selfish to think she could have it all. When he was better, things were going to change. She would make sure this was a new beginning for them.

She got out her phone and gave Aaron a call.

'What time did you leave him last night?' she asked after she'd told him how Scott was now. He'd wanted to come straight to the hospital when she'd called him, but she'd put him off. There was no point in them both hanging around waiting for news. In fact, she hadn't told any of her friends until this morning, not wanting to burden them after the news of Kit.

'It was just before ten, I think.'

'And you had no worries about him at all?'

'No, he seemed fine to me.'

'So how the hell is he lying in a hospital bed, having had surgery to his leg?'

'You don't think it was deliberate, do you?'

'I keep thinking it was.'

'Shit, what are the police saying?'

'Nothing yet, but they're looking into it.'

'Leanne, is he going to be okay? There isn't anything you're keeping from me?'

'That's rich coming from you.' She ignored his first question. 'There's something you're not telling me, isn't there?'

'What? No. I honestly have no idea.'

'Is this all to do with Car Wash City?'

His pause told her everything, his answer not so much.

'If it is, they didn't tell me about it.'

CHAPTER FIFTY

Aaron hoped Gemma wouldn't think he was out to cause trouble, but he had to tell her what he'd found out. He'd called her after speaking to Leanne, asking if he could visit.

He knocked on her front door, thankful not to see Ben's car. Gemma let him in without a word.

'How are you?' she asked when they were in the kitchen. 'I bet your head is in a spin after what's happened to Kit, and now Scott.'

'Yeah, I can't get it out of my mind. Has Leanne been in touch?' He didn't mention he'd spoken to her on the phone.

'I sent her a message earlier, and she replied to say he's doing well.' She paused. 'Is everything else okay?'

'We need to talk.'

'And by the look on your face, it seems like some pretty serious stuff.' She pointed to a chair. 'Want a coffee?'

'No, thanks.' He sat down. 'Before you have a go at me for what I'm about to say, you need to hear me out.'

Gemma narrowed her eyes. 'I don't like the sound of that.'

'It's about Ben.' Aaron took a deep breath. 'Since I had

that chat with Charlotte, I've felt uncomfortable about him. I can't explain why.'

'That was ages ago.'

'Maybe. I don't know what Scott and Kit were arguing about on Saturday because I'd just come back from the loo, and they were at each other's throats. But I'm sure Ben was stirring. He'd been throwing sarky comments around all evening.'

'Like what?'

'Oh, this and that. Harmless stuff, but lots of things with double meanings. So I... when he left your house yesterday, I was parked outside and followed him.'

Gemma's mouth dropped open. 'What on earth for?'

'Like I say, it was a gut feeling.' He reached across the table for her hand. 'He visited a house in Stoke and he stayed there last night, Gem.'

'What?' She pulled away from him.

'I think he lives on the Ivy House Estate. I also Googled him and can't find him.'

'If you Googled me, you'd probably find nothing.'

'Your point being?'

'That can't be right.' Gemma shook her head. 'He's already called me from Birmingham this morning. He's on his way back, actually. I was going to talk to him about a few things.'

'He didn't leave Stoke, I'm telling you.'

'How do you know?'

'I... I was sat outside the house.'

'All night?' Gemma's tone was one of incredulity.

'Most of it. They went out for an hour. I had a drink with Scott and when I went back to the property later to check, both cars were parked outside the house.'

'But he has no family here, and he said he hadn't made many close friends as he was always travelling around.'

Aaron paused, unsure how Gemma was going to react to what he was about to say next. He wouldn't reach across for her hand again, in case she rebuffed him, but he really wanted to comfort her. Take the pain away from the heart he was about to break in two.

'Gem, Ben wasn't alone,' he went on. 'He came out of the house with a woman. They were chatting and laughing. They got into what I assume was her car, and then they drove off.' Aaron took out his phone. 'I took these. Have you met any of his family or friends?' Aaron tapped the screen, pinching an image to enlarge it. Then he showed it to Gemma.

She looked carefully, then frowned. 'Are you serious?'

He nodded. 'Do you know her?' Perhaps there was a valid explanation after all.

'That's Carmen, Nicky's friend. Are you saying that Ben is *with* her?'

'I don't want to jump to the wrong conclusion. I think you should ask him yourself.'

'But why isn't he in Birmingham, like he told me? Like he *tricked* me into believing.' She gasped. 'Do you think he does this every week? Are they a couple and he's leading a double life?'

'I don't know, but he spent the night in that house.'

'He can't have! We FaceTimed. He was in his flat.'

'Are you sure?'

'No, but...'

'Have you visited it to see what it's like?'

She shook her head, her chin dropping. 'He wouldn't do this to me.'

'Have you ever been with Ben and Carmen at the same time?'

'No, but I don't see her that often. I don't know what to make of this. I mean, if she is with him, why would he be with me? And why wouldn't she have told me?'

Aaron shrugged. 'I wasn't really expecting you to know the woman.'

Gemma's hurt turned to anger. 'The conniving bastard.'

'So you're not mad at me for telling you?'

'For following him when it was none of your business, yes, I am. But at least I have time to digest this and think about why he'd do that to me.' Her eyes brimmed with tears again. 'I'm not sure it matters now anyway. I was going to finish things with him last weekend.'

'Oh.' Aaron hadn't been expecting her to say that.

'It wasn't working for me anymore, but with what happened to Kit, I didn't feel comfortable calling it off. I wish you'd told me sooner what was going on. I wouldn't have felt so guilty.'

'I didn't know until yesterday.'

'So he's tricked me, *lied* to me, and yet I can't work out why.'

'I can't understand it either because he seemed to be so into you.' He glanced at her sheepishly. 'Sorry, but he did.'

'That's the thing I don't understand. Why would he be dating me if he–'

They heard a key in the front door and both turned to see Ben coming in.

'Get out of my house!' Gemma cried. 'You're not welcome here anymore.'

'What's going on? This looks a bit cosy.' Ben came towards her.

She put up a hand to stop him. 'Where did you stay last night?'

'I was in Birmingham. I've just driven back to see you as you were upset about Kit and—'

'Don't lie to her, Ben,' Aaron said quietly.

'I know your address, on the Ivy House Estate,' Gemma went on. 'And it seems you don't live there on your own!'

'I don't know where you got that from.' Ben shook his head. 'You've got it wrong.'

'I saw you,' Aaron admitted.

'You've been following me?'

Aaron nodded. 'You were with a woman.'

'What do you do?' Gemma retorted. 'Spend the week with her and the weekend with me? I bet you don't even have a flat in Birmingham.'

'Of course I do. Let me—'

'I don't want to hear another word. In fact, I don't ever want to see you again.'

'But, Gemma, it's not what you think, and I—'

'You heard her.' Aaron walked towards him. 'Piss off before I take great pleasure in throwing you out.'

'I wouldn't do that if I were you.' Ben stepped forward, his fists clenched, his tone menacing.

'She wants you to leave!' Aaron grabbed Ben's arm and walked with him to the door, still open. He pushed Ben outside.

Ben fell forwards but stayed on his feet. He turned to Aaron.

'You'll pay for that.'

'No, I won't. And give her back the key to the front door.'

Ben snatched it from the ring and threw it to the ground. 'Don't worry, I won't be visiting here again.'

Aaron picked it up and went inside, slamming the door. He and Gemma stood in silence, their ragged breath the only noise.

'Do you think he was telling the truth, about not coming back?' Gemma asked after a few moments.

'I'm not sure. Would you like me to stay, in case?'

'No, I'll be fine, thanks.'

On impulse, Aaron gave Gemma a hug. This time she didn't pull away. He sniffed, the scent of her overwhelming his senses. How he would love to be with her again, although he knew it was probably too late.

So for now, he'd keep her as safe as he could until things died down. He'd do anything to protect her.

After all, that's what he'd done in the past.

CHAPTER FIFTY-ONE

Allie had just got back from the hospital. Sam waved her over as she walked into the room.

'CCTV's come in from the hit-and-run,' she said.

'Please tell me we have a good view.' Allie rolled a chair over and sat next to her to look at the screen.

'Yes, re the vehicle, but not the driver. The windows are blacked out, but I might be able to enhance it. Guess what? It's a dark Range Rover.' She pressed a button, and the footage began to play.

Allie watched as Scott Milton walked across a road, his phone in his hand. He clearly wasn't concentrating, but there wasn't a car in sight to be fair.

From out of nowhere, the vehicle drove at him, the driver almost mounting the pavement in their hurry not to miss him.

It wasn't comfortable watching a man fly into the air and land a few metres in front.

'Ouch, that was intended, wasn't it? I wonder who was driving.' Allie leaned forwards. 'I can't see anything, can you? Apart from a hand on the steering wheel and a shadow.'

'I can't make anything else out,' Sam replied. 'However, wait for it... The car is on lease to one Mr Ben Grant.'

Allie gasped.

'Address was given as twenty-seven Herbert Road. It's on the Ivy House Estate.'

Allie wrote it down and ripped the paper from the notepad. 'Time to pay Mr Grant a visit. Perry, you're with me.'

'Do you believe the cases are linked, boss?' Perry asked, driving out of the station. 'It can't be a coincidence that Kit Harper and Scott Milton are friends, and one is murdered, the other run over.'

'I'm wondering more about them both working at Car Wash City.'

'You think there's something deeper at play?'

'I do, but I can't put my finger on it yet.'

'Want me to talk to Martin?'

'Yes, perhaps ring him, sound him out. It'll get back to Kenny that way.' She snarled. 'That man is like the proverbial bad penny. I thought Terry Ryder was awful, but Kenny seems to have taken his place. I'm sure he's working for him, though. I don't think Webb is smart enough to run the operation like Ryder did.'

Terry Ryder had been the bane of Allie's life for years. As a sergeant, she and her team put him away for the murder of several people and, although they hadn't been able to prove he'd killed his wife, she was certain of it. Even from his prison cell, his empire was run by people who he controlled.

Twenty-seven Herbert Road was a smart semi-detached property. Perry parked in front of it and killed the engine.

Allie released her seatbelt. 'Let's go and see what Mr Grant has to say for himself.'

They knocked on the door, but there was no answer.

While Allie tried again, Perry disappeared around the side of the property. There was a garage at the end of the drive.

Still no answer, so she went round to join him.

Perry was peering through a small window. 'The Range Rover is here,' he said.

'Let's see if we can get inside.'

The roller shutter door seemed new and expensive. There was no lock, so it must be activated by a key fob.

'We'll need an enforcer.' Allie got out her phone. 'See if—'

The back door opened.

'Hey, what the hell do you think you're doing?' Ben came towards them.

'You mustn't have heard us knocking, Mr Grant, so we assumed no one was in.' Allie pointed to the garage. 'We have reason to believe that your vehicle was involved in a hit-and-run last night. May we see it, please?'

'No. Besides, I didn't go out anywhere in it last night, so you must have the wrong one.'

'If we can just take a look then we can eliminate you from our enquiries. It won't take a minute, or we can come back with a warrant, if you prefer?' She stared at him, letting him know they were going nowhere.

Ben gave out a dramatic sigh and disappeared into the house. He returned with a set of keys, pressed a fob, and the garage door went up.

Allie held out her hands for the keys. After a moment's hesitation, he gave them to her.

'Thank you for your co-operation.' She smiled sweetly at him before disappearing inside.

The Range Rover had been driven into the garage forwards. It was dark, so she searched around for a light switch. Perry beat her to it, spotting it on the wall, and flicked it on.

She followed him around to the front of the vehicle,

noticing a bull bar. It would have taken the brunt of the damage.

Perry nodded at the headlight on the far side. When she drew level with it, she could see it was broken, and there were several scratches on the paintwork and chrome.

She raised her eyebrows at Ben. 'You didn't go out, you say?'

Ben came round to see and frowned. 'That wasn't there the last time I looked.' He ran a hand over the damage.

'Does anyone else have access to this vehicle?'

'No.' He shook his head vehemently. He walked round to the back of it. Then he made a run for it.

Allie shot after him. At the end of the drive, she shouted to Perry.

'Grab the car!'

Allie followed Ben along Herbert Road, much to the amusement of numerous families who were enjoying another sunny day. Some of them egged Ben on as she tore past them, keeping him in her sights.

'Slow down, there's nowhere to go!' Allie shouted.

Ben slipped into the cut-through that would take them to the next street. She hoped Perry would make it in time before he could get out the other end. The estates were like rabbit warrens. They could easily lose him.

Slowing to negotiate the turnstile fitted to stop the bikers speeding up and down, Ben faltered, tripping over his own feet, but he righted himself and continued running.

Allie was flat out but nowhere near catching him.

Perry screeched to a halt in front of them and got out of the car, leaving the door open.

Cornered, Ben slowed to a stop. Allie pushed him up against the hedge, reached for her handcuffs, and snapped them on his wrists.

'Ben Grant, I'm arresting you on suspicion of attempted murder for the hit-and-run on Scott Milton.'

'It wasn't me!' Ben insisted as she turned him. 'I swear it wasn't me.'

She finished reading him the rest of his rights and they bundled him into the car. Then she high-fived Perry before driving back to the nick.

CHAPTER FIFTY-TWO

Allie was upstairs in the office. Perry was booking Ben Grant in with the custody sergeant while she caught up with Sam.

'I'm way too old for this kind of stuff,' she said. 'I'm knackered.'

'Get off with you,' Sam cried. 'It's too bloody hot for anything today, never mind him running you ragged.'

Perry came striding across the room, his face like an excited child. 'Boss, you have to hear this. Ben was causing a right fuss about having his fingerprints done. That's probably because he's not who he says he is.'

Allie frowned. 'He gave us a false name?'

Perry nodded, his smile widening. 'When we ran him through the database, he came up as Ricky Fletcher.'

'As in the son of recently deceased Jack Fletcher?' Allie said.

'And younger brother of Peter Fletcher?' Sam added.

'That's the one.'

'Interesting,' Allie mused. 'The family definitely moved off the estate some years ago, but Ben could have come back, too.'

'He has a flat in Birmingham,' Sam reminded them.

'And a job, apparently.' Allie nodded. 'Let's check into that. If he's using an alias, he might be known there as Ben Grant, so enquire about both names. Or he might not be known at all if it's fake.'

'It's strange why he hasn't come forward about his dad, though,' Perry said.

'Hmm. I wonder,' Allie thought out loud. 'According to our records, Ricky has been in and out of prison since his twenties. Maybe he's holding a grudge, and he thinks that Kit, Scott, and Aaron are involved in Peter's death?'

'He could be. Although, why would he befriend them?'

'To get closer, for revenge, perhaps?'

'So, Kit and Scott might have been involved in the fire?' Frankie asked. 'Aaron, too?'

A bubble of adrenaline rushed up Allie's spine. 'When exactly did he get out of prison?'

'Eight months ago.'

'Frankie, check with the voting register to see who's renting the property. I'll ask Ben in the interview, but let's see if he's there on his own, if he's cohabiting or sofa surfing.' Allie gnawed at her bottom lip. 'This *has* to tie up with the hit-and-run, and perhaps it's linked to Kit Harper's murder, too.' She stood up. 'Perry, I think now will be a good time to go and have a talk to Mr Grant.'

'Absolutely. Do you have a plan of action?'

'No, let's see where he leads us. I'll be interested to see him wriggle out of this one.'

CHAPTER FIFTY-THREE

'Knock, knock.'

Leanne and Scott looked towards the door. Nicky came into the room, carrying a couple of magazines and a box of chocolates.

'How's the wounded soldier?' She greeted them with a smile.

'I'm doing great, thanks.' Scott winced as he pulled himself up the bed. 'You didn't have to come, you know, with what's happened. But I appreciate it.'

Nicky placed the items on the bedside cabinet. 'That's what friends are for.'

Leanne's bottom lip trembled. How could Nicky be so nice to them when she had lost Kit? There didn't seem an ounce of envy, and what had Leanne done to her? Betrayed her, both of them, in the most awful of ways.

All of a sudden, it became too much for her, and before she knew it, she was crying in Nicky's arms.

'Hey, it's okay,' Nicky soothed. 'Why don't we grab a drink? Do you want one bringing back, Scott?'

'I'd love a hot chocolate, ta.'

Once out of the ward, Leanne turned to Nicky. She had to come clean to clear her conscience. She couldn't keep what she'd done to herself anymore. Secrets ate away at you until they poisoned your system.

But her nerves got the better of her, realising the damage it would do, so she said the first thing she thought of instead.

'I have something to tell you,' she started. 'You know Kit was working at Car Wash City? Did he ever mention the name Kenny Webb to you?'

'No.'

'Well, he's a drug dealer and he's their boss.'

Nicky balked. 'What?'

They slowed down to let two porters come past with a patient in a bed.

'Let's find somewhere quieter,' Leanne suggested.

'We're in a hospital. I don't think they do quiet.'

Leanne glanced up and down to see people everywhere. 'Outside, then.'

Minutes later, they were sitting on a bench. There were still folk about, but at least they were at a distance, so it felt safer to talk.

'Kit and Scott have been helping to store drugs on the premises as a pick-up and collect point,' Leanne told her.

Nicky's jaw dropped. 'How did you find out?'

'Because he brought some home, too.' Leanne went over what had happened when she'd found the drugs in their bedroom.

'There was two thousand pounds with them, as well.'

Nicky seemed surprised. 'What did you do?'

'I went ballistic! I told him to get them out of the house. I had no bloody idea.'

Nicky rested a hand on Leanne's for comfort. 'I noticed you'd been cagey with each other for a few weeks. I just expected a lover's tiff. Kit never said anything to me. Oh God.'

Her face paled. 'Do you think someone killed him and then tried to run Scott over so they would keep their mouths shut?'

Leanne blew air over her face. 'I don't know what to think.'

'We have to tell the police.'

'No!' She lowered her voice. 'We can't.'

'But they could come after us next. Are they looking for the drugs?'

'There aren't any now. I told him to get rid of them.'

'And did he?'

'Yes.'

'Are you sure about that?'

Leanne paused. Was she certain? If Scott had lied to her for years about dealing drugs, he could be lying about moving them on, too.

'As far as I'm concerned, he took them away from the house. But what if he didn't?' She burst into tears again. 'Why is this happening to us, Nicky? For all the trouble he brings to me, I love Scott and I don't...' She was about to say she didn't want to lose him but realised at the last minute how insensitive it would sound.

Nicky drew her into her arms. 'I understand. But I don't know what to do either.'

Leanne took her friend's hands in her own. 'I wanted to mention the drugs so you could look out for yourself. I know it's hard for you at the moment and I'm sorry to burden you with this as well. But I thought you had a right to know what had been going on before Kit died.'

Then Nicky pulled away. 'Was this to do with a text message I saw on Kit's phone? It said: "Don't ever tell her what's been going on." Could it have come from Scott? Was it about me?'

'I don't know,' Leanne lied. It was the text message she'd

sent to Kit after she'd ended it. At the time she'd wanted to come clean. She hadn't realised Nicky had seen it.

Almost at once, her skin heated up. She had to hold it together or else she'd give herself away.

But it was too late. Nicky was already eyeing her suspiciously.

'What's going on, Leanne?' she asked.

'Nothing. I...'

'What is it?' Nicky stared at her. 'Tell me.'

They say that action speaks louder than words, but equally staying quiet could be just as damaging. Leanne put her head down.

'The message wasn't from Scott?' Nicky frowned, deep in thought. Then her eyes widened in horror. 'What are you saying, Leanne? Did you send it? You knew about the drugs ages ago, and you didn't tell me?'

'No!'

'Well, if it wasn't about the drugs then what else should he have told me?' She stared at Leanne. '*Was* the message from you?'

Leanne didn't know what to say.

'Were you and Kit... you were, weren't you? You were having an affair!'

'Oh, Nicky, I'm so sorry.'

Nicky withdrew her hand. 'How could you?'

'I'm sorry. It just happened.'

'*When* did it happen?'

'It doesn't matter.'

'It does to me!'

Leanne knew it would break Nicky's heart to know that she had been seeing Kit for so long. All through his marriage to Brooke, their break-up, and then through his marriage to Nicky, too. She shook her head.

'I won't tell you,' she replied. 'It's bad enough what we did, so I won't add to it.'

'Tell me, or I will tell Scott everything!'

Even with that threat, Leanne refused to confess.

'You're pathetic.' Nicky stood up. 'Our friendship is over, do you hear me? It's over.'

'But, Nicky, wait!' Leanne raced after her, reaching out to touch her arm.

Nicky brushed her hand aside. 'Leave me alone. You've done enough damage.'

'I've wanted to tell you—'

'That you were fucking my husband?'

'No! Yes, I don't know. But you need to know that we didn't set out to hurt you.'

Nicky slapped Leanne. The ring of it reverberated in the air, the women staring at each other. Emotions bubbled up, but neither of them spoke. Until Nicky dropped her bombshell.

'I'm pregnant.'

Tears fell down Leanne's cheeks as her world fell apart. Just those words said so much. It meant that Kit had planned to stay with Nicky. And pregnant? A part of Kit had been left behind, but she would never be glad about that.

Tears streamed down Nicky's face, too. 'I've a good mind to tell the police everything.'

'No, please don't. Scott will be in so much trouble.'

'There you go again, thinking about yourself.' She stabbed a finger at her. 'You brought all this on. I hate you with a passion. I thought I could trust you with anything!'

'You can!'

'But not with my husband it seemed.'

Leanne knew she was beat. 'I'm so sorry.'

Nicky glared at her. 'I will let you come to the funeral

because of Scott, but you will never set foot inside my house again.'

She turned and left, her walk changing to a run in her haste to get away.

Leanne sat down again before her legs failed her. What was going to become of their conversation? Would Nicky tell Scott to get her revenge? She clearly hadn't taken it well, nor could she blame her either.

Leanne would never have forgiven her if it had been the other way round.

CHAPTER FIFTY-FOUR

'Sorry to keep you waiting, Ben,' Allie said as she entered the interview room with Perry. She slid a chair out and sat down. 'Or should I say Ricky?'

Ben folded his arms. 'It's not a crime to use a different name. I did it legally.'

'After you last came out of prison?'

'Yes, because someone offered me a job and I wanted a fresh start.'

'That's very admirable of you. Depending on what the job was.'

'I've already told you. I work in Birmingham, in property development.'

'Really? Then why are you registered as unemployed?'

That wiped the smile off his face.

'You live in Stoke, don't you? The property we arrested you at earlier belongs to Mr Jeff Farrington. Do you live there with him, or are you lodging? Or is he an acquaintance?'

'What's that got to do with you?'

'Let's say I'm being friendly.' Allie smiled. 'I'm not quite clear on a few things, though. Can you tell me your where-abouts last night, please?'

'I was in the house, the one you found me at earlier.'

'Can anyone vouch for you?'

Ben shook his head.

'Jeff not home?'

'He's away.'

'And your relationship with Gemma Clarke?'

'I met her a few months ago and I see her most weekends. Why?'

'Does she know that you live in Stoke?' Allie watched him squirm in his seat.

'It isn't a crime if I bend the truth a little,' Ben snapped.

'But why?' Allie sat forward. 'What's in it for you?'

'I can't see how that's relevant.'

'I'm just trying to work out what kind of a man changes his name and pretends to be someone else, living somewhere else. It's quite strange, don't you agree?'

'Like I said, it's none of your business.'

'Okay. Moving on, then, tell me about your relationship with the men in this group. In The Wheatsheaf on Saturday evening, you were with Kit Harper, Scott Milton, and Aaron Clarke. Are you sure there's nothing else you can tell us about the disagreement that took place at approximately eleven-thirty? Perhaps you've remembered something now, with a bit more time to think about it?'

'Everything I said was how it happened.'

'The first version you gave us or the second?'

Ben said nothing, choosing to stare at her instead.

'Does anyone else have access to your vehicle?' she pushed.

There was a further pause before Ben replied with the shake of his head.

'So can you tell me how, if you were at home all evening

last night, your vehicle was involved in an accident that mowed Scott Milton over? The driver sped off, failing to report an accident, and leaving the scene of a crime.'

Ben wriggled in his seat. 'It wasn't me.'

'You're saying someone stole your vehicle, hit Scott deliberately, left him lying injured, possibly deceased, drove away and then put it back?'

'I don't know, all right!' Ben sat forward, banging the palm of his hand on the table. 'Look, I lied. I wasn't in all evening, but I didn't take my car out either.'

Finally, they were getting somewhere. Not what Allie had expected, but all the same. He was rattled.

'Where were you?' She was eager to know.

'I was out with friends. We were in The Albatross from half past seven until ten. Then I walked home.'

Allie groaned inwardly. Why was he messing them about? If he'd told them earlier, there would have been no point in him running. Unless he was telling them this to stall them while they checked into something that wasn't true.

'So you have people who can vouch for you?'

'Yes.'

'Why didn't you tell me this at the beginning?'

'I panicked when you called.' Ben's eyes flitted from her to Perry and back. 'I hid at first, thinking you would go away, but then I saw you in the back garden. I'd seen the damage to my Rover when I got up, so I put it in the garage out of sight. Then I heard about Scott from Leanne – she sent me a message. I knew you'd blame me for it, but I left the Rover at home.'

'Who else has access to it?'

Ben stopped talking then.

'Jeff Farrington, perhaps?'

'No, he's in Spain.'

'We're dusting for prints right now, so we're bound to find

out who it was that helped themselves to your vehicle to commit a crime. Which, incidentally, now seems that this person was trying to set you up for the injuries caused to Scott Milton. And yet you'll still shield them?'

'I don't know what happened!'

'So it wasn't you driving the Range Rover?' Allie repeated her earlier question for clarification.

'No.'

'When we enhance the image, we won't find you behind the wheel?'

'How many times do I have to say no?'

'But you won't tell us who it might be.'

'I'm not saying another word.' Ben sat back and folded his arms. 'You have nothing to hold me here for. You only need to check with the pub. I can't be in two places at once.'

Allie kept her sigh to herself. He was right. They would have to let him go, for now. But she would leave him to stew in the cell while she checked out his alibi.

There was one more thing she needed to ask him.

'Are you aware of what's happened to your father?' She changed her tone in case he hadn't heard.

'Yeah, I am.' Ben ran a hand through his hair. 'It was a shock. Not a loss, though. We hadn't seen him in years.'

'We've been trying to contact relatives but with no luck. Why didn't you come forward when you heard about him?'

'Because he got what he deserved. I hope he died a long and painful death.'

Allie could almost feel the anger coming from him. Something terrible had gone on between him and his father for Ben to hate him so much. It could be the reason why he'd had such a wayward past.

'Were you aware Jack had moved back to Stoke?' she asked, knowing her next line of questioning was going to be controversial.

'No.'

'Where were you when—'

'Don't try and blame me for that as well. I despise the man, but I wouldn't waste my energy on killing him. I haven't seen him since I was eighteen.'

Allie nodded her understanding. She'd been getting nowhere until this final stretch of conversation.

'Okay, Ben, one more thing before we close down the interview.' She looked him straight in the eye. 'Who's the "we" you mentioned?'

CHAPTER FIFTY-FIVE

Allie rested her head on the desk momentarily. Ben Grant had been released. It hadn't been the news she wanted to hear, and even if Ben wouldn't tell them who was driving his vehicle last night, there wasn't enough to hold him on.

The CCTV footage from The Albatross showed him there at the time of the hit-and-run. He'd been sitting with three men and a woman. None of them were from the group they were interested in.

'We can bring him back in if we get more evidence,' she mused. There was clearly something going on. He hadn't told her who the 'we' was. Ben had been reluctant to talk to them after she'd mentioned that.

Allie was sitting next to Sam while she went over Ricky Fletcher's background again. She sipped a fresh mug of tea and gave out a satisfactory sigh.

'You seem like you needed that.' Sam grinned.

'Oh, I did. It's hit just the spot.' Allie smiled. 'I must admit, it was quite a find, Ben being Ricky Fletcher. I'm just looking at his file. I'm surprised we haven't bumped into him before now if he's been in Stoke for a while. Ah.' She clicked on a couple of buttons. 'He only came back after his last spell in prison. His previous address was in Derby.'

'I wonder why he did come back?' Frankie said, sitting down across from her. 'He obviously wanted a new start because he changed his name. But he hasn't been working anywhere so far as we know, and he's been getting money from somewhere. That car is worth a fortune, even to lease.'

'Maybe he hired it to impress Gemma?' Sam suggested. 'He might not seem like the big businessman in a clapped-out Fiesta.'

'But why would he be lying to her about everything?' Allie couldn't work it out.

'Because of his past?' Frankie offered. 'He found a nice woman and didn't want her finding out?'

'Perhaps.' She reached for a digestive biscuit and dunked it in her mug.

An hour later, her mobile rang. It was Dave Barnett.

'I thought you might like to know there are two sets of fingerprints coming up from the black Range Rover. We have a match on the system – Ricky Fletcher.'

'Yes, we know that. We've had Grant in for questioning and—'

'Let me finish, Ms Impatient.'

'Dave!' She laughed. 'Go on.'

'The others belong to Suzanne Fletcher.'

'Wait. You're saying it's his sister?'

'I am indeed.'

'Ooh. I owe you doughnuts!'

'I'll hold you to that.'

Allie disconnected the call and pulled up the records for Suzanne Fletcher, the youngest member of the Fletcher clan. There were photos of her starting from her teens. She had twelve prior convictions. Petty theft and shoplifting mostly. She'd done three short spells in prison.

But as the images changed with age, Allie's eyes widened. Because she recognised the woman in the last photo.

She'd met her only days ago, in Nicky Harper's home.

It was her friend, Carmen.

Ben walked out of the police station and called for a taxi. While he waited for it, he called his sister.

'It was you, wasn't it?' he yelled down the phone, his voice drowned out by the sound of nearby traffic.

'What was?'

'You killed Kit! And you tried to run Scott off the road.'

'Of course I didn't. You know it's Kenny Webb who's behind it all.'

'Don't lie to me! What the hell are you playing at it?'

There was a pause down the line and he thought she'd hung up on him. But the words she came back with were chilling.

'They had to pay – all of them.'

'They would have done, if you'd left it to me. I was sorting it.'

'You were taking too long!'

Ben closed his eyes momentarily, hoping to open them and for all of this to be a dream. But it wasn't.

'What happened last night?' he wanted to know.

'I don't know! Things got out of control.'

'All the trust I've earned over the past few months has gone. No one will believe I had nothing to do with what happened to Scott, and then they'll blame me for Kit's death, too.'

'There's no evidence. All you need to do is stick to what we discussed.'

'Are you mad?' Ben paced up and down the pavement.

'I've just come out of the police station. You used my fucking Rover to run Scott down!'

'It was a spur-of-the-moment thing.'

'You've landed me right in it.' Ben couldn't believe how calm she sounded. 'I need to get away from here.'

'You *need* to stay calm.'

'How the fuck can I do that?'

'Just act normal.'

'After what you've done? No, you're on your own now.'

'Oh, get over yourself. You're sounding like a baby, whinging all the time. I'm tired of having to do everything—'

'Listen to me,' he butted in.

'No, you listen to me! We're doing this for the family. For what they did to Peter.'

The phone went dead, and he cursed loudly. A woman walking past tutted, and he glared at her.

'What are you staring at?'

She soon dropped her eyes, scuttling away.

Ben had been so close, and now she'd ruined everything. Rather than get his story straight for when the cops came sniffing around again, he would leave. At least once he was home, he had his own car to use now that the Range Rover had been impounded.

Everything he'd worked towards had fallen apart anyway. Kenny would be furious.

And that could never be a good thing.

CHAPTER FIFTY-SIX

Allie quickly gathered the team around.

'Ben Grant and Nicky's friend, Carmen, are Ricky and Suzanne Fletcher,' she said. 'They could be in this together, whatever *this* is.'

'So is Carmen the hit-and-run driver?' Perry questioned. 'That's why Ben was being sheepish in his interview, if his sister had taken the vehicle.'

'Either way, they both need speaking to. According to our records, Carmen's last known address is fifteen Worthington Drive, West Brom. Sam, try the phone number we have. It's a long shot as she's not been in trouble for a few years, and she's more than likely in Stoke, but it's worth a go.

'Also, get on to Traffic and see if we can find further images of the Range Rover. I know you'll be doing this too, but time is of the essence.' She ran a hand through her hair. 'You know this means one of them might have killed their father on Sunday? Despite what Ben said to us, he could be lying to cover up what his sister's done. Plus he has no alibi for what time he got home on the night Kit was murdered.'

'It's too much of a coincidence for it not to be, but without a confession there's no evidence,' Perry replied.

'Then we'll *find* the evidence or *get* the confession.'

'That number's disconnected, Allie,' Sam told her.

'Okay, team. Our top priority is to find Carmen. We need to speak to her immediately, to rule her in or out. Frankie, ring Simon and ask him to put it out on *Stoke News* social media. I'll do a press release, flood our channels with it. Let's see if we can flush her out. See if you can pick up Ben again, too. Bloody sod's law we let him go.'

Leanne was feeling fragile after her argument with Nicky, so she'd offered to nip home to collect Scott's laptop. Even though she'd had the morning from hell, she felt better now she'd seen the consultant. Scott's operation had gone well, and he would be able to come home soon, possibly tomorrow evening. If not, another night and he would be out.

He'd been lucky, even though they didn't yet know who'd tried to run him down. To kill him, most probably.

She was putting the laptop in a bag when there was a knock at the front door. She opened it to find Ben. He pushed past her and went through to the kitchen.

'Hey, you can't just barge into my home.' Purposely leaving the door on the latch, she followed him.

He turned to her. 'Where are they?'

'I don't know what you're talking about,' she bluffed.

'The drugs.'

'We don't do drugs.'

He sliced his hand across her face and then grabbed her hair. 'Tell me where they are or I'll hurt you like you've never been hurt before.'

'I honestly don't know.' She tried to pull his hands away. 'I found them yesterday and told him to get them out of the house. He took them with him.'

'Did he have them on him when he was hit?'

'You're hurting me!'

'I intend to. Did he?'

'No. The police didn't mention it.'

Ben faltered. 'They've talked to you?'

'This morning. DI Shenton came to the hospital.'

'What did you say?'

'Nothing, because I don't know!' Leanne screwed up her face in pain. 'He could have been meeting someone last night to hand them over, but they weren't on him when he had the accident.'

'If you're lying, I will come back for you.' Ben released his grip and went through to the living room.

Even though thankful to be free of his grip, Leanne tore after him. He was rummaging through her bag.

'I'm telling the truth,' she cried.

'You'd keep them close after what happened to Scott.' He tipped the contents onto the carpet.

'There's nothing here!'

'Then give me money instead. Scott was always bragging he was loaded.'

'We don't have any.'

'He never mentioned fetching and carrying? Or running a county line?'

'What?' She stepped forward, but he pushed her away. Her leg caught the coffee table, and she fell to the floor. As she sat bewildered, he searched the room.

'Please, stop,' she tried again.

'I need money to get out of here. There's no way I'm going back to prison.'

'Prison?' Leanne paled.

'Mum, what's the front door doing on the...?'

'Amy!' Leanne screamed as her daughter came into the room. 'Run!'

Ben raced towards her, pulling her into the room. He pushed her down onto the settee.

'Stay there and be quiet,' he demanded. 'Me and your mum are having a little chat. Unless you know about the drugs, too.'

'Drugs?' Amy frowned.

'Leave her out of this,' Leanne cried. 'Please... go.'

Ben was about to speak again, but instead he glared at her.

'You haven't heard the last of this,' he said. 'I'll be back.' Then he ran out of the room.

'Mum!' Amy went to Leanne. 'Are you okay?'

'Yes, I'm fine.' Leanne burst into tears of relief.

'What was he doing? Why did he mention drugs? Was that what Dad was talking about on the phone?'

'No.' Leanne needed to nip that in the bud straight away. Even though it was true, she couldn't tell Amy. She might let it slip, and they'd all be in trouble.

Gemma's instincts about Ben had been true. It seemed they'd both had a lucky escape. It could have been much worse for her if Amy hadn't come home when she had.

With the help of her daughter, she got to her feet, a little shaken but unharmed. She needed to warn Scott without letting on to Amy how much trouble they might be in. Because the only way Ben would know so much about what Scott and Kit had been up to would be if he was in cahoots with Kenny Webb.

CHAPTER FIFTY-SEVEN

Leanne tried desperately to keep her tears at bay. Not only had she lost Kit, but her husband had been run off the road by Lord knows who, Nicky had found out about her affair, she had reason to believe Scott was more involved with drugs than he'd said, and now Ben had threatened her.

Despite worrying about it, she needed to talk to Scott about what Ben had said. He'd kept her in the dark for far too long, about everything. She had to find out what had been going on, and just how much danger she and her family might be in. Because it could be someone else who came to see her the next time.

She wished she could roll the clock back to Saturday afternoon. She had been lounging in the sun with Scott, Amy and her friend, Marnie, lying on towels on the lawn. It had been bliss. Little did she know what was coming.

She managed to find a parking space and made her way to the ward again. Scott was sitting up in bed when she walked into his room.

'Hey.' He smiled. 'I've had some painkillers and feel on top of the world.'

She pulled up a chair, sat down, and folded her arms. 'I've just had a visit from Ben. He was demanding money and threatening me if I didn't give him any. He told me about you running a county line. Is that true?'

Scott grimaced. 'It doesn't matter now. It's over. I'm finished with it.'

'But how did he find out? Do you think he's working for Kenny?'

'I don't know anything anymore. I can't trust anyone.'

'The drugs are gone, aren't they? You did get rid of them?'

'Yeah, course.' Scott gnawed at his lip.

'You're lying. I can always tell.' Scott didn't speak but she needed more information. 'I want to know how deep *you're* in with Kenny Webb. I know something's going on.'

Scott hesitated. 'I've been helping out a bit behind the scenes. But I've also been thieving and selling some on.'

'What!'

'Kenny must have found out. I think it was him who tried to kill me last night.'

'My God, you idiot! What have you got yourself involved in?' Leanne sat forwards. 'You have to tell the police. You could set Kenny up so they catch him with the drugs, and he'll go to prison, and then we can move off the estate and—'

'That's not how it works. He'll come after me, even if he does get sent down.' He pointed to his legs. 'Look what he did to me. His boss is worse than him too. This was just a warning.'

'You're certain he was responsible?'

'Who else would it be?'

'You tell me. You seem to have kept a lot of secrets.' Her voice broke with emotion. 'So we're stuck? We'll have to live with this for the rest of our lives. What happens if they come after you again?' Her questions came so fast, but she didn't let him answer any of them. 'Why did you get yourself into this? We were doing okay, weren't we?'

Scott huffed. 'Ben said you and Kit were having an affair.'

Leanne faltered but managed to keep her nerve. She laughed to show her absurdity.

'You can't be serious. There's no way—'

'That's what the fight was over in the pub. Ben said something to Kit, I don't know what. It was loud, there was a band on. The next thing I knew, Kit hit out at me. Aaron tried to stop it, calm it down. That's when Ben said that about you.'

'Surely you don't believe him? He's trying to cause trouble.'

Scott paused. '*Have* you and Kit—'

'I told Nicky what you and Kit have been doing,' she interrupted to take him from the scent.

'For fuck's sake, Lee. I'm in enough trouble without anyone else hearing about it.'

'She had a right to know. It's not fair what you and Kit have got us into.' She glared at him. 'Tell me the truth. Was Kit killed because of the drugs?'

'I don't know.'

'Then that's what we'll find out. If we come clean with the police now, they'll be more lenient with you.'

Scott buried his head in his hands. 'It's not the police I'm worried about.'

CHAPTER FIFTY-EIGHT

Allie put her key in the front door, glad to be home. The afternoon and evening had been frustrating. Despite a social media campaign and a further press release, no one had come forward about either Ben Grant, or even Ricky Fletcher. Neither could anyone tell them the whereabouts of Suzanne Fletcher.

She'd spoken to Gemma Clarke, warning her of the dangers but Gemma had been adamant she would be fine, having seen Ben that morning. She'd also said things were over between them, although she hadn't elaborated on why.

Allie pulled the key from the door, closed it, and was about to go through to the kitchen, when a waft of something caught her nose. Was that paint she could smell?'

'Mark?'

'Up here!'

Allie found him in the spare room. They'd cleared it in readiness to create a bedroom suitable for a child. Gone was all the junk that had been stored there since forever and the room had been empty for about a month now.

Mark had covered the carpet with a dust sheet and was

busy walloping the walls with a neutral colour. Oatmeal. They both knew it was boring for a child, but equally they planned on buying several sets of brightly coloured bedding suitable for children of all ages.

'What are you doing?' she said, a stupid statement really because she could see for herself.

Mark had a line of paint on his cheek, and spots of it covering his hands, alongside a huge grin.

'Surprise!' he cried. 'I thought I'd make a start.'

'But we agreed we wouldn't. Not until we'd–'

'I know, but I couldn't wait any longer. And we're going to get approval.' He shrugged. 'So, what do you think?'

She glanced around. It was a lot tidier than before, despite it being so... bland.

Mark was waiting for her approval, so she smiled. 'It's perfect,' she said, moving forward to kiss him. 'I can't wait to jazz it up.'

'It's going to be fit for a girl or a boy.' He began to paint again, the roller swooshing up and down the wall. 'Or maybe a girl *and* a boy, if we get a brother and sister to stay for a while. We don't want to split them up, if we can help it. Remember the special bond you and your sister had?'

Allie did remember. It wasn't as painful as it used to be to think about Karen. Karen had been twenty-four, and Allie twenty-one when the attack happened. Before the assault, their bond had been unbreakable, and they'd been so close.

Afterwards, when Karen had been left unable to speak, or care for herself, Allie had felt robbed. All she had were memories of before. But no one could take them away from her.

And then suddenly, she thought of Suzanne and Ricky. They would have had a connection that no one should have broken.

Perhaps after the death of Peter, *their* bond was shattered too.

Maybe that's why they were after revenge on the group of friends. It had to be connected to Peter Fletcher's death.

She needed to speak to Aaron Clarke. He was the only one left of the group that hadn't been hurt.

And she wanted to look at those images on file again.

'Allie?' Mark waved a hand in front of her face.

'Sorry,' she replied. 'It's this case. Something has been bugging me, but you've just given me food for thought.'

'Speaking of which.' He put down the roller. 'I have a pizza ready to slide in the oven, a bag of salad to pop on a plate, and a nice white chilling. Why don't you have a shower while I get it ready?'

As the water washed away her weariness, Allie's thoughts went into overdrive. She was onto something, she was certain. It was too late to go back to work now and besides, she knew from experience that her mind would go to work on the finer detail as she slept.

But she would make sure she was at the station super early tomorrow.

CHAPTER FIFTY-NINE

Wednesday

As soon as she'd got into work that morning, Allie checked in to see what information had come in overnight. The search for Ben and Carmen was still ongoing – they'd obviously gone to ground.

Allie pulled up Peter Fletcher's case, clicking through some of the images that had been uploaded online.

The scenes were pretty horrific. The shed had been hidden in bushes, which had set alight, too. It had taken the fire brigade a while to realise anyone was inside the shed, it was so far gone when they arrived.

Then she came to some further evidence and stopped to examine one image closer. It was of three teenagers seen running away. This was what she'd remembered.

She stepped straight back into the past, recalling it clearly. No one had come forward, despite pleas in umpteen press conferences, and Peter's murder had gone unsolved after the case ran dry.

She went to chat to Jenny about her thoughts and then shared them with the team during the eight a.m. briefing.

'The images that were captured twenty years ago?' she went on. 'I think they could be Kit Harper, Scott Milton, and Aaron Clarke.'

Sam moved closer and peered at the digital screen. 'It's going to be hard to prove, though.'

'I'm sure it would be dismissed in court if either Scott or Aaron deny it was them,' Allie concurred. 'But I've spoken to the DCI and I'm going to bring Aaron in, show him the image and see if he cracks. He's the only one in that group who hasn't been hurt. *He* could be the key to all this, to tell us what happened to Peter Fletcher and why his brother and sister are taking out a group of friends.'

A rush of adrenaline raced through her as her team agreed.

'In the meantime, keep searching for Carmen. Perry, talk to Nicky. She's going to be upset finding out her friend isn't who she says she is. But she might know where we can find her.'

'Boss, I've had a call from one of the men I spoke to at The Wheatsheaf,' Frankie butted in. 'He says he knows Jack Fletcher, was at a party with him a while back and a mate of his has a few photos on his phone. I said I'd pop by as he can't work out how to send them to me.'

'Great. Go now.' Allie shooed him out of the room. 'Ben denied seeing his father. Fingers crossed there will be an image of him and Jack.'

Allie had brought in Aaron Clarke. She was now sitting in the interview room with him. He'd been read his rights under caution. She'd also told him he could stop at any time for legal advice.

For now, she wanted to tread carefully to get him to admit as much as she could. She was going to play on the one thing she knew he'd be concerned about. Gemma's safety.

'Aaron, things as you know have spiralled out of control over the past few days,' she began. 'First Kit Harper was murdered, and now Scott Milton has been involved in a hit-and-run. We can only assume that this was an attempt on his life. We've brought you in, more for your own safety really as we're wondering if there's anything you can tell us about why someone would target your friends.'

Aaron sat upright. 'Wait, you think I'll be next?'

'We're not certain but we have to take everything into account. I need to ask you some questions about something that happened twenty years ago. What can you tell me about the death of Peter Fletcher?'

'He died in a fire.'

Allie took the photos she'd printed out and slid them across to him.

'Do you know who these three youths are?'

Aaron shook his head. 'No.'

'Is this you?' She tapped one of them with her index finger.

Aaron peered at the images for the slightest of moments before shaking his head. 'I don't think so. Where was it taken?'

'This still was from a camera in Seddon Street on the night that Peter was murdered. After what's been happening over the past few days, we think Ben Grant is connected to it. Because we've found out that Grant is Peter Fletcher's younger brother, Ricky.'

Aaron's eyed widened. 'But Gemma has been seeing Ben.'

'We believe Ricky, as Ben, got close to Gemma, to get to

know more about you, Kit, and Scott. What we haven't quite worked out yet, although we have assumptions, is why. Why would Ricky Fletcher pretend to be someone else?'

'I— I don't know.'

'Were you involved in Peter's death?'

'No.'

She tapped the photo again. 'Is this you, Kit, and Scott?'

'No.'

'Because if it is and you don't come clean with us, then Gemma's life may be in danger. If you were there, then we need you to tell us *everything*. We can't ask Kit, and we will be interviewing Scott formally as soon as he is fit to be released from hospital. So it's down to you. Were you there on the night Peter Fletcher was killed?'

Aaron paused, and then lowered his eyes. 'I think I need some advice before saying anything else.'

Allie arrested him on suspicion of murder and arson and then paused the interview.

CHAPTER SIXTY

Gemma had been crying on and off since Aaron had left the day before. How could she have been such a fool about Ben? How could he have done that to her?

Even though things were over, she'd cared for him, and she thought he'd felt the same way. She'd even allowed him to get to know Charlotte, to stay in their home for days on end around them both. But he had another woman on the side. He hadn't even denied it.

She'd fallen for all his lies. He was certainly a smooth-talker.

So she was surprised when a message came in from him.

Can I see you? There's something I need to tell you and I don't want to do it over the phone.

She replied quickly.

I don't want to see you.

Please, hear me out. I'll only be with you for a few minutes.

No.

I have to see you.

Gemma paused. She didn't want to see him, but maybe it would be the only thing she could do to get him off her back.

And for some reason, she wasn't wary of him anymore. She was so angry, there was no room.

You have half an hour.

Be with you soon.

When she came downstairs, the back door was open. She hadn't left it like that. She always locked it when she was in the house.

She walked slowly towards the kitchen and stepped inside.

Carmen was standing in the middle of the room.

'Oh, you gave me a fright.' Gemma held her hand to her chest. 'How did you get in?'

'I have a copy of your keys.'

'How?' Gemma didn't wait for an answer. 'You can give them to me and get the hell out of my house. I don't know how you have the audacity to show up here after what you and Ben have been—'

Carmen punched her in the face.

Gemma gasped, shock registering before the pain. Carmen came towards her once more, and it was then she saw the knife in her hand. She stepped back.

'I'm not afraid to use it.' Carmen noticed her staring at it. 'So you'd better sit down.'

She eyed the door, wondering whether it was worth making a dash for it.

Carmen pointed at the seat with the knife.

Gemma shook her head.

'I said sit!' Carmen yelled. 'And if you don't, for every time you annoy me, I'll hurt that girl of yours. Charlotte, isn't it?'

The venom in Carmen's voice forced Gemma to react, and she sat down.

'What's going on?' she dared to ask.

Carmen pulled out a chair and sat across from her. 'Tell me what you know about Peter Fletcher.'

Carmen's stare unnerved Gemma, and she swallowed. She hadn't heard that name for years, nor did she want to. Painful memories came rushing back at her.

'Tell me!' Carmen cried.

'I don't know what you're talking about.'

'Of course you do. You were responsible for his death.'

'I wasn't.'

'So you know what happened to him?'

Gemma nodded. She remembered what had happened to herself, too.

'I bet you don't know that it was twenty years ago tomorrow since the fire.'

Gemma had no idea. She hadn't exactly been keeping a score. She hated Peter Fletcher.

'It's easy to ruin someone if you think about it. It's all about the planning. Although why I thought Ben would be capable of helping out and not getting anything wrong was beyond me.' Carmen rolled her eyes. 'You see, it wasn't supposed to have been like this. He was taking too long, and I'd had enough of waiting around to see if he had a backbone. It seems he doesn't. And now I have to cover for him again, like I've done for so many years.' She leaned forward. 'I know everyone talked about the Fletchers. We'd always been known as a rough family so, of course, we lived up to our reputation. I'm sure you knew that I had three older brothers. Ben is two years younger than you, even though he told you he was the same age. Peter, as you know, was two years older, and Stuart was twenty-one when Peter was murdered.'

'He wasn't murdered,' Gemma said, confused. 'He died in a fire.'

'You weren't there so how would you know?'

'Were you?' Gemma went to speak again, but the look Carmen gave her quietened her.

'I was eleven when Peter was killed. When I was twelve,

our mum died, leaving us in the care of our father. Jack was never out of the pub, and then he left, so we mostly fended for ourselves. I relied on my brothers to take care of me, but they didn't do a very good job. They were always out, leaving me alone in the house. I had to do all the cooking, cleaning, and washing for them. If I didn't do it, I'd get a good hiding. They treated me like a skivvy, at their beck and call.

'As soon as I was sixteen, Stuart upped and left without a word, too. We never told the council. They found out eventually when we went into rent arrears. We lied for months until they evicted us.'

Gemma didn't understand why she was telling her this. But she listened, hoping Carmen would leave soon. All she wanted was to get her out of the house. She didn't want to make the situation any worse.

'I lived here and there for several years until I met Jeff,' Carmen went on. 'I was hooked on every drug you could think of by that time. I'd lived rough, too, but it didn't put him off. Jeff took me under his wing. He's fifteen years older than me, and very rich. He treated me well. But in the end, I ruined what love he had for me. I messed about. I took him to the edge, where he couldn't cope with me anymore and he told me to leave. I wouldn't, though. So he let me stay in one of his houses, rent free.

'You see, as I grew older, I realised I could make things work to my advantage. So when Ricky came out of prison, I wanted to wreak revenge on the close-knit group of friends that I know killed my brother.'

Gemma frowned. 'What? I don't understand.'

'All that time they got away with murder.'

But then she twigged. Kit's murder. Scott's accident. Ben befriending her. Was it all to do with the fire? She didn't want to believe it.

'Aaron, Kit, and Scott destroyed our family, so I thought

we should ruin their lives, too. In whatever way we could.' Carmen scoffed. 'If only Ben had been more controllable.'

Bile rose in Gemma's throat. 'You mean Ben was only seeing me to get to the men?'

'Got it in one.' Carmen chuckled. 'Do you honestly think he enjoyed screwing you? He did it to get his own back. Peter's death was a long time ago, but he still held a grudge. We both did.'

'But you don't know what Peter did to me!'

CHAPTER SIXTY-ONE

A duty solicitor had arrived for Aaron, so Allie could go ahead with the second part of her interview. The woman was in her mid-twenties, fresh and keen, which was good to see. Her navy suit and white shirt combination embraced her professionalism. Red-rimmed glasses and a pierced nose showed her fun side.

'Tell me what happened, Aaron,' Allie said. 'I know you need to get it off your chest. There's only you and Scott who know what went on.'

'Scott had nothing to do with Peter's death. Nor did Kit.'

'Go on,' she urged after he stopped talking.

'Me and Gemma had been going out for a few months. It was quite serious – well, as serious as you can be when you're both sixteen. Peter Fletcher didn't like it. He'd seen us together, hanging around the shops with Scott and Leanne who were a couple, too.

'Peter wasn't at our school, and he was a few years older than us anyway. We didn't know him well, but we *did* know of the Fletcher family's reputation as troublemakers.

'One night, me and Scott got into a fight with Peter. He

was calling Leanne names, saying she was a slag, a whore et cetera. Scott was livid, so he punched him. Peter hit him back, and then I joined in, and we laid into him. Gemma and Leanne were screaming for us to stop. In the end, it all fizzled out and Peter walked off. But he threatened us as he was going.

'We thought it was the last we'd hear as we'd given him a right seeing to. What we hadn't planned on was him getting his own back through Gemma.'

Allie noted tears in his eyes as he went back in time. One fell, and he flicked it away.

She had no sympathy for him right now.

'What happened, Aaron?' She encouraged him to continue.

'He waited for Gemma one night and he… he raped her.'

Allie couldn't help but give out a deep sigh. What that poor woman must have gone through as a sixteen-year-old girl.

'Did Gemma tell you that?' she enquired.

'Yes, and I believed her.'

'I didn't mean to imply that you didn't. I wanted to know Gemma's take on events. Did she say anything to her parents?'

Aaron shook his head. 'She was traumatised and wouldn't tell anyone. I only found out because she changed when she was around me. When we… you know, she wouldn't let me near her. She kept saying she was having heavy periods. I thought she wanted to finish things with me, and that's when it all came out.' He thumped the desk, causing both Allie and the duty solicitor to jump. 'He followed her home one night, pulled her into the bushes, and fucking raped her.'

'What about her friends?' Did Leanne and Nicky know?'

'Not to my knowledge.'

'But you told Kit and Scott.'

He nodded this time. 'I couldn't help it. I was so angry I wanted to go and sort him out, but the others said it would be too dangerous. They thought I wouldn't be able to stop.' He looked up at her with a pained expression. 'I'm not really a fighter, and I didn't want to drag Kit and Scott into it.'

'But by telling them, you already had.'

'Yes. Scott said we should get revenge another way. We knew that Peter and a couple of his mates hung around in the woods at the back of the school. There's a clearing at the far end that comes out on the allotments, and an old shed. It was practically falling down, and it leaked when it rained. You could hardly open or close the door.

'I watched Peter for weeks. He'd often get wasted, and if it rained, he'd shelter inside the shed. One night, we decided to set it on fire.'

'Watch what you're doing with that can, Kit,' Aaron said as they crept through the woods. 'We'll have no petrol to use if you keep spilling it. Where did you get it from anyway?'

'My old man keeps it in the garage for the lawn mower. He'll never know if I take the can back.'

'Do you think there's enough?' Scott pointed at it. 'It's not very big.'

'There's tons of rubbish inside the shed. Once we pour this over everything, it'll soon go up.'

They laughed, continuing along the path towards their target.

They drew closer, coming out into a larger area where there was a settee and a deckchair huddled around a pile of pallets used as a makeshift table. The shed was behind them.

They checked around to see if anyone was there and when they found they were alone, Aaron took the petrol from Kit and poured it over the settee.

'Don't use too much on there,' Scott said. 'That'll go up in flames easily. Use the most for the shed.'

Aaron nodded, walking over to it.

He popped the can on the floor while he forced open the door. The noise was enough to wake the dead, and he picked the can up again.

Something scraped across the floor. He squinted into the dark until a figure loomed out of the shadows. It was Peter. He was sitting down, clearly out of it, on some drug or another. He didn't even acknowledge anyone was there.

'I snapped,' Aaron explained. 'I poured petrol over the floor and the stuff inside, and then I trailed it back to the settee.'

'Who lit the match that started the fire?'

'I did.' His face creased up. 'I was so angry with him for what had happened to Gemma. He had no right to do that.'

'And you had no right to get revenge in that way either. The crime should have been reported, and we would have dealt with it.'

'But everyone would know what had happened to Gemma. She didn't want that, and neither did I.'

Allie glanced at the duty solicitor surreptitiously, unable to believe that Aaron thought his reasoning was okay. An eye for an eye, so to speak.

The woman remained impartial. Allie could never understand how. Professionalism, she supposed.

'What happened then?' she asked.

'We ran.'

'So it is you in the photograph?'

Aaron nodded.

'And Kit and Scott.'

'Yes. When they heard someone had died, they were furious. I told them I didn't see anyone in the shed, and they believed me. When it was confirmed to be Peter, we made a pact not to tell anyone about it, and we never did.'

'You killed a man, hid it for over twenty years, and were

disloyal to your friends by lying about what happened. Do you have any idea how much trouble you've left Scott in?'

'He had nothing to do with it, I swear,' Aaron insisted. 'Nor Kit. They didn't know Peter was in the shed. It was my fault.'

'All three of you went there with the intention of committing arson.'

'Yes, but not to kill anyone!' He looked at Allie with pleading eyes. 'I can't let Scott take the blame, not after all this time.'

Allie wasn't thinking about Scott. She had to see that Gemma was safe. With Ben and Carmen out there, she was their priority. Because she was now the remaining link to it all.

Gemma could be in real danger.

CHAPTER SIXTY-TWO

Gemma looked up as Ben went past the kitchen window. He stepped inside when he saw the door open. For once, she was glad to see him.

His eyes grew dark when he took in the scenario in front of him.

'What're you doing?' he asked Carmen.

'What you should have done ages ago,' Carmen snapped. 'I'm tired of waiting around for you so I decided to do it myself, again.'

He glanced at Gemma. 'Are you okay?'

She nodded, although she was far from it. Perhaps Ben could find out why Carmen had turned up at her home uninvited, let herself in even. Because, she realised then, he must have given her a key to copy.

'Are you going to tell her or should I?' Carmen giggled. 'I think it would be better coming from you.'

'I think *you* should leave Gemma out of this and calm down,' Ben retorted. 'You've done enough damage over the past few days.'

'Not nearly as much as I intend to.' Carmen picked up the

knife and held it in the air. 'You know I'm not afraid to use this, and I will, if you don't stick to the plan.'

Gemma didn't understand. What plan was Carmen talking about?

'Well, you've gone a little off-piste, haven't you?' Ben held out his hand. 'Give me the knife.'

Carmen got up, stepped towards him, and sliced it in the air.

'Watch it, you stupid cow. I'm trying to help you.' Ben stepped out of the way.

'Oh, you're so good at that, aren't you?' Carmen pointed the knife at Gemma. 'Tell her how this was all a game to you, and how much you hated sleeping with her.'

'No, because it wasn't true. Gemma doesn't deserve this.'

'You should be protecting *me*.'

'Will one of you tell me what's happening?' Gemma found her voice at last.

They ignored her.

Ben stepped closer to Carmen. 'This needs to stop. You'll end up in prison again. You don't want that, do you?'

'*You* wanted revenge as much as I did.' Carmen pouted like a child. 'Are you going to tell her how you killed our father?'

Gemma gasped. What did she mean by that?

'Shut up, Carmen.' Ben ran a hand through his hair as he paced the room.

Carmen laughed hysterically. 'That's right, you can't say too much, or you'll land yourself in it, too.'

A rush of nausea rolled through Gemma, and she fought to keep it at bay. Not only had Carmen attacked her, but she was arguing with Ben, and she still had the knife. Yet she was saying that Ben had killed their father. If so, when?

And could it mean he'd murdered Kit too?

'It was you, wasn't it?' Gemma looked at Ben. 'You killed Kit.'

'No! I—'

'He was getting in the way,' Carmen griped.

'It was you?' Gemma's voice cracked.

'Yes, it was me!' Carmen scoffed as if it had been nothing. 'Everything was taking so long. Ricky was supposed to be setting them up so that they could go to prison for a long stretch.'

'Ricky?' Gemma frowned at Ben.

'Give me the knife.' Ben held out his hand again.

'I wanted to kill them all, after what they did to Peter. But *he* got them a job at Car Wash City.' Carmen pointed the knife at Ben again. 'Did you know your precious friend, Scott, has been dealing drugs for years? We were going to set him up, get him caught with a large quantity of gear, so he would be sent down. Kit, too.'

'You didn't have to tell her that.' Ben stared at Carmen. 'And we were doing fine until you got too heavy.'

'They should pay for what they did!'

'And they would have done! But not like this. I wanted them to suffer.'

Carmen glanced at Ben and then back at Gemma. Then realisation hit her.

'You stupid fool. You've fallen in love with her.'

'Is that a crime now?'

'I told you not to get too close! You're emotionally involved and can't think straight.'

'Me and Gemma are over.'

'Oh, you poor thing.' Carmen laughed hysterically. 'Has your life come crashing down around you yet again? You really are a waste of space, a pathetic specimen of a man. You had one job and—'

'That's enough.' Ben moved towards Carmen. 'You've gone too far and ruined everything. Give me the knife.'

'You don't get to tell me what to do.'

'Give me the fucking knife!' Ben stepped nearer to Carmen.

Carmen struck out with it, cutting his hand as he tried to grab it from her. He cried out in pain and smashed a fist into Carmen's face. She staggered, then dropped to the floor, dazed.

Ben went to Gemma. 'Are you okay?'

Gemma shook her head and then found her voice. 'Get her out of here.'

Carmen was back on her feet. She raised her hand in the air.

'Watch out!' Gemma screamed.

Ben turned, and Carmen plunged the knife in his chest.

Gemma screamed.

Ben's face contorted in pain. A pool of blood appeared on his T-shirt, growing larger by the second.

'Carmen, what have you done?' Gemma sobbed.

Ben dropped to the floor, pain etched on his face.

'Help him,' she cried. 'He's going to die!'

Carmen walked towards her.

Gemma cowered, squeezing her eyes tightly shut, knowing the knife was going to come at her next. But Carmen grabbed her arm and pulled her towards the door.

'Come with me.'

'He needs an ambulance.'

Ben was now lying on his back, his fingers covering his wound. He was losing so much blood.

'Help me,' he said, lifting a hand in the air.

Carmen ignored him. 'He'll be fine. Come on.'

'You can't leave him. He'll die!'

'He deserves to die. They *all* deserve to die.' She grabbed

Gemma and pushed her towards the door. The tip of the knife was pressed into her back.

'But Ben is hurt! You can't leave him.'

'Do as I tell you!'

Gemma's breath came in spurts, a feeling of light-headedness washing over her. She wanted desperately to wriggle from Carmen's grip, but the knife was scaring her. Carmen was too. It was as if she was in a trance, unable to see the wrong in what she was doing. How could she leave Ben alone, her own brother, without getting help? It clearly showed her state of mind. She had lost it.

'If only everyone listened to me, we wouldn't be in this predicament,' Carmen said. 'But they didn't. No one did. Ever. And now you have to pay instead.'

They stepped outside. Gemma cried out when Carmen picked up a petrol can. That wasn't hers. She must have brought it purposely.

With thoughts of what Carmen was proposing to do racing around her head, she tried to free herself as she was pulled along the garden path. They were heading for the shed and there was no one around to shout to. She had to think of something to do to get away. But her mind was full of other things.

She thought of Ben alone in her kitchen and gave out a sob.

She thought of what had happened to Peter in the shed twenty years ago.

She thought of the petrol can that Carmen had brought with her, showing her intention. The knife she had behind her back.

She thought of her daughter, beautiful Charlotte.

The padlock was open on the shed door. Gemma hadn't left it that way. Carmen must have a key to that too.

In fear of her life, she punched out and wrenched her arm from Carmen's grip.

But Carmen was too quick, grabbing her again. She shoved her inside the shed.

Gemma fell to the floor, her hands sliding along the wood. Scrambling to get back up again, she turned to face Carmen.

'I had nothing to do with anything. Please, you have to let me out.'

Carmen punched her on the side of her face.

Gemma fell onto the floor, losing consciousness just after Carmen slammed the door and locked it.

CHAPTER SIXTY-THREE

Allie was out of the interview room and racing up the corridor. She called Perry.

'Where are you?'

'I'm still upstairs. I've been going through –'

'I've had a confession from Aaron. The lads did go to burn the shed down, but Aaron found Peter inside and set it alight anyway. He never told anyone. Ben and Carmen must have found out and—' She was wasting time. 'Meet me in the car park. I'll explain everything else on the way, but we need to get to Gemma's house.'

Allie raced out to her car, Perry joining her. She flicked on blues and twos, updated Control as to the situation, and then filled him in on what they'd found out.

'So this has nothing to do with Car Wash City?' he said, holding on as she took a corner a tad too fast.

'It doesn't look like it.'

Ten minutes later, she screeched to a halt outside the property, thankful to see Gemma's car on the drive.

With no answer at the front door, they went around the back. The landscaped garden with a mixture of decking, slabs and a lawn, looked inviting with a bright blue sky above. But it was the open back door that first caught her attention. She raced towards it.

'Staffordshire Police. Show yourself,' Allie shouted into the kitchen.

Nothing.

Snapping out their batons, she and Perry stepped inside.

The body of Ben Grant was on the floor. Allie stooped down at his side, tried to find a pulse on his neck, but there was nothing.

'He's gone. Fuck! Be careful, Perry,' she said to his disappearing back. He was already halfway up the stairs, checking the rest of the house.

She went into the living room. Everything seemed to be in its usual place. Where was Gemma?

'All clear, boss,' Perry rejoined her and they went back into the kitchen.

'Call it in,' Allie told him. 'Get forensics down here. And then we need to think where Gemma is. She *must* be with Carmen.'

'You think Carmen killed Ben?'

'Not entirely sure, but until we've located both her and Gemma, we treat it as so. We should try the place where Peter died first.'

A movement from outside caught their eyes and they turned. Carmen was standing at the bottom of the garden.

Allie narrowed her eyes. 'Christ, is that a petrol can she's holding?'

They stepped outside again, but Carmen yelled.

'Don't come any closer.' She held up the can. 'It's full. Well, it was.'

'Where's Gemma, Carmen?' Allie asked, advancing slowly.

'She's safe.' Carmen laughed.

The smell of petrol wafted towards Allie. Then she

realised Carmen's clothes were wet. Had she doused herself in the liquid?

She glanced at Perry, who stood at her side. Then she took a tentative step forward, hands held out in front.

'Whatever help you need, Carmen, we can get it for you,' she said.

'I told you to stay where you are!' Carmen screamed.

'We just want to talk,' Allie reassured her. 'Please, put down the can. You don't want to do yourself any harm.'

'They did it to Peter. I saw them.'

'Who did you see?'

'Them – Kit, Aaron and Scott.'

'Why don't you tell me what happened?' Another step.

'I woke up all alone in the house and I was frightened. It was late, and Peter wasn't home. I knew he'd probably be at the back of the allotments, so I sneaked out of the house to look for him. That's when I saw Kit, Aaron, and Scott walking into the woods.

'They were laughing. Kit was carrying one of these.' Carmen raised the can up high. 'I ran and hid and then I followed them when they'd gone past. I stayed hidden but I saw what happened! I saw Aaron pour petrol inside the shed. Then I saw the flames, and they all ran away. I panicked and I ran, too.' She let out an animalistic scream. 'I didn't help Peter. I ran away because I was scared.'

'It wasn't your fault,' Allie tried to appease her while she moved forward inch by inch, hearing Perry doing the same. 'You couldn't have saved him.'

'I should have tried harder! But they killed him. That's why I hated them all. They deserved what they got. And I haven't finished yet.' She pointed to the shed. 'She and her precious Aaron set the whole thing up. *She* wanted Peter dead.'

'It had nothing to do with Gemma. Aaron was trying to

protect her, like your brother tried to shield you. That's why he killed your father, isn't it?'

Carmen laughed. 'Ten out of ten for effort, Inspector. I didn't see why *Ricky* should have all the fun, so I set about hurting Kit.'

'Did you mean to kill him?'

'Not so quickly. I was going to throw petrol in his face, light it and watch him burn. But I must have hit him so hard first that I knocked him out, or so I thought. There didn't seem any point in doing anything if he wasn't going to scream.'

A shiver ran through Allie, despite the heat of the day. Carmen's words were so chilling.

'What did you hit him with?' she asked next, eager to keep her talking.

'The wooden handle of a hammer. I didn't have the courage to use the head as I'm squeamish.' She laughed.

It wasn't a pretty sound. Allie glanced at Perry who was still inching closer with her.

'And Scott – did you intend to kill him too?' she asked.

'Yes. I can't believe he survived. I wanted him to die!'

Carmen threw down the can and pulled a Zippo from her pocket. She flicked it on, the flame igniting.

'Wait!' Allie cried. 'Did you know Gemma has a daughter? Charlotte, she's only nine. She doesn't deserve to lose her mum. You don't want her to grow up like you, do you?'

'Why should I care?'

'Because you loved your family. No matter what they did. You stood by them. Family is important to you. It is for Gemma, too.' Allie dared to take a step closer. 'Please, give me the lighter.'

Carmen stared at her. 'I don't want to live like this anymore.'

'So let's get you some help. We can—'

Carmen threw the lighter on the ground. The grass, soaked with petrol, caught fire and a ball of flames rose in an instant, taking hold of her body.

'No!' Allie yelled.

She and Perry tried to get closer but were forced back. There was nothing to douse the flames with. If the weather wasn't so hot, they'd have jackets and coats, but they couldn't get near enough to roll her over. Then she recalled seeing a blanket at the end of a garden settee. She ran to grab it, then threw it over Carmen to smother the flames.

Carmen was writhing in pain and screaming.

A few seconds later, the fire was out, but it was clear the damage to Carmen would be life-threatening. Her arms, face and legs were burnt, some of her hair gone; hands pulled into fists that might never straighten again.

Her screams had turned to mumbles. They sounded just as harrowing. Allie knew she would hear both in her dreams that night.

'The shed,' Perry said.

Allie turned to see flames licking at its door. Carmen must have trailed the petrol from there, indicating that Gemma could be inside. There wasn't anything else she could do for Carmen, so she went to Perry.

'There's a padlock. I can't get in.' He kicked at the door.

Allie looked around, spotted a brick from a rockery, and used it to break the side window.

'Gemma!' she shouted. She could see a figure standing as far back as she could.

Gemma stepped forward and put a hand through the gap. 'I'm here. Get me out,' she cried. 'I don't want to die!'

The door gave way enough for Gemma to squeeze through. Allie pulled her to safety while Perry held the door back.

The three of them ran down the garden, away from the

flames that had now engulfed the shed, and collapsed on the grass.

While Perry rang it in, Allie went back to Carmen. She wasn't in a good way, but she was alive.

Allie wished she could take her in her arms, comfort her, but knew it would cause her too much pain.

Instead she went to sit with Gemma, whose tears were falling freely.

She could hug her, and she did. But she knew it was too late to take away the fear, the hurt, the pain. Gemma's life had been shattered by the Fletcher family once more.

CHAPTER SIXTY-FOUR

With two ambulances taking away the injured, Allie and Perry were in Gemma's rear garden catching their breath. The next-door neighbour had offered them tea to soothe their nerves and, once they'd drunk it, had given them bottles of water.

The past few hours had been one hell of an experience. Allie flopped back on the grass, shielding her eyes from the blazing sun.

'I didn't expect to solve three cases today,' she told Perry, who was sitting beside her. 'Two ongoing and a cold one. That's some terrific teamwork, right there.'

'Yeah, definite job satisfaction.' He lay back too. 'I hope Carmen makes it.'

'I'm shocked that she'd kill Ben. Not after all they'd been through.'

'I can't believe it was Ben who killed his dad.'

'Well, unless Frankie has anything good from the photos he was fetching, we only have Carmen's word on that. I expect that's what happened though.'

Perry pointed upwards. 'I can see a bunny rabbit in that cloud.'

Allie squinted. 'Where?'

'There!'

'All I can see is a big cloud and a little cloud.'

'That's its head and tail.' Perry squinted too. 'Maybe not.'

They laughed. It was needed after the horror.

There was so much going on around them, but they lay in silence for a few minutes.

Finally, Perry headed off to the station and Allie made her way to the hospital, thinking again of the two women.

Gemma's eyes had swollen due to the beating from Carmen, and she was clearly in shock.

Carmen had still been alive, but with so many burns to her body, including some internal damage, the paramedics had said it was unlikely she'd survive. She'd be given every possible treatment, though.

Before going inside, Allie gave Mark a quick call.

'Hey,' she greeted.

'Hey, I'm watching *Celebrity Garden Makeover*. It's such a pile of crap.'

She roared with laughter, knowing he had sensed from that one word she'd spoken how much she was struggling. She loved how he always had her back.

'Which celeb is on it?'

'I have no idea. Some reality TV star, I guess. I barely know any of the so-called celebrities anyway. How are you?'

'It's been a rough day.' She told him what she could. 'I have to do a couple of interviews before I'm able to come home. What did you have in mind for tea?'

'Beans on toast. Ever the gourmet chef.'

'I might grab chips on the way home. Want some?'

'You sweet-talker. I'll have mushy peas, too.'

She finished the call, taking time to sit on her own. What

a week, and it wasn't over yet. Not by a long shot. But, she hoped, the danger had gone; that no one else would be killed.

Ten minutes later, she checked on the women. There was no news on Carmen; she suspected that was a bad sign. But Gemma was sitting up on a trolley bed in cubicle five.

'Hi.' Allie smiled as she went into her. 'How are you feeling?'

'My eyes are sore, and I need a shower, but I'm okay.' She shook her head. 'I had no idea what Aaron had done.'

'I know.'

'How could he do that and not tell anyone? No wonder the family couldn't move on. He had them stuck for nearly twenty years, not knowing what had happened to Peter.'

'I must admit to being shocked about his reasons why. He said he was protecting you.'

'The only person he was safeguarding was himself. What on earth am I going to tell Charlotte?'

Allie gave her a half-smile. She wouldn't like to be the one to break the news to her either.

'I can't believe Ben is dead too,' Gemma added.

'I'm so sorry. I know you were fond of him.'

'I was, but it all makes sense now. Anyone looking in on mine and Ben's relationship wouldn't notice anything was wrong. But when we were on our own, he often changed. Sometimes I'd see the Ben I was fond of, and life would be great. Then he'd be in a dark mood, and I'd feel as if I was walking on ice. Now I know why. It had all been an act. He didn't want to be with me.

'It had all gone wrong before I told him to leave. I found out he was seeing Carmen. At first, I thought it was his partner and he was seeing both of us. Even then, I had no idea they were related.'

'How did you find out?'

'Aaron followed him.' She pulled a face. 'I'm sorry. Perhaps we should have told you that Ben and Carmen knew each other. Aaron told me yesterday.'

'We already knew.'

Gemma's shoulders visibly drooped with relief. 'I didn't think for a moment they were brother and sister, let alone Ricky and Suzanne Fletcher. I just thought he was doing the dirty on me.'

Allie pulled up a chair, realising Gemma needed to talk. And she really wanted some answers as the people who could give them to her were both dead.

'Ben told me he'd lived in Stoke for most of his life but had been in the Army for twelve years,' Gemma began. 'He said he lived in Birmingham, in a city-centre flat with amazing views. He showed me photos of it and sent lots of selfies of himself there. I lost count of how many times he said I could visit, but when I asked, he'd always say he preferred to come and see me. He said he loved my house and being with me and Charlotte there. Said it felt like home to him.' She smirked. 'What a liar.'

'I'm so sorry. It must be awful for you to find out, especially as you were in a relationship with him.'

'For five months! How stupid was I?' Gemma dabbed at her eyes with a tissue, wincing. 'He said he loved me; that he'd never had the chance to find anyone special enough until now.'

'I suppose he told you a pack of lies about his background?' Allie questioned.

'I didn't know he'd been to prison. Leanne told me; she saw the details about it online after he'd mentioned it to her.'

Even though she had heard it from Aaron, Allie wanted to hear Gemma's side of things. 'What really happened when you were sixteen?'

'I was at the school disco one evening, with Leanne and Nicky. Aaron and Scott wouldn't be seen dead there, so we were having a laugh on our own for a change. Leanne had a small bottle of vodka, and we added it to the Coke we bought. Ever the sophisticated girls.' She laughed and then stopped.

'I began to feel ill so went outside to get some air. Peter Fletcher was hanging around. I'd been dating Aaron for a few months, and he knew we were an item. But he found me sitting on the steps a bit the worse for wear. He was nice to me at first and then forced me to give him a blow job.' A tear escaped Gemma's eye, and she wiped it away. 'Afterwards, Peter threatened me. He said that if I mentioned it to anyone, he'd tell Aaron that I'd come on to him, and about how much I'd enjoyed it. I ran back inside to my friends.'

Allie's heart sank. Yet another stupid man who had ruined a young girl's life before it had started. She had no doubt the effects of what Peter had done, even without the consequences of the men afterwards, would have stayed with Gemma for years, if not all her life. And she knew there was worse to come.

'I never said anything to Aaron about what had gone on,' Gemma continued. 'I thought it would be a one-off, but then Peter followed me home one night. Me and Aaron used to say goodnight at the entry to the cut-through. I'd walked that path for years and felt safe. But Peter was waiting for me.

'He stepped out from behind a tree and said he wanted to show me something. I told him I wasn't interested. He said he didn't care what I thought and then he dragged me into the bushes.'

'Oh, Gemma,' Allie sympathised, reaching for her hand.

CHAPTER SIXTY-FIVE

Allie tried to soothe Gemma who was crying openly now.

'He pawed at my clothes, and I tried to push him off, but he was too strong. I scratched and I slapped, but he grabbed my hands. His face was so angry, and he said if I didn't do what he wanted he'd do it anyway and it would hurt much more. All I could see in my mind was Aaron and how he would never want to be with me after he found out what had happened.' She gulped in a deep breath of air.

'Afterwards, I told no one. I was so embarrassed and thought everyone would blame me. They wouldn't believe me over Peter. But Aaron sensed something had happened and got it out of me in the end.

'As you can imagine, he was furious. And when Peter died in that fire, I asked him about it, and he swore he wasn't involved. It was months after it happened anyway.' She glanced at Allie. 'I didn't know they were all in on it.'

'Aaron told me that Scott and Kit had no idea he'd seen Peter.'

They were silent for a while, listening to the noises of the hospital. People talking, hurrying from one place to another.

Machines beeping, a baby crying. A soothing mother's voice. An angry one too.

'I'm tired of it all. No more lies. No more secrets.' Gemma rested her head back. 'When Carmen and Ben were arguing, she mentioned something about drugs and Car Wash City.'

Allie's ears pricked up. 'What about?'

Gemma filled her in, and Allie took down the details. It might be too late now, but she'd check in with the drugs team. The information would be good intel either way.

'I'll leave you to it,' she said. 'I can see you're tired. Get some rest. An officer will give you a lift home, and also, we'll need to take a statement from you tomorrow. Is there someone who'll look after you tonight?'

Gemma nodded. 'I've rung Nicky.'

She smiled. At least Gemma had friends who she could rely on.

Allie was certain all three women had no idea what had happened to Peter. Of course, they all would by tomorrow.

There would be a lot of pain, a lot of anger and angst to deal with, but she believed, from what she had seen of them, that these women would stick by each other and get through the mess their men had created. That is, if Leanne's secret about Kit remained hidden.

She left Gemma then and headed over to talk to Scott. She hoped to find him alone because she wanted to chat to him without Leanne being present. She'd have to record his statement until she could get him into the station.

Scott was watching TV when she went into his room. One look at her face, and he could tell something was wrong.

'No more secrets, that's what Gemma's just said to me,' Allie said to him. 'She's told me all about what Peter Fletcher did to her. Aaron told us the rest.' She quickly updated him.

'It was a stupid prank that went wrong,' Scott insisted.

'Arson is way more than that. And it had fatal consequences.'

'He never told us.' Scott looked away. 'All those years, and not a word.'

Allie believed he didn't know. She could tell by his body language, the shock mixed in with the disappointment.

He turned back to her. 'And that's why Kit died? Why I was run over. She wanted to kill us?'

'It's possible.' Allie thought back to her conversation with Carmen. She did believe she had set out to kill them, no matter what she'd said. Carmen had suffered all her life for something the men had done. She wanted her revenge much more than her brother.

She speculated who had set the ball rolling. Her guess was on Carmen. She would have been able to manipulate Ben far more than the other way around.

'Wow,' Scott said, his eyes brimming with tears.

He said nothing else. Allie wondered if he was thinking himself lucky for surviving or worried about his future.

'You'll be arrested once you're released from hospital,' she said. 'There will be an officer outside your door until then. Now, are you sure you don't want to tell me about Car Wash City before I leave?'

For a moment, Allie believed Scott was going to say something.

He opened his mouth, but then thought better of it.

'Yes, I'm sure,' he replied.

She left then, her frustration hidden away. She would get to question him again later.

CHAPTER SIXTY-SIX

One week later

Nicky came off the phone and sighed with relief. She'd just been talking to the mortgage company and found out that the mortgage would be paid off in full. Luckily, she and Kit had taken out insurance against one of them dying before the term had ended. At least she didn't have to worry about that large chunk of money going out every month now.

She made a coffee and went to sit in the living room. The funeral had been arranged for next week. She was dreading walking behind the coffin into the chapel of rest, playing the devoted widower when all the time Kit had been carrying on with one of her best friends.

Her thoughts turned to Leanne. She'd been inconsolable about what had happened, but equally because of Kit's death, too.

Nicky had been torturing herself about what Kit would

have done if he hadn't been killed. Did he love Leanne more than her, enough to have left everything to start again?

Despite her hurt and anger, she hadn't said anything to Scott about the affair between their spouses. Admittedly, she battled with her conscience, but Scott had thought the world of Kit. Finding out he was being disloyal would break him more.

Having said that, even without what happened putting a stop to it, Ben would have come on the scene anyway. Leanne and Kit might have continued their affair until they were found out. They could have chosen to leave their partners. There was nothing to say they would have stayed loyal.

Ben Grant and his sister, Carmen, had set out to ruin their lives. They'd been successful, too. Nothing would ever be the same for the gang now. Kit was dead. Aaron was on remand, and Scott conditional bail while further investigations were made.

She and Gemma didn't want to see Leanne at the moment. She questioned if they ever would again. No doubt Scott would wonder why their friendship was over, but that would be up to Leanne to come up with an excuse.

All this because of something that had happened at school. Nicky hadn't even been a part of it, yet Ben, or Ricky, had come after them. So, too, had Carmen, or Suzanne, and yet it was nothing to do with her.

Nicky pondered what would have happened if Kit hadn't got drunk that night. What Ben and Carmen had done to them all before the truth came out.

She'd never realised a thing, Leanne neither, she suspected, although she would never ask her now. Back then, she was as shocked as anyone to hear of Peter's death. But she didn't know him. She'd heard of him but he didn't go to their school, nor hang around with any of them.

But what hurt the most was realising that everything Carmen had told her was a lie. She couldn't believe how she'd tricked her. She'd made her background out to be so different. And all that stuff about domestic violence with Jeff? She'd never know now if it was the truth or lies, but she suspected the latter.

She'd used the story to reel her in, make her feel sorry for her. It hadn't worked, simply because Nicky had liked Carmen for who she was. Well, who she thought she was.

Nicky hadn't mentioned the money she'd found in the loft either. If anyone came looking for it, she was ready. She was going to deny its existence, and then if pushed further by Kenny Webb, or any of his cronies, she would say she gave it to the police.

She wasn't going to spend it all in one go, just a little here and there when she needed it. Two thousand pounds would go a long way to buy the remaining baby things she'd need. She deserved that, now that she had to go through it all alone.

She rested a hand on her tummy, flat for now but one day she knew she would feel the life growing inside her. So far, it was still her secret, although she might confide in Gemma after the funeral. She would always be there for her, she was sure.

'I'll look after you, little one,' she said. 'You'll always have me.'

Gemma laughed as Charlotte pranced around the living room in her mum's high heels. It reminded her of when she'd done the same with Leanne and Nicky. Now their strong friendship, that had stood the test of time for over twenty years, had been ruined.

How could Aaron have set that shed on fire knowing that Peter was still inside? And then to marry her, continue their life on a big fat lie.

She had been enraged at first. But gradually, she'd realised it was him, and not her, that was at fault.

Gemma had confided in Nicky about what had happened to her, but it still didn't take away the guilt she now felt. People had died through something that had started with her.

She still hadn't been able to speak to Scott about it. She wasn't sure she ever would.

Their whole friendship circle had been fractured in a matter of days.

Ben had been scary at times, but she hadn't ever felt he was that dangerous. So to learn that he'd been in prison, and then what he'd done to his father, had floored her.

Add that to what Aaron had done and she wondered if she'd ever trust a man again.

The house had gone up for sale as soon as the crime scene had been cleared. She hated going into the kitchen, recalling how Ben had died right there on the floor.

She hadn't even told Charlotte about her dad yet. She'd chickened out and said he'd gone to work away for a few days. Already, Charlotte had questioned why she couldn't FaceTime him. How could Gemma say that Aaron wasn't allowed to do that from prison?

And now everyone in the city knew what had happened to her. It had been written about in the *Stoke News,* and beyond. Simon Cole, the local crime reporter, had done a really good article from her side though. It had been caring, compassionate. But still, everyone knew. And her nightmares, the ones she'd hidden deep inside, had come back.

Kit's funeral was next week, and she was worried about Charlotte. She was too young to go to the service. And besides, she didn't want people looking at her with pity. Neither did she want anyone to question her about her dad.

So there was no putting off what she needed to do.

'Charlotte, come and sit with me for a minute,' Gemma said, wiping away a single tear. 'I have something I need to tell you.'

CHAPTER SIXTY-SEVEN

Leanne answered the door to find a man in his mid-forties, smart and trendy, with a shaved head and tanned skin.

He smiled. 'It's Leanne, isn't it?'

'Yes.' She frowned, not recognising him.

'I'm Kenny, Scott's boss.'

Leanne froze, trying not to show the fear that was coursing through her. 'Scott's upstairs, asleep. He's still in a lot of pain after—'

Kenny held up his hands. 'Relax. I want to talk to you. It won't take a moment.' He stepped past her and into the kitchen. 'Nice place you have here.'

'What do you want?' She failed to keep the tremble from her voice.

Kenny folded his arms and leaned against the worktop. 'You know he was doing some extra stuff for me?'

'Not until his accident.'

'His last delivery never made it. I was wondering if you knew where it went.'

She couldn't help the blush appearing on her cheeks, but she shook her head regardless.

He stepped towards her, and she moved away from him.

'I need you to let him get on with his job at Car Wash City when he comes back.' Kenny's voice demanded authority. 'All of it. Do you understand?'

'Yes,' she managed to say.

'And don't go blabbing to the police either, nor trying to leave. Because if you do, I'll be coming after that pretty daughter of yours.'

She nodded vehemently. All she wanted was for him to leave. How had she come to have a crime lord, or whatever Scott would call him, in her kitchen? She was not a part of the criminal world, never would be.

'Good.' Kenny smiled again. 'I'll see myself out, but one more thing. I wouldn't mention my visit to Scott, if you know what's best for you. And Amy.'

Leanne waited until he was out of sight before rushing upstairs into the bathroom. She lifted the toilet lid and threw up.

She'd thought the nightmare was over when Scott had been granted bail, and when Nicky had chosen not to say anything about her and Kit. Now, it seemed, she would have to live the rest of her life looking over her shoulder.

'You okay?'

She turned to see Scott standing in the doorway, using crutches.

'I'm fine,' she said.

'Did I hear someone at the door?'

'Just some idiot trying to get odd job business.'

Scott looked at her, and she averted her eyes. She knew he was thankful to her for sticking by him after what he'd told her. But, even so, she hadn't made her mind up if her marriage was worth saving once she'd learned the full truth.

Now she realised she had no choice but to stay. She certainly didn't know how she felt about that.

. . .

Kenny was now enjoying a cappuccino from the coffee machine that had arrived at Car Wash City. He had no idea how it had got here as he hadn't ordered it, but he could hazard a guess who was behind it. Someone was trying to keep the boys sweet. And it had worked as they were all over it, too.

His phone rang.

'Everything going okay?' the caller asked.

'Yeah, I think it will blow over now,' Kenny replied. 'They didn't have anything on us here, nor any of the other branches. They checked them all, you know.'

'But you managed to shift it all out?'

'Yes, I did. As soon as I heard Kit Harper had been murdered, actually. They weren't impressed.'

The two men laughed.

'So Scott's still with us?'

'Oh, yes.' Kenny snorted. 'If he knows what's good for him.'

'Maybe you should give him a gentle reminder to keep his mouth shut when he returns.'

'Minus the gentle?'

'Exactly.'

'Sounds like a plan. At least we can sort everything else out at a later date.'

They ran through a few business items before it was time for the call to end.

'When are you out?' Kenny asked. 'Do you have a release date?'

'A few more months at the most. And then I'm going to sort things once and for all.'

'I'll come and pick you up.'

'Cheers, Kenny.'
'No worries, Terry. See you soon.'

CHAPTER SIXTY-EIGHT

The team were having an oatcake breakfast. Perry was collecting their order from Six Town Oatcakes on his way in.

While they waited for him to arrive, Allie went through the paperwork that had built up on her recent cases. It had been good to solve two at the same time, plus a cold case. Who would have thought they would be linked when they'd first come in?

Jack, Ricky, and Suzanne Fletcher would be laid to rest together at a joint funeral. Their brother, Stuart, who had been living and working in Australia for the past fifteen years, had come over to arrange their funerals.

It hadn't been pleasant explaining everything to him. Understandably, there had been tears of remorse, regret, as well as grief.

He told Allie that he'd left to get away from the family, because he knew he would have gone bad if he'd stayed. He was married with three children, had a good life, and not a hint of a Potteries accent left.

Allie couldn't begin to understand the pain he was going

through. Even though they hadn't been close, his whole family over here had been wiped out in one go.

Frankie had come good with his photos from Bob's friend's phone. They had captured shots of Ricky with his dad so that would have been their next line of enquiry.

Yet they still hadn't finished with Kenny Webb.

They'd raided the car wash franchise and arrested him shortly after Gemma Clarke had told her what Carmen had said. But they had found no drugs. Not in the Longton branch, nor any of the others. It was obvious they had been warned or had the forethought to hide them in case they were swooped upon.

'Allie.' Perry waved a hand in front of her face to get her attention. 'Your oatcakes?'

'Oh, thanks,' she replied and held out her hand for her bag of delight. 'Come to mama.'

Over breakfast, the chatter continued, Perry and Frankie having the usual banter about their generational gaps. Old man, young pup. It was a joy to listen to.

'What do kids find so fascinating about dens?' she mused, thinking back to the fire in the shed. 'Me and Karen used to make so many indoors with a sheet across the top of a couple of dining chairs.'

'I had a wigwam for my tenth birthday,' Perry recalled.

'Only you could have a wigwam,' Frankie scoffed. 'I had a tent and pretended to be a soldier.'

Sam was giggling beside her. 'I had a Wendy House for years. Teatime with my dolls was my favourite pastime.'

Allie looked at them all in turn, their normality grounding her once more, and they caught her.

'What?' Perry wanted to know.

She shrugged. 'Just thankful to have you guys on my side, that's all.'

'Oh, she's coming over all emotional.' Walking past, Sam

stopped to put an arm around her shoulders, giving her a quick squeeze. 'We'd be nothing without you, Allie. You run us ragged, but you run us well.'

Allie laughed. 'I'll remember that when I catch you moaning that you can't go home.'

'We would never do that.' Frankie laughed, too. 'Actually, we would.'

'Stop looking at that phone,' Perry chastised Allie as she picked it up again.

Allie looked up guiltily. They all knew she was waiting for an email from Mark.

'I think you're going to make great foster parents,' Sam said, sitting down at her desk again. 'I know it took me a long while to get pregnant with Emily but I'm quite glad about it now. We were more settled in our home and a lot of the mortgage was paid. Luckily, we didn't have to struggle while I was off work because we had savings.'

'I bet you'll miss your holidays, though,' Perry teased.

Allie and Mark went away at least twice a year. In her job, she found she wanted nothing more than to switch off, lying on a hot beach somewhere near to a bar that sold cocktails. It would suit children, that was for sure. Apart from the cocktails.

'We can take them away with us,' she replied, 'if we have permission, and *if* we feel there won't be any safety issues.'

An email pinged in from Mark. Allie's eyes widened.

'Is it here, boss?' Frankie asked as they all stared at her.

Allie picked up her phone, skimmed the email, and beamed. 'We have a date for the panel to talk to some of the foster children who have been through the system.'

'They have a panel?'

'Yes. A focus group made up of teens who've been through the system. Apparently, they can be brutal.'

'You'll fly it, Allie.' Perry chuckled. 'We all know you're made of the strong stuff.'

Allie laughed, doubting that. But all the same, she couldn't wait to talk to Mark about it again. Not that they'd done anything but over the past few weeks.

If they got through this stage, there were only two more things to pass. And then her life might really fall into chaos.

And, hell, was she looking forward to it.

A LETTER FROM MEL

First of all, I'd like to say a huge thank you for choosing to read Hidden Secrets. I hope you enjoyed my fifth outing with Allie Shenton and the team.

If you did enjoy Hidden Secrets, I would be grateful if you would leave a small review or a star rating on your Kindle. I'd love to know what you thought. It's always good to hear from you.

The next book in the series will be on preorder late summer/early autumn. Why not join my reader group to be the first to hear? I love to keep in touch with my readers, and send a newsletter every few weeks. I also reveal covers, titles and blurbs exclusively to you first.

Join Team Sherratt

ALL BOOKS BY MEL SHERRATT

These books are continually added to so please
Click here for details about all my books on one page

DS Allie Shenton Trilogy

Taunting the Dead

Follow the Leader

Only the Brave

Broken Promises

Hidden Secrets

The Estate Series (4 book series)

Somewhere to Hide

Behind a Closed Door

Fighting for Survival

Written in the Scars

DS Eden Berrisford Series (2 book series)

The Girls Next Door

Don't Look Behind You

DS Grace Allendale Series (4 book series)

Hush Hush

Tick Tock

Liar Liar

Good Girl

Standalone Psychological Thrillers

Watching over You

The Lies You Tell

ACKNOWLEDGMENTS

To all my fellow Stokies, my apologies if you don't gel with any of the Stoke references that I've changed throughout the book. Obviously writing about local things such as *The Sentinel* and Hanley Police Station would make it seem a little too close to home, and I wasn't comfortable leaving everything authentic. So, I took a leaf out of Arnold Bennett's 'book' and changed some things slightly. However, there were no oatcakes harmed in the process.

Thanks to my amazing fella, Chris, who looks out for me so that I can do the writing. I wish I could take credit for all the twists in my books but he's actually more devious than I am when it comes down to it – in the nicest possible way. We're a great team – a perfect combination.

Thanks to Alison Niebieszczanski, Caroline Mitchell, Louise Ross, Talli Roland and Sharon Sant, who give me far more friendship, support and encouragement than I deserve.

Thanks to my amazing early reader team - you know who you are! I'm so blessed to have you on board.

Finally, thanks to all my readers who keep in touch with me via Twitter and Facebook. Your kind words always make me smile – and get out my laptop. Long may it continue.

ABOUT THE AUTHOR

Ever since I can remember, I've been a meddler of words. Born and raised in Stoke-on-Trent, Staffordshire, I used the city as a backdrop for my first novel, TAUNTING THE DEAD, and it went on to be a Kindle #1 bestseller. I couldn't believe my eyes when it became the number 8 UK Kindle KDP bestselling books of 2012.

Since then, I've sold over 1.8 million books. My writing has come under a few different headings - grit-lit, thriller, whydunnit, police procedural, emotional thriller to name a few. I like writing about fear and emotion – the cause and effect of crime – what makes a character do something. I also like to add a mixture of topics to each book. Working as a housing officer for eight years gave me the background to create a fictional estate with good and bad characters, and they are all perfect for murder and mayhem.

But I'm a romantic at heart and have always wanted to write about characters that are not necessarily involved in the darker side of life. Coffee, cakes and friends are three of my favourite things, hence I write women's fiction under the pen name of Marcie Steele.

Printed in Great Britain
by Amazon

84570137R00181